VALLEY
OF THE
TIGER

BY

RAYLAN WAYNE

ISBN: 979-8-9867084-3-0 PAPERBACK

Publishing Date 2023

ACKNOWLEDGEMENTS

My first acknowledgement is to my readers. Thank you to everyone who purchased my first novel and said all the wonderful things that inspired me to write a sequel. I worked hard to make this book as good or better than *Broken Covenant*.

As for my biggest fan, thank you Sweetheart for all the support. It has been a wild year, not one either of us want to repeat, but you showed me the depths of your love and I am in awe of it. It is cliché to say I am the luckiest man alive for having you as my wife, but it is the truth. You have my whole heart, and you always will.

A special acknowledgement for my friend Lee B. He and I have travelled to some remote places around the world. We've met with different leaders and advised them on improving the rule of law. Part of the idea for this book came from a discussion we had about one of his mission trips to Central America. More of it developed as we travelled the back roads and barrios of Panama and Nicaragua.

Another special acknowledgement goes out to my "aviation consultant" Don P. He and I have gotten ourselves into some tight spots on some short strips. Don always manages to get us out in one piece. He taught me a lot about flying and that is probably why aviation features so predominantly in my novels and certainly why Sam Harrington flies a Citation.

A big acknowledgement goes out to my copy editor Paul M. He is not just my editor, but a great dive buddy and fellow outdoorsman. He is a gem of a human and one of the smartest people I have ever had the pleasure of calling a friend. We've made a lot of money together and done a lot of good for the world. It is no exaggeration to say there are people alive today that wouldn't be if not for our efforts.

My final acknowledgement is for my buddy Bill P. Bill is my advanced copy reader. Bill tells me where the story needs improvement and provides suggestions for critical thinking about the characters and the plot. He is a great film maker and I really value his insights. Some rough stuff happens in *Valley*. You may not like it. Blame Bill.

MESSAGE TO THE READER

While *Valley of the Tiger* stands on its own, it is a sequel to *Broken Covenant*. You will have a deeper appreciation of the characters if you read *Broken* Covenant first, but each character grows and matures on the pages that follow. Sam, Johannes, Dan, Morne and the whole ARC crew are about to run headlong into the Azteca drug cartel. It is going to be exciting. As always, I bring real world elements into the story and try to show the reader things from far off lands they have not been exposed to in most cases. Some things are difficult to believe, but they are true.

I drew heavily from my professional background for this book. I spent time with the head of the Houston Gang Task Force. When a guy meets you in a restaurant because he is afraid a hit squad might follow you to his office, you know things are serious. He gave me a lot of insight into the precarious relationship between US Law Enforcement and the cartels. The cartels control the southern border, and nobody crosses without paying them. Our recent border policies (2020 to 2024) have made the cartels incredibly wealthy. I spent time with Texas DPS and US Border Patrol discussing the situation. If felt for them. I talked with many of the thirty-two sheriffs whose counties border Mexico. Some of them have as few as six deputies, but they stand up for law and order and do their best to protect their citizens. Listening to them was like a TED Talk on cartel violence and gang tactics. I saw a lot of things that would turn your stomach and learned about how cartels and gangs operate. I found the religious side of gang culture with the Santa Muerte, the death saint, fascinating.

I spent time in Nicaragua with some high-level leaders who told me how they manage the gangs and cartels. They assured me the cartels had honor, whereas the gangs did not. You must remember the Sandinistas welcomed Pablo Escobar and the Medellín cartel into Nicaragua after they took control of the country. That relationship with the cartels exists today regardless of what the government says publicly. When I asked how they managed the gangs, the reply was "We fumigate them." That is one of the reasons Sam brings the Afrikaners to Nicaragua, because they have control.

Finally, I spent some time with Javier Peña of *Narcos* fame. Javier and his partner Steve tracked down and killed Pablo Escobar in Colombia. We had a good laugh about how Netflix made him out to be dirty. He said they asked him if they could do it and his response was "As much money as you are paying me, do whatever you want." It was nice to see a DEA agent that risked everything to bring one of the world's biggest terrorists to justice cash in a little on his celebrity.

I hope you enjoy *Valley of the Tiger*. It is a wild ride about a group of people trying to get along in an area you will find on the maps called *the ungoverned zone*. As always, if you like the book, please tell a friend.

All my best,

Raylan

CHAPTER 1

Inspired by my conversation with an African bush war veteran.

Sam heard the rattle of automatic weapons over the roar of the engine. Time slowed. He saw three holes in the hood that were not there a second ago. The rear end of the Jeep slewed as Johannes jammed the accelerator to the floor. Sam could see a line of Angolan soldiers standing on a rise to his right. Long flames spewed from their AK-47s. His ears were filled with the supersonic cracks of 7.62 caliber bullets whizzing by. The air was full of them and then seemingly the hell around them ceased as suddenly as it began. He saw the soldiers disengage and retreat behind the rise. He figured they must have a truck. Steam was wafting from the Jeep's radiator. He and Johannes exchanged glances. Their vehicle's life was limited, and all they could do was drive it until it died then hide, run, or fight. Neither was willing to be taken alive. The ancient tribal atrocities still visited upon those captured made Sam and Johannes decide over beers months ago, if it came to that, they would go down fighting.

The problem with this part of Africa was there were very few places to hide. It was rock and desert with occasional sparce scrubby plants and no real cover. Sam looked in the back for the radio. Air support was what they needed. What he saw was devastating. The radio took a round.

"Radio is dead," he said.

"Damn it," Johannes replied as he glanced at the steam blowing back towards them.

"We stay on this road we're dead too."

"Suggestions, Lieutenant?" Johannes asked.

"Head for the ocean," Sam barked as he calculated how long it would be before the engine seized up.

Johannes jerked the wheel and crossed onto the desert sands. He kept his foot on the accelerator. Slowing down wasn't going to delay the

1

inevitable, but crossing the sands was going to leave a clear trail. Sam hoped the sands were firm enough for their Jeep to skirt across, yet soft enough to bog down a heavy truck.

Captain Lugu saw the tracks leaving the road. His patrol was the advanced scout for the main artillery unit of the MPLA commanded by South African MK Colonel Okar. The MPLA was the communist backed army in Angola and the MK was the military arm of the African National Congress from South Africa. They were united in their fight against the government forces of South Africa, South West Africa and their Angolan tribal allies who fought for control against the MPLA. The artillery was moving south to shell the forward fire bases of the South African Defense Forces. He told his driver to follow the tracks and the Soviet-made truck started replacing them with its own.

Sam and Johannes were lucky. Neither were hit and the hole in the radiator was caused by a fragment instead of a whole bullet. If the puncture was larger, the engine would have seized five miles back in the middle of the barren sands that led to the ocean. They would be dead or captured by now.

Sam turned around in his seat as he held on to keep from being thrown from the wild ride. An adrenalin powered dread overtook him as he saw a truck appear through the cloud of dust behind their vehicle.

"They are behind us," he said.

"What is that ahead?" Johannes asked.

Sam turned back around. It must be some kind of mirage he thought. It looked like a ship coming towards them in the desert. It disappeared as they dipped into a low spot and re-appeared as they crested. Johannes changed course heading directly towards the object. He glanced at the temperature gauge. It was far into the red. As they closed the distance, they could see the mirage was a ship. A ghost ship. A solitary inhabitant of the Skeleton Coast. Lost long ago, currents drifted it here and it sat listing to its starboard side above the tidal line on what is one of the great graveyards for lost ships. It was an old freighter, and it was the only cover for the upcoming firefight.

"We are going to make it," Johannes declared.

The radiator steam was all but gone. The temperature gauge was pegged to the right. When they were two hundred meters from the ship the engine seized and the 4x4 stopped. Both men jumped from the vehicle. They glanced back to see the truck coming toward them. Johannes grabbed his pack, Heckler and Koch G3 rifle and the water bag they carried. Sam grabbed his M-16, pack, and rifle bag which also contained his M-24 sniper rifle. Sam took a hand grenade from his pack and handed the bag to Johannes.

"Go for the ship. I will slow them down a bit."

Johannes took off running towards the rusted ship. Sam tied a piece of paracord to the ring on the pin and tied the other end to a lashing grommet of the Jeep. He rested his sniper rifle on the rear of the vehicle. The truck was closing, but it was more than a quarter mile away. He adjusted the distance compensating ring on his Uberti scope, lined up with the driver and fired. The truck swerved. He launched three more rounds down range hitting the truck each time. He placed the grenade atop the rear tire. He pulled the pin almost out but left just enough in to keep the spoon from arming it.

Sam followed Johannes' footprints through a rusty hole in the side of the ship and made his way up some stairs that led to the main deck. Johannes found two good vantage points for them and was laying out ammunition. As Sam approached, he handed Sam his canteen.

"There might not be time to drink later."

The ship was canted, and nothing seemed comfortable. They watched as the truck approached. It stopped beyond their disabled Jeep and as it did soldiers spread out on each side.

Captain Lugu was surprised when the bullet came through the windshield. His driver panicked and turned to the right. Lugu grabbed the wheel and turned back towards their quarry. Another round slammed into the truck as the two fought for control of the wheel. The driver was intent on getting out of there, the captain on catching his prey. Two more rounds slammed into the truck before the captain struck his driver in the nose and pointed the truck back towards the ship in the distance. He screamed at the driver and brandished his sidearm. The driver held his bloody nose in one hand and drove slowly forward until the captain said stop. As the truck came to a stop, Captain Lugu hollered for his men to fan out. Exiting, he yelled for the gunner atop the truck manning the machine gun to get ready.

He commanded twenty-five men, twice as many as should have ridden in the old truck. He raised his Soviet-made binoculars. He could see the footprints from the vehicle to the ship. He could not see his quarry. He ordered the machine gunner to cover the advance of five of his men to the enemy's abandoned vehicle.

Sam surveyed the scene through his scope. He was well hidden, and his scope carried a shade that kept it from glinting in the sunlight.

"They've got a Dushka." Sam said.

"That is not good."

"I hear that means sweetheart in Russian," Sam said.

"It can shoot holes through this ship," Johannes replied.

"Not if there is nobody to pull the trigger. You know what the NRA says, guns don't kill people, people kill people."

"What is the NRA?"

"Never mind, they are on the move," Sam said as he saw five soldiers zig zagging towards their abandoned Jeep.

The soldiers took cover behind the Jeep and peered over it looking for any sign of the men they hunted. Sam could see their heads nervously popping up and down peering over the top. He never took his eye away from the scope.

"I'm going to blow up the Jeep, so if you left your purse in there, I'm sorry."

"It didn't match my outfit anyway. What do you want me to do?" Johannes asked with a nervous chuckle as he wiped the sweat from his forehead.

"Take out the radiator on their truck. I'll get the gun."

"I was hoping to drive out of here in their truck, Johannes said.

"It is their big advantage other than numbers right now. Let's put them afoot," Sam said as he pulled a magazine with armor piercing rounds from his bag and reloaded his weapon. He grinned at Johannes before he raised above the railing and fired.

Sam's first round put a hole in the gas tank of the jeep. The second blew out the rear tire and the hand grenade fell. The chord jerked the pin out. There was a three-second delay. Those three seconds were filled with the deafening sound of twenty-three AK-47s opening up in fully automatic mode punctuated by the heavy thumping of the DShK machine gun firing at a rate of six hundred rounds per minute. The 7.62mm AK rounds striking the rusty ship sounded like a storm of hailstones on a tin roof. The 12.7mm DShK rounds punched through the rusted steel and left burning holes of daylight behind. Sam and Johannes ducked behind the most solid things around. Then the grenade went off. The Jeep exploded sending the bodies of the five men behind it flying. The DShK was silenced by the blast. Immediately, Sam was up and drove a round through the chest of the man operating the machine gun. He took careful aim and drove two more rounds into the side of the gun itself. Johannes peppered the truck with several rounds going through the radiator.

Like his troops, Captain Lugu was startled by the explosion. He knew he just lost the five men behind the Jeep. The rest were firing wildly or simply looking around wondering what to do. The DShK was silent. He looked up and saw it was unmanned. He saw the truck's radiator pouring coolant into the sand. He blew his whistle and commanded everyone to rally on him. He pulled back behind the truck. He had not seen the trail of a rocket or heard the whistle of a mortar. Somehow the men had blown up their own vehicle remotely. He grabbed his sergeant by the elbow.

"Get the mortar. I want you to shell that ship. Corporal, when the sergeant has the range, you and I will lead the attack."

Sam reloaded his M-14 with regular rounds after taking out the big gun. Johannes exchanged his partially spent magazine for a fresh one. The soldiers had taken refuge behind the truck.

"What do you think their next move is?" Johannes asked.

"They will attack I suspect. Maybe wait for dark, but that is awhile from now."

"What is our plan?"

"Shoot the hell out of them. When they try to cross the open sand, we bury 'em in it. If it all goes bad, we pop smoke for cover and go into the ocean. Get out of rifle range as quickly as we can."

Sam watched the truck through his scope. There was activity behind it. He felt the ship's rusty iron burning hot spots on his knees and elbows. He was shifting to a different spot when he heard the telltale thump of a 60mm mortar. He and Johannes both flung themselves to the deck as the whistle started and a sudden explosion blew sand all over them. Acrid black smoke hung in the air. They jumped up and were instantly surrounded by a swarm of bullets being fired from the soldiers. They scurried back down the stairs to look for shelter. The second shell hit the front of the ship and the entire vessel shook. After the second round, more bullets struck the ship. Sam and Johannes were below deck working their way towards the stern when the third mortar round hit above them shattering the structure above and showering them in jagged pieces of the rusted ship.

"What do you think?" Johannes asked.

"We can go astern for the bridge or back the way we came figuring he is walking those shells down the ship."

"The assault will be coming next," Johannes yelled above the noise.

"I'd rather get them in the sand than let them onboard," Sam yelled back.

"Agreed."

Sam and Johannes ran the best they could back the way they came as mortar shells continued to pound the ship. They stayed below the main deck in the stairwell until the shelling stopped. They heard a whistle and then a tribal yell called out continuously by many voices. Sam bolted up onto the deck and peered over the rail. Nine soldiers were running at the starboard side of the ship. They had crossed the sand under the cover of the mortar.

Captain Lugu split his forces. When the first mortar round hit in front of the ship, he knew his sergeant found his range correctly and would walk the shells down the rusted vessel. He sent his corporal and half his men to the left, the side their quarry entered the ship upon. He took the other half to the right. There was no way to enter the ship on that side, but he had a plan, and he strapped the only explosive he had, a TM-46 Soviet anti-tank mine, on the back of one of his men. He instructed the sergeant to fire ten shells and then try to get the DShK operational. As soon as the tenth round stopped, the corporal and his troops were to storm the opening into the ship with one firing at the railing as they ran to keep the heads of the defenders down. With any luck, the two men would be distracted by the attack on the starboard side and his group would be able to advance without suppressing fire. Once there, he would create an opening into the ship, and they would overwhelm their prey.

AK-47 rounds peppered the railing as Sam stuck his head up. The soldiers were coming fast for the opening in the side of the ship. Sam looked back towards the truck. Nothing was moving there. Sam changed positions, popped up and drove two 5.56 mm rounds through the man firing his AK-47. Another took his place, and thirty Russian-made bullets sporadically struck the ship around Sam. Johannes pulled the pin on a grenade and tossed it into charging men. They ran faster trying to get away from it, but the shrapnel took down the two men in the back. Sam put bullets into each of them to make sure they stayed down. The six remaining soldiers were nearly at the opening to the ship. Johannes cut down the last man in line. Now they were under the overhang of the listing ship where Sam and Johannes could not see them. Johannes eased behind some cover at the top of the stairs.

The first head appeared through the opening and Johannes put a round through it. A rifle followed and a pair of hands indiscriminately sprayed bullets into and up the stairwell. Johannes returned the favor by tossing a grenade down the stairs. There was some hollering in a tribal tongue. Before the grenade exploded, the ship was rocked by an explosion on the port side that threw a cloud of black smoke into the air.

Captain Lugu led his team quickly down to the beach under the distraction of the mortar rounds. His sergeant was one of the best mortar men in the MK, the fighting faction of the African National Congress and was doing an excellent job of walking the explosive shells down the ship. If they were lucky, they would find the two men dead. When the last shell fell and it was possible to advance towards the ship, he led his men in a dead run toward the port side. He heard the AK rounds striking the ship from the other side. He knew the defenders were still alive. More shots rang out and a scream. The scream served to boost his men's adrenalin. There was an explosion and more gunfire. He heard his corporal yelling that they had reached the entrance to the ship. It was his turn to create his own opening. He called the man carrying the tank mine forward. He placed it at the edge of the ship and armed it. His men ran back down the ship out of the blast radius, and he had one of his men shoot the mine. It exploded and ripped a hole in the side of the rusted ship. His men poured through the hole like a snake going into a mouse's den.

Sam scampered up the listing deck to the railing where the black smoke hung. He looked down in time to see the second group of men entering the ship.

"We gotta go," he yelled as he ran to where his sniper rifle and ammunition were stashed.

A haphazard stream of gunfire was coming up the stairwell towards Johannes. Sam pulled a grenade from his pack and tossed it down the hole as Johannes grabbed his pack. Together they ran across the slanted deck towards the stern dodging the twisted metal and jagged holes left by the mortar. The second group of men came up the stairwell opposite the one where their comrades had been battling Sam and Johannes. They saw their two opponents running towards the superstructure of the bridge. They opened up on them in fully automatic mode. Bullets filled the air around Sam and Johannes. Sam felt the burn of a bullet grazing his over-developed right bicep. They slid behind cover as the remaining bullets pock-marked the rusting metal around them. As it lulled, Sam yelled for Johannes to move.

Johannes sprinted up the outside stairs towards the bridge as Sam laid down covering fire on the men who just fired on them. Johannes jerked open the rusty door and prepared to cover Sam's retreat. He started firing at the soldiers as Sam extracted himself from cover. As Sam neared the top of the stairs, gunfire followed him up the steps. The first group they engaged had emerged on deck and Johannes now had two groups firing back at him from opposite sides of the bow.

The bridge was a mess. Scavengers had ripped open the cabinets to pull out the electronics. The windows were gone and blown sand drifted into the corners. There were identical doors on each side that opened to exposed stairwells leading down to the deck. There was an open door in back that led down into the bowels of the ship. Sam looked around as he reloaded his M-16. He peaked over the windowsill and saw both groups advancing on each side of the deck. He counted roughly ten in the port group and five in the starboard. He placed the crosshairs of his sniper rifle ahead of a man moving quickly around a gaping hole left by one of the mortar shells. He timed his shot to put the bullet where the man would be in a second. He heard the bullet thump as it hit the man's chest and he fell through the hole. A hail of bullets riddled the bridge. Johannes wiped the blood and sweat from his forehead, popped up and killed one of the starboard five. Sam took another of the port nine before switching rifles. The hail of bullets seemed non-stop at this point. When there was a pause, Sam leaned out the door and took another of the nine with a headshot. The bullets began again.

"I counted twelve," Sam said as he picked up the M-16 and slammed a new magazine home.

"Six to one odds," Johannes replied while reloading his own rifle.

"The kill rate at the Alamo was seven to one."

"Yeah, but they all died, right?"

"Minor detail. We have automatic weapons. And they are down half their force by my count," Sam said with a smile over his heavy breathing.

Captain Lugu was determined to succeed but was dismayed at his losses. He'd lost half of his command in a half hour to two men. He turned to the man behind him to give an order and saw he was gone. He cursed the coward for running in the middle of a fight. He would make an example of him when this was over. He scanned the bridge. He would catch a movement here or there, but neither of these men were staying still enough to allow a shot at them. Besides, their ancient Soviet AKs were not that accurate anyway. Overwhelming fire was their best use. He saw the head of the man two in front of him blow apart and his body fell onto the hot rusted deck. *If we stay here, they will pick us off,* he thought. *We must attack.* He called out his orders to the corporal across the boat. They would take turns advancing under the protection of the other group's fire. When they reached the foot of the superstructure, they would lob grenades into the bridge and rush up both sets of stairs.

"They are on the move," Sam yelled.

"I count seven port and four starboard," Johannes said.

He and Johannes wedged themselves into spaces on opposite sides of the bridge. The men on Sam's side were moving forward. The men on the other side were shooting into the bridge. Sam grabbed a piece of metal laying on the floor. He put his hat atop it and moved to the window so the soldiers would have something to focus on other than Johannes. The bullets began sizzling around Sam's hat. Johannes leaned forward. The starboard attackers were moving quickly and unfortunately for them, too close together. Johannes flipped the selector to fully automatic and hosed down the group. Two fell. The suppressing group stopped firing to reload. Sam peeked out the door and dropped one of them with three rounds through the head and torso.

"What's the count?"

"Seven port, two starboard."

"I like our odds," Sam replied as he took a peek over the sill.

Seven point six two millimeter rounds slammed into the ceiling and ricocheted around the bridge.

"They are right underneath us," Sam said as he stood.

His eyes caught sight of an object coming through the window. With the hand-eye coordination that made him a standout on the football field back home, he reached out and swatted the hand grenade mid-air back through the window. It fell to the deck and exploded. There was a moment of pause and then a tribal war cry came from below and sent chills up the men's spines. They heard feet running up both sets of metal stairs.

Sam flipped his rifle to full-auto and stuck it out the door pointed down the stairs exposing only his hands to enemy fire. He depressed the trigger and emptied it. When it ran dry two seconds later, he dropped it, pulled his combat bowie, launched himself out the door and was prepared to dive down the stairs onto the two men. It was not needed though. They were bloody piles at the bottom of the stairs.

Johannes adopted a different approach. He moved forward of the door along the windows and as each man ran up, he shot them in the back and ended up shooting straight down on them out of the window. The captain was last in line and as he saw the two men in front of him fall, he turned back. Johannes exited the door to the top of the landing. He sighted the captain and as he approached a hole left by the mortar shells, Johannes dropped him.

Sam turned back into the bridge and could not believe the sight before him. A fierce looking man with skin as black and shiny as alabaster had just emerged from the door leading below deck and was leveling his AK-47 at Johannes. The man the captain thought was a deserter found a way to the bridge though the ship and for a split second, Sam thought he was the Specter of Death. Sam took a single step and launched himself just as he had against several All-American running backs in college. The tackle was perfect. Sam and the soldier bounced off the bulkhead and the AK went scattering across the deck. The soldier grabbed ahold of Sam's head driving his finger into Sam's left eye. Sam slung him sideways, put his arm in a bind and ripped his left shoulder out of the socket. The man screamed in pain as Sam threw him across the bridge. They turned towards each other. The soldier's face was a mask of pain and anger. He was the scariest man Sam had ever seen in life, but he was injured, and his left arm hung at his side. He drew a large knife from its scabbard with his right. It flashed in the beam of sunlight coming through the window as he positioned it. Johannes was in the doorway, but his rifle was empty. He tossed it to Sam as the soldier charged. Sam sidestepped the hard swing of the knife and bashed the soldier in the face with the stock of the gun. The soldier swung wildly at Sam, who deftly moved back and jabbed him in the stomach with the barrel of the rifle. The man rushed forward with a howling war cry and Johannes shot him in the chest with Sam's sniper rifle. At point blank range, it hurled him backwards and he never moved again.

Sam and Johannes looked at each other. They took stock for a moment. Both were bloody, but they were alive. Sam's arm was completely covered in blood from the bullet grazing him and his left eye was bloody and starting to swell. Both had cuts on their faces and heads from the rusty shrapnel of the ship. Sam reached out and hugged Johannes. It startled him, but he hugged Sam back. He had never been hugged by an officer before, but he realized rank didn't matter in a firefight. The two were bonded in that moment. They would be friends for the rest of their lives whether they died today or in seventy years.

Sam started to say something as the first rounds from the DShK started penetrating the bridge. They dropped to the floor as the machine gun began dismantling the bridge one inch at time. Johannes passed Sam the sniper rifle. He grabbed his own and they crawled on their bellies to the rear door and got off the bridge.

They split up when they got into the bowels of the ship. They were making their way forward, Sam on the starboard side, Johannes on the port. Sam passed the hole where they entered and climbed the stairs. In a minute, he heard Johannes' whistle. He returned it. Johannes raised himself above the deck and started shooting at the truck. The sergeant on the DShK responded with withering fire. Sam leaned against the scalding iron for a brace and aimed for the gunner's chest. With the lightest of touches, he felt the trigger break. The recoil jolted him, but he recovered in time to see the man fly backwards.

"Did you get him?"

"I think so. I'll keep watch. You check the rest."

Johannes kept low and checked the soldiers laying on the deck. They had all bled out. He went below and checked the captain and the other man who fell through the holes. They were dead too. He approached Sam from behind.

"I brought you a souvenir," he said as came up the stairs behind Sam and handed him the captain's red beret.

"Let's get patched up. Unless there is a radio in that truck, we've got a long walk," Sam said.

Sam roused from his half-conscious state remembering the firefight and opened his eyes. He reached over and felt the scar on his right bicep. It faded over time but was still a reminder of that day. A battle tattoo of sorts. He reached up and felt the scar on his neck. That one was from Afghanistan. It almost killed him, but it too had faded. Finally, he laid his hand on the ivory cross that hung around his neck. It was the symbol of his greatest scar, the death of his wife Sarah. Time had filled in the deepest parts, but he could not think too much about it for fear of reopening the wound he still carried in his heart. He looked over at Katherine lying asleep next to him. She was beautiful and this was a different life, but sometimes in the ether between sleep and awake he kept a toehold in his past life. His barely conscious mind hoped beyond reason he would see Sarah's ghost when he opened his eyes as he had twice before. Once she came to him in the midst of the most dramatic Mozambique lightning storm and once more while he was standing alone on a Nicaraguan beach after releasing a grand African bull elephant and a few others into the rainforest and promising to protect them from all men.

Few would ever believe he saw her ghost, but his adopted son, Patson, saw her too. Patson was an orphan from a remote Mozambique village. Sam met him when he and Johannes were summoned to protect the village from a rogue elephant killing the local inhabitants and raiding the crops to a point where the villagers would starve in the coming season. Reluctantly, Sam dispatched the marauder, but found himself alone in the bush except for the exceptionally brave orphan. In the night, the ex-Army Ranger and a nine-year old boy faced down a big black maned lion and his pride. Sam ended up adopting Patson at the end of the ordeal and he and Johannes agreed Patson should stay under Johannes and his wife Anna's charge in South Africa. He was enrolled in school with tutors Sam paid to get him up to speed. He proved to be a quick study, a math wizard, and a star on the school rugby team.

Sam smiled as he thought about Patson then he thought about the wild ride of the past few years. Johannes asked Sam to return to Africa and meet with an eclectic group of Afrikaners who wanted to save their culture from being erased. Morne Delport was the leader and explained to Sam how the vision of Nelson Mandela was but a dying ember in the darkness for the Afrikaner people. They had no voice in the new government. Laws were being passed to strip them of their land, their friends and families were being murdered in their homes by hit squads and the schools teaching their native tongue were being systematically burned. Universally, they were sending their children out of the country when they turned eighteen, mostly to Canada, Australia, and the United States. The Afrikaners were aging out and resulting knowledge drain was setting the foundation for the collapse of the country and ultimately the entire southern half of Africa. The policies of the South African government, or more exactly the African National Congress, were casting the die for what was destined to become the greatest humanitarian crisis of the 21st Century.

The Afrikaners, for all the faults of their ancestors, simply wanted a place to call their own. A place to speak their language, worship their brand of Christianity and live in peace. They asked Sam's opinion as a former soldier, an energy magnet, and nation builder. Sam convinced them to look at Central America, which was a mess economically and politically, but in chaos he told them there was opportunity. The Sandinistas won the Nicaraguan revolution after the US Congress tied Oliver North and Ronald Reagan's hands. They brought a level of misery to the population that can only be achieved by totalitarians spouting the purest of communist propaganda. They offered state level protection to the biggest and most enterprising of the narcotics producers, including Pablo Escobar's Medellin Cartel. Like other strongman run states, the oligarchs got rich, and the rest of the population suffered. But, for all their failings, the Sandinistas did some things right. They had a zero-tolerance policy on the gangs that ran nearly half of the Central America's economies. This level of control is what drew Sam and his group of eclectic Afrikaners to the country. The Nicaraguans had a level of control where nobody else really did, or at least so they thought. Times were tough and resistance to the government in Managua seemed to be growing daily.

Sam and Morne created the American Resource Corporation, or ARC as it was affectionately known, and they struck a deal with the Nicaraguan president to build a nuclear power plant on the eastern side of the country far away from the majority of the population. In return, the government provided a twenty-five-mile by twenty-five mile square of relatively unpopulated land just below the Honduran border and along the unspoiled coast of the Gulf of Mexico. This area was labeled *the ungoverned zone* on maps. They also gave the company transmission rights through Nicaragua to the surrounding countries. In return, the government took a twenty-five percent ownership in ARC and a royalty on electricity sold outside of Nicaragua. President Beto Duran forced ARC to give up a monthly board seat stipend of one million US dollars to Vice President Isabella De La Cortez Duran, who was also the wife.

ARC was going to bring the people of Nicaragua into the 21st Century by giving them badly needed electricity, telephony, and broadband connectivity better than or equal to any developed country. But ARC was also a 21st Century Trojan horse, for ARC was also an ark, a lifeboat for the Afrikaner people. Sam and Morne did not divulge the true nature of the company to Beto Duran. The plan was to bring as many Afrikaner people to Central America as possible and give them a new place to live. This would be seen as a huge threat to the Sandinistas if they knew the true mission. It was not just the Afrikaners who were looking at this place as a lifeboat. The Israelis put forth capital to buy up additional territory and with that money, ARC bought up many more parcels of surrounding land. Ansel Van Dyk was the Afrikaner mastermind behind the land acquisitions. He more than doubled the amount of land under ARC's control by creating dozens of shell corporations and buying out the little farms that were hidden throughout the surrounding lands. He also bribed the Nicaraguan bank presidents into loaning far more money than they were allowed under the International Monetary fund and World Bank regulations to the shell companies. Now he had every bank in Nicaragua under his thumb and they did not even know they were in danger. If the shell companies stopped making payments, the banks would default on their IMF and World Bank loans. The country's entire economic system would collapse.

ARC's project was opposed by more than a few. The CIA expressed some concerns with ARC's nuclear program given a radical sect of Wahabi Muslims inhabited the tri-border region of Brazil, Argentinian and Paraguay. The thought of them getting ahold of nuclear materials for a dirty bomb within two hours flying distance of a major US city made the CIA nervous. Sam tried to calm their fears by discussing the intensity of the security of the site.

The drug cartels were very upset. ARC came in and discretely bought out the farmers growing crops for them. Those farmers fled the area, grateful for being freed of what was essentially economic slavery to the cartels. Also, there was now a heavily fortified nuclear power plant going in along their eastern smuggling routes to the United States. Sam heard they were voicing their displeasure with the President as of late.

The "Greenies" in the United States were furious a nuclear power plant was being built near, and cutting transmission paths through, the world's second largest rainforest. Their ire cost Sam his CEO job at MADEC, a company he built into a stock market jewel by combining an electrical utility company with an oil and gas exploration corporation that was also pioneering wind and solar. He was still on the board of directors, which was one more way he kept a toe in his past life. He maintained an impressive estate west of Fort Worth and big ranch in South Texas. When the airport was finished across the Coco River in Honduras, another venture of ARC, he could be back in Texas in less than three hours on his private jet.

The early light of dawn's glow was peaking around the curtains. He softly rolled out of the bed trying not to disturb Katherine. She was one of the ARC Board Members, an Austrian woman widowed from an Afrikaner. She was soft and feminine as well as smart and more than a bit stubborn. She challenged him and he liked it. While he was constructing the power plant, she was building the airport, bridges, and roads. Together they were an impressive duo.

He found his shorts and shirt and crept out into the main living area. It was a beautiful room ornately decorated. One would never know it used to be cabins on a cruise liner. Katherine's living quarters comprised what used to be twenty cabins in length, the hallways outside and the corresponding twenty interior cabins. Gone were the individual balconies and they were replaced with grand glass windows and a beautiful outdoor veranda. The cabins above were removed and the ceilings stood nearly twenty feet high. Sam's residence was similar in design and was on the other side of the ship. All of the original members of the ARC project were housed about this ship as were hundreds of others. Morne Delport and his wife had a beautiful residence in the forward part of the ship. Marcus Odendaal and his wife were near the stern. Ansel Van Dyk, the only other bachelor, had a place near Sam and Jayden Hocks and his wife and children were quartered near Johannes and Anna. The only original conspirator not quartered on the ship was Father Matthew Hoffman, the head of the Dutch Reform Church in South Africa who chose to stay in South Africa and serve the Lord there.

Sam passed Johannes' quarters on his way to his own. A smile crossed his lips. He thought about the day they all moved in. Each of the conspirators spent large sums of money renovating their own spaces. After all, the ship would be their home for a couple of years, but Anna would not bring her piano. It had been in her family for several generations, and she refused to put it on a rocking and rolling ship rounding the Cape of Good Hope and crossing the turbulent Atlantic. She would wait for a real house and then send for it. Sam flew them and Katherine to the United States for a visit in Texas before they went down to Nicaragua on his private jet. They all went to see Johannes and Anna's quarters and when Anna opened the door, she was overcome by what she saw. Sam had a baby grand piano installed prior to sailing. She cried saying it was the most beautiful thing she had ever seen. She rushed to it, got a feel for the keys, and started playing *Auld Lang Syne*. They all sang along.

Sam stopped at the cabin door for Dan Weston. Dan was Sam's old army buddy and more than a bit of a wild man. Where Sam used his time in the military to advance his education between combat assignments, Dan simply volunteered for more combat. They both straddled the line between military and intelligence work with the CIA, but Dan crossed the line so many times it was hard to know where one began and the other ended. When he exited the military, he sold his gun for hire. Sometimes he worked for the "the company," other times it was the Brits or even a corporate gig or two. When Sam looked him up to run security for ARC, he was vested in a venture selling guns to private ship security trying to fight off the pirates around the Horn of Africa. There was no answer to his knock, so Sam knew Dan was out and about.

Sam entered his code into the electric door lock and then placed his forefinger on the print reader. The door clicked and he entered. He hit the button on the coffee pot and got in the shower. After he shaved and dressed, he grabbed his tablet and mug. He went onto his balcony to read his emails. His view this week was of the land and up on the plateau he could see the nuclear power plant under construction. On Thursdays, the ship captains would put the ships to sea to keep things operational, run higher salinity water through the desalination process and discharge the waste. Upon return they would face the ships in the opposite direction. The result for the residents was an ocean view for a week and a land view for the next. Sam could see the open buses that transported the construction crews from the three cruise ships up to the construction site coming down the escarpment. The third shift was ending. Those workers would disembark the buses and first shift would soon board to head up to the construction site.

Sam opened his e-mail. His daily reports were waiting on him. The plant construction manager copied Sam on all emails concerning the construction process. They were three weeks ahead of what was already an aggressive schedule. The men and women worked twenty-four hours a day building the nuclear reactor except for Sundays. All work stopped at dawn and the day was reserved for worship, relaxation, and family.

Sam and Morne got a daily update from the admiral of the fleet. Admiral Jon Sharpe was a former British admiral who had seen action around the globe and while each ship had a captain, they were all subordinate to Sharpe. It may have been his smallest command since he got his stars, but he took it very seriously. His fleet consisted of three cruise liners, a diesel tanker that kept the ships and construction equipment supplied with fuel, a commercial landing craft and a couple of patrol boats. He took the Santa Maria as his flagship since that is where the organizers of this little experiment were quartered. He oversaw the alterations of the ship for their quarters, and they allowed him freedom to create his own space. As a result, he possessed very comfortable living quarters complete with dark hardwood paneling and great paintings of ancient sailing ships. Some sat anchored calmly in a bay, while others crested great waves as if escaping the clutches of an ancient evil. His favorite was Admiral Nelson at the battle of Trafalgar. Nelson died in the battle, but his fleet destroyed the French and Spanish armadas to set the stage for total British domination of the seas. Sam and Dan enjoyed visiting his quarters. They all agreed it was the manliest place on the ship and they could enjoy the vices of tobacco and whisky while they swapped tales from their military careers.

Morne and Sam quickly realized the admiral's capabilities were extensive and they expanded his areas of responsibility. He was now responsible for all shipments coming to the colony via freighter and controlled the wharf and loading docks. He was Lord and Master over all ship matters from ship readiness to bilge dumping. This included the massive galleys that fed the volunteer population and ship security. Dan Weston was in charge of overall security for the operation, but what happened on the ship was purview of the admiral and his captains. They had their own security personnel, who mostly stood around and opened doors for ladies during the day but were called upon from time to time to break up a fight or settle a dispute. They all desperately wanted to be on the marine patrol detail. Those lucky souls spent their days driving their patrol boats up and down the coast scanning for any signs of human activity. It was rumored a fair amount of fishing was done amidst the patrols.

Dan's nightly e-mail was its usual short and terse verse. All it said was *All Good*. That message was sent at ten. There was another at three am. *Caught more smugglers. Need to talk first thing in the morning* was all it said. Sam was about to check his watch when the balcony door next to his opened. He saw Patson emerge in a pair of shorts. His adopted son stretched a sleepy stretch. Sam could see the muscles in his arms and back become taught and then relax. He was becoming quite the beast of a boy. His father was a Chinese engineer working projects in Africa and his mother was African. His skin was a honey-brown color, and his eyes gave a hint of being elongated. He was one of the brightest young men Sam had ever known and when they met, he was a nine-year old orphan who kept the fires burning in Werner Van Schultz's safari camp. Now he was at the top of his academic class and a fan favorite rugby player at boarding school in South Africa.

"You keep yawning like that and you are going to make me sleepy," Sam said.

"I'm sorry, Father. I didn't see you."

"No problem, Son. You gonna make it to work this morning?"

"Oh, Yes Sir. I have twenty-minutes."

"Don't be late."

"No, Sir," Patson said as he ducked back into his room.

Sam smiled to himself. It was December and Patson was on his summer break from school. Sam had him working the tool room under the tutelage of a good man who thought it was his personal responsibility to account for every nut and bolt of the project. It gave Patson exposure to responsibility and structure, but also the everyday working man. His mentor was there to teach him, but also to watch out for him. Sam and the man had a secret agreement that he would not protect him too much, just keep him from getting into any real trouble. He wanted Patson to know what it was like to work with real men, tough men and grow personally to hold his own. The tool manager was reaping benefits of having Patson there. He was far better at the computer systems than the man and helped keep everything organized. Patson was likeable and he developed many friends among the construction workers, but there were a few who gave him a hard time. The volunteers were vetted by the Dutch Reform Church of South Africa, but some of their adult children who joined the mission had not been entirely vetted. A few were bullies and Patson was an easy target being the only black person in the operation. There were little jibes here and there and even outright rudeness at other times. For his part, Patson held his own. Boarding school made him tough and far more socially adept than others his age. He was polite to even the roughest of characters, but never showed a hint of fear. Things never got out of hand because there were usually others who would step in on Patson's behalf and the tool manager never let it go very far. Patson had his own little ways of getting even. He would give the agitators the worst tools in the collection. The wrenches that slipped and the pliers that pinched their hands. He kept a special box just for those fellows and the tool manager tried to hide his grin every time he handed one out to them with a polite smile. Patson never mentioned a thing to Sam, but a quiet word from the tool manager and the agitators found themselves on the third shift working in the middle of the night.

Sam finished the rest of his coffee and called Dan.

"Weston."

"Where are you, Boogie Man?" Sam asked.

"At the jail."

"You need me down there?"

"Yeah. You need to see this, Boss," Dan replied.

Sam tossed his tablet into his backpack, put on his hat, slipped his 1911's paddle holster inside his belt and headed out the door. He exited the gang plank onto the dock and found his Toyota Land Cruiser pickup waiting on him. The third shift washed it and made sure it was full of diesel every evening. Sam took the main road towards the plant but turned off onto a dirt track that led inland through the coastal vegetation toward the rainforest. He braked as he pulled up to a shipping container set in the jungle. Windows were cut into it and metal grating welded over the openings. Dan was standing outside with his Oakley sunglasses on, and his pistol holster strapped to his leg like a modern-day gunfighter, which he was.

"Captured another group of smugglers," Dan said.

"How many?"

"Eighteen males, all military age and a dozen donkeys. Their stuff is piled up over there."

Sam looked at the burlap sacks piled up under a tree. Each contained bags of cocaine neatly packaged and wrapped in packing tape. The donkeys were half-starved and their ribs showed through their hides. They were carrying millions of dollars in drugs and the smugglers didn't spend enough to keep their animals fed properly. It made no sense to Sam. The smugglers would carry their loads on their backs and strapped to the donkeys up into Honduras and return with sacks of US dollars from the gangs. Sam was starting to re-think their policy towards these smugglers. To this point, they had been detaining them for two days in the makeshift jail and then giving them back their contraband and sending them back the way they came. They were blindfolded, so they never knew exactly where they were, but it was obvious people speaking English or Afrikaans grabbed them in the jungle and hauled them away. A moron could put two and two together. It was a policy designed to not antagonize the cartels, but also to let them know to find a different way around the colony. He would bring it up with Morne.

"This is our biggest group yet. Ever see any of them before?" Sam asked.

"Yep. Four of them," Dan replied.

"Were they armed?"

"No."

"Did you ask them why there are so many of them this time?"

"We did. They just looked at us. Wouldn't say a thing. I know the policy against 'enhanced interrogation,' but if you would just let me…" Dan trailed off.

"Tell them not to come back. Find another way," Sam said.

Morne Delport stepped out of his vehicle. Katherine was holding court with her airport construction supervisors. Blueprints were spread on the tailgate of her pickup, and she was pointing out things to the men. She turned around to point across the new runway when she saw Morne. Her smile beamed.

"How are things progressing?" He asked.

"Very nicely," she said as she stepped towards him leaving her cadre behind. "I was just talking to the boys about starting the terminal. Did you notice the new bridge columns when you came across?"

Morne indeed saw the new suspension columns being built as he traversed the dilapidated bridge built by the governments of Nicaragua and Honduras. They nicknamed it the dragon because it was so uneven vehicles pitched up and down as if they were driving on the back of a great serpent. The new bridge design was a thing of beauty and it would be the most beautiful bridge in Central America when completed. Since ARC controlled the land south of the Coco River through a Nicaraguan land grant and purchased the land to the north in Honduras, Sam was able to convince both governments to allow ARC to control the crossing between the two countries. ARC employees now crossed back and forth as needed and without restriction. They truly were making this land into their own.

"What problems are you having?" Morne asked.

"We need more concrete capacity. I am planning on bringing it up at the next council meeting."

"What else?"

"The weather. The rain is slowing us down."

Morne nodded and looked to the sky.

"Any…visitors?"

"Only a few locals selling vegetables. Dan has kept the gangs out of my hair."

Dan briefed everyone on how the gangs ran the illicit economy of Honduras. They ran a significant part of the legitimate economy as well. There were no moral limits on how they operated and nothing in the country was untouchable in their eyes. Dan devised a system of controlling the roads in and out of the territory owned by ARC. All of Dan's patrols were professionals and armed. They were a serious deterrent, but still the gangs probed for weaknesses. Instinctively, they could smell a chance to make money.

Morne crossed the dragon again and headed inland to find Marcus Odendaal. Marcus was in charge of agriculture for the group, and he was making great strides in getting his feet underneath him in this new land. Morne passed fields of cattle grazing on coastal grass. They were fat and the cows were springing. There would be lots of calves born in March and April. Different winter crops grew in fields near the road. The transformation from what the farms previously were to what they are now was truly amazing. It was all thanks to Marcus, his farmers, and their ability to invest heavily in fertilizers, irrigation and pesticides. But as amazed as Morne was with the turnaround of the farmlands, he was truly impressed with the hydroponics and aeroponics operation being built.

Up the escarpment, tucked in a spot protected from a hurricane, was the hydroponic and aeroponic facility. It consisted of three enormous round buildings with room to triple the total size of the facility. Morne wandered through the first building amongst the workers running pipes and fitting joints. He found Marcus conferring with the Frenchman who was the lead engineer on the project. They were staring at a large tank full of Mozambique tilapia.

"Good Morning, Gentlemen," Morne said as he approached.

The Frenchman smiled. Marcus offered his hand.

"Our fish are doing well. We are using their waste to start the bacteria growing in the systems for the plants."

"Wonderful. Is everything on schedule?"

"Of course not! We must wait in queue behind Sam and his damn power plant for everything! If we need concrete, we are forced to wait until a day they are not pouring concrete. And they are always pouring concrete! We must wait to get pipe and wait to get bulldozers. We must wait for everything!"

"And despite all of that, you have built something wonderful."

"Wonderful? We have started something wonderful, but it is just a shell. It will be magnificent if we can get what we need."

"You will. I will make sure you do. But you know the priorities of the mission. We can buy food. We can't buy electricity. We must have the plant operational when the lines are connected. Besides, I suspect you have your ways."

Marcus huffed and walked off towards his office. The Frenchman smiled. Morne smiled back. They both knew Marcus' people were very good at acquiring what they needed to keep their project moving forward. Piping regularly disappeared from other projects and concrete trucks got diverted occasionally, especially on third shift.

Jayden Hocks was the overlord of a race. The greatest infrastructure race since the transcontinental railroad linked the East Coast of the United States to the West and the biggest construction project in Central America since the Panama Canal. He oversaw the transmission tower project. He personally felt completely unqualified for the job. He was an IT guy, a tech wizard, and a bit of nerd at heart, but the transmission tower project was forced upon him by the others. He may have felt underqualified to do the job, but he was succeeding. Mostly because he surrounded himself with a very qualified staff. Hard driving men and women who understood construction, managed big projects and were arrogant enough to be fearless about the task ahead when they should have been scared to death. Their false assurances gave him comfort and to their credit, they were performing. There were four transmission paths under construction currently. Two outbound from the plant and two inbound from the capital cities of Nicaragua and Honduras. President Beto Duran took a victory lap expounding to the entire population of

Nicaragua the revolutionary progress and dominance of the region when first towers were placed on the edge of Managua. Isabella De La Corte Duran, the president's wife, a board member of ARC, and the Vice President of Nicaragua christened the first tower with a bottle of champagne as if she were launching a ship. President Orlando Rodriguez of Honduras did the same when the first tower was placed in Tegucigalpa. That set of towers was running across Honduras and would meet its connection in the Bosawas rainforest in Nicaragua.

Each tower was a modern marvel of engineering. The towers were tall cylindrical structures that would last over a hundred years before needing replacement. They were impervious to the elements and were nearly impervious to human tampering. Their real secret though was the routers and electrical transmission capability residing atop them. ARC was setting itself up to become the major player in Central America in not only electrical production, but also in wireless broadband. The capabilities within these towers would allow ARC to monitor communications of anyone on their network and selectively provide or deny electrical service to anyone without disrupting the rest. The capabilities were designed by Jayden Hocks and once deployed, would give ARC state-level power few other companies held.

Each leg of the tower race had its own crew. The crews leaving the power plant were almost entirely Afrikaners, although Jayden brought in some experienced leadership from the United States and there were two French environmental experts employed to make sure the rainforest was protected when the towers were being installed. The leg originating in Tegucigalpa, was comprised mostly of Hondurans with an Afrikaner as their leader. The leg originating in Managua was entirely Nicaraguans, except for the ARC managers on the ground. The projects originating from the capital cities were something akin to a travelling circus or a nineteenth century army encampment, complete with military protection. As the work got farther and farther away from the cities, a mobile makeshift encampment followed the works. ARC brought in large tents and cots for housing of the workers, and they brought in more when it was obvious the workers were bringing their families. They would be sleeping in all manner of makeshift housing if left up to their own means. Jans Vroom was the head ramrod on the Tegucigalpa leg. He found a capable foreman in Jose Valdez and made him Quartermaster General in charge of housing and personnel logistics. It was a grand title Jose loved, but what it really meant was he was to make sure the tents were deployed properly, and housing assigned as best as possible. He had no control of the camp followers. The merchants, food vendors, scavengers and entertainers had a camp unto themselves. Jose's job was to keep the workforce healthy and working while limiting the drama associated with the circus following. It was not only impossible to prevent interaction between the workers and the camp followers, it was necessary for the people to interact as the followers provided necessary services including clothing, tools, food, medicine and stress relief in all manner of vices.

Jans tried not to look behind him at the semi-ordered chaos that was the camp followers and focused mainly on the path ahead. He focused on where the next tower was to be erected and where the next bridge was to be built. Luckily for him, Jayden assigned an American to provide security for the group. Javier Cordova was a Puerto Rican who joined the US Army at the age of seventeen. He was a tough boy from the barrios of San Juan and the Army had been his only hope to get out of Puerto Rico and what would have been a short life in crime. The hardship of his youth helped him in the grueling selection process for Ranger School. He became one of the elite, earned his bachelor's degree online and became a mustang, making the transition from enlisted to a second lieutenant. He retired as a Major and now was the head of security for this leg of the Great Central American Tower Race as it was being called. He knew the gangs from his youth, and he knew combat from America's wars against the Arabs. Few knew his closet at home contained two silver stars for heroism, but those in camp knew he was not someone to be trifled with. The gangs were his biggest problems. They tried to get hired onto the work force. He managed to stop that by making every applicant strip to the waist. One gang tattoo and you were disqualified. The last thing he needed was gang members stealing ARC property and selling drugs to the other workers. He held an advantage in that he spoke Spanish and could converse with anyone fluently, but the gangs played a continual game of cat and mouse working people in and out of the camp followers. Legally, he had no authority, but he did have a Honduran Army detachment assigned to the project and the problems he could not resolve with an enormous amount of profanity laced yelling, or his fists, he called upon them for assistance. They controlled the road to and from the work site and they maintained a presence to ward off attacks by the gangs and enforce some sort of order. They were commanded by a lieutenant and the day he showed up with his detachment, Javier greeted him in his BDU blouse with the bronze oak leaves on the collar. It worked and the lieutenant took orders fairly well, although Javier did not trust any of them. He arranged for them to have separate billeting, better food and even a TV with a DVD player and a stack of movies. Still, he caught them turning a blind eye to some of the gang activities and even some of the workers trading ARC property to vendors for personal items or favors. Jans told him not to worry, just keep the losses to a minimum and don't let anything slow down the construction pace. They were in a race against the Managua tower set, and if they connected to their towers to their mates coming from the power plant through the rainforest before the Managua towers connected to their outbound mates, he would win the $500,000 prize money offered by ARC. The challenge was that his path was longer, so Jayden and Morne gave him a head start. A head start Jans Vroom hoped would give his crew the edge. They made mistakes on the early towers. Mistakes he intentionally hid from ARC so his opposite number in Managua would not know. He wasn't about to help them learn. He now ran a well-oiled machine of tower installers, cable pullers and electricians. He did share his secrets and solutions with his partner racing through the rainforest to meet him. He wanted every edge they could get, but in the end, the only edge that mattered was could you outwork your competition. Could you get more done today and tomorrow than your competitor. He was sure he could, and he worked his men hard from sunup to sundown. ARC mandated Sundays were no-work days, but Jans used his cash fund to pay workers off books to go ahead of crews and prepare more sites for the next towers. Come Monday, he was ready to pour more concrete pads than the Managua line and it was showing in their progress.

Back on the ships, a weekly newsletter was circulated showing the progress of the four lines. All manner of gambling was taking place on who would win, where would they meet and on what day they would finish. Odds were all over the place and everyone followed the progress of the tower builds with great enthusiasm.

Sam's pickup emerged from the dim road onto the dirt track leading from the food production area towards the ships. He heard a honk and looked back to see Morne's pickup behind him. Morne greeted him enthusiastically as they shook hands. It was nice to be away from the hustle of the ships and construction sites, just two friends on the side of a dirt road in a beautiful country. They caught up on the morning's events and ran things past each other for opinion and advice. Eventually, they got to the pressing matters.

"What do you think about these smugglers?" Sam asked.

"Seems to be an escalation. It is twice as many as we have ever seen before."

Sam looked thoughtfully down the road.

"The fact we have always sent them back with their drugs has probably kept it peaceful to this point. But these guys are not used to being pushed around."

"We should ask El Presidente for some assistance before this turns ugly."

"Agreed. We also need to get some better intel. Dan and I can reach out to some of our three-letter agency friends in the US."

"Good. Speaking of El Presidente and his wife, I got a note last night from Isabella. She wants to be paid in cash going forward, No more wire transfers to her bank in Switzerland."

Sam raised his eyebrows.

"I know it has been getting tough on them with the protest and riots and pressure from the States. I hope it doesn't mean they are looking to run."

"Quite the opposite. I think they need untraceable money to pay off people. Say what you want about the Durans and the Sandinistas, they are ruthless survivors."

"She is due $500,000 in three days. I'll take Dan and deliver it."

"Get Ansel to arrange the funds. You should be able to pick it up from one of the banks in Managua."

Sam and Dan waited patiently in the bank president's outer office. Señor Sedrick Guzman, the bank president was busy in the vault supervising the filling of Dan's duffle bag with five-hundred thousand US Dollars. Sam watched the traffic out the window while Dan made time with the banker's administrative assistant. She was a beautiful dark-haired woman and Dan was clearly trying to score some points while they waited. Sam tried to hide his grin as he could not avoid hearing the banter between the two. Dan was trying overly hard, and she was coyly turning him down. Sam had seen Dan operate before though. He knew it was only a matter of time before he wore her down.

The bank president returned with the duffle bag full of cash. He was extremely professional and accommodating. He knew these men had business with the President and he wanted everything to go smoothly. He also knew they were somehow connected to at least a few of the Mexican and Panamanian lawyers who gave him the account codes and passwords to nearly ten million US dollars in numbered Swiss bank accounts. His life had been greatly enriched in the last two years. He and Sam counted the money out on his desk before returning it to the bag. Dan winked at the secretary as he opened the door for Sam, then jumped ahead of him before entering the foyer. Julio, Dan's old Contra contact, was waiting outside for them in his Toyota Hilux pickup. His nephew was riding shotgun in the front seat with a folding stock AK-47. Dan got Sam into the pickup quickly and climbed in after him. Julio let them off at the Presidential Palace and waited for them to return.

Ernesto Ruiz, the President's chief of staff was waiting inside the main doors for them. The greeting was warm and friendly. He escorted them to the security window and looked at Dan. Dan grinned and produced the 1911 from his rear waistband. He handed it to the man behind the window and looked at the chief of staff who simply cocked his head and raised a single eyebrow. Dan lifted his pants leg and removed the Walther PPK from his ankle holster. Satisfied, the chief of staff led them through a side door towards the vice president's office.

Isabella De La Corte Duran smiled broadly when her secretary announced Sam and Dan just inside her door. She embraced Sam and kissed him on both cheeks. Sam handed her the bag which she placed inside a lateral file cabinet.

"How are things progressing at the construction site?"

"We are ahead of schedule."

"That is excellent news…for the people."

"Yes, Ma'am. Excellent news for the people."

"And the towers?"

"I have a map here to show the progress. I thought you would like to see it," Sam said handing her a tri-folded piece of paper from inside his jacket. She looked at the dots showing the progress of the different paths the towers were cutting through Nicaragua. When they met, Nicaragua would be the most powerful energy producer in Central America.

"You are doing amazingly well. Is there anything I or the President can do to assist you?"

"There is one thing. The cartels were not supposed to be coming through the lands the government appropriated for the power plant. We keep catching their people transporting their product north. We have been detaining them and then sending them back. It was small groups. Now, they are sending larger groups. We fear they are going to start arming them."

"I see."

"Do you think you or the President can have a word with them and ask them to stay to the western side of the country?"

"Yes. Of course. No problem," she said with a wrinkled brow. The leader of the cartel was on the President's calendar for later in the day. He requested the meeting. Isabella wondered if this was the reason.

Julio took Sam and Dan back to the airport. Jayden was waiting for them at the FBO with one of ARC's Airbus helicopters, still affectionately known as a Eurocopter. He tagged along to inspect the towers leaving Managua. The helo flew slowly along the route of the towers letting the men examine everything from the air. When they got to the newest towers being erected, the pilot spotted the area designated by the crew for him to land. They had cleared it and even created a makeshift windsock for him.

Henry Claassen, the project lead ran crouched under the slowly spinning blades of the Eurocopter to open Jayden's door.

"Mr. Van Dyk, Dr. Harrington, Mr. Weston, so nice to see all of you," he hollered as the blades whipped overhead.

"How goes it?" Jayden asked.

"Going along proper I must say. A hiccup here and there, but nothing we have not been able to get sorted."

There was a growing crowd encircling the helicopter. All locals, mostly camp followers, and some of the workers. The Nicaraguan military escort was also present. The towers had left Managua to the west and were deep into the countryside now. There was no police presence this far out to speak of, so the military assigned a permanent escort. Henry looked behind him to see the crowd and suggested they move the conversation into his trailer.

Henry's construction trailer was the most secure facility in the traveling circus that was the Managua tower construction project. Welded rebar over the windows protected the documents within and a safe protected the payroll.

"Tell us about things as of late," Jayden said.

"We are in a good rhythm. The road crew clears a path and improves the road to the next location. Makes it good enough for the concrete trucks and the pumper to get along. The framers frame and reinforce the concrete pad and the concrete crews fill it. They all stay one week ahead of each other. The pads need to cure for a month, so our operation is quite strung out. The cranes and the tower crews are getting faster but are somewhat bound by the month cure time on the concrete."

"What about security?" Dan asked.

"Minor things mostly. Something small stolen here and there. No big threats. Just like Jans up in Honduras, I have a travelling circus behind us complete with everything a man could want."

"No gang or heavy criminal activity?" Sam asked.

"Not really. A slight incident here or there with drugs, but all and all a pretty good bunch of people I have to say. They like to drink on Saturday nights a bit too much, but who doesn't?"

They all chuckled at the comment. Henry arranged for two of his trucks to be washed and ready for their visit. He took them down the road to view the different stages of construction. They watched the men working high above them welding the towers together, the pumper truck pumping gallon upon gallon of concrete into the base for a new tower and the road crews knocking down trees and cutting roads with bulldozers for the trucks to follow. They went further ahead to where a temporary bridge was being built to get the trucks across a small river. It was an impressive operation. It was even more impressive that there were three other identical operations underway at the same time.

Chapter II

A black Mercedes sedan followed by a black Land Rover stopped in front of the Presidential Palace. Two security guards exited the Rover, checked the surroundings and then one opened the back door of the sedan. Gabriel Perez walked briskly towards the front doors of the palace with his bodyguard in tow. Once inside, he went to the security window and withdrew his gold-plated Desert Eagle from its shoulder holster. He casually handed it across the threshold to the security officer without saying a word. The security officer held it as he would a newborn. Dropping the pistol of the most powerful drug lord in Nicaragua was not something he wanted to do. El Tigre, as Perez was known, held a reputation of a man with a violent temper. The guard gently placed the gaudy pistol on the desk and dialed the phone.

Ernesto Ruiz, the President's chief of staff appeared nearly instantly beside the drug lord.

"Buenos Dios, Senor Perez. Please follow me. As always, your man must stay here."

President Beto Duran rose to meet his old friend as he entered the office with Ruiz closing the door behind him.

"Como Esta, Mi Amigo?" The President said.

"I am troubled by your pet project," El Tigre said.

"Please, tell me."

"You came to me and said you were going to partner with a Hong Kong company to build a power plant and you had given them twenty-five miles of land south of Honduras as part of the deal. That is nothing unusual for a deal with the Chinese, but you also asked me to discontinue the routes we use to transport our product into Eastern Honduras and up to Belize and Mexico. I agreed for the betterment of you and your pet project, but the American DEA seems to know we have abandoned the eastern routes and they are hitting us hard in the west. I've lost millions of dollars in merchandise over the last year. I have had enough. I am resuming transporting through my eastern routes."

President Duran sat forward in his chair.

"You would cross me?"

"The deal is not as you said. These are not Chinese people. These are gringos. Gringos from Africa that speak that funny language. These African Gringos have taken more than the twenty-five miles you granted them. I have lost production in that part of the country. The farmers are gone. Poof! Disappeared a year ago!"

"What do you mean they have taken more land than was granted them?"

"I mean I have already started using my eastern routes. I sent trucks at first and they were intercepted at roadblocks well outside the twenty-five mile grant."

"Did they take your merchandise?"

"No. They simply turned the trucks around."

President Duran leaned back in his chair contemplating.

"Now we transport our couriers near the roadblocks by truck and then set them on different footpaths leading to Honduras. The problem is these African gringos have been capturing my couriers and imprisoning them," the drug lord declared.

"For how long?"

"Two days, at which time they release them, return their merchandise and send them back to me."

"So, you have lost nothing?"

"That is not the point! I need my eastern trade routes reopened. The DEA has me in a box in the west. My visit is a courtesy to you to tell you our deal is off!"

"You have already violated our agreement by sending your people through that area without telling me!"

"Let us not forget your large stipend my cartel pays you each month."

President Duran's nostrils flared at the statement.

"Let us also not forget you exist with my protection. My protection from the Americans and my protection from prosecution here," the president said calmly. He was not about to be pushed around by a man who operated his illegal business with impunity within his country's borders.

The two stared at each other with soulless eyes. Both were sociopaths. Both were killers. Both wondered if they really tangled, if they pushed all of their chips into the middle, who would come out on top. Thus, neither was willing to show weakness. President Duran offered a de-escalation.

"The ARC people have complained about you as well. I will talk with them and see if they will allow your shipments to proceed."

"They must. The Hondurans give the Americans whatever they want in exchange for their financial assistance. The US Navy is in the Pacific and the Coast Guard is in the Gulf looking for my boats and submarines. The damn DEA and CIA are everywhere looking for my planes. My product must go by land."

The President pushed a button under his desk. The meeting was over. He said he would be in touch.

The Presidential helicopter violently beat the air around the Santa Maria into submission. It was old and Russian, Soviet to be more precise. It had two huge engine air intakes that looked like ugly nostrils poised above a cyclopic crystal eye that was its bulbous glass cockpit. It was painted blue on top and yellow below and part of the skin looked as if someone used a sledgehammer to conform it to shape. Sam offered to send one of ARC's sleek Eurocopters when Isabella's chief of staff called the day before saying the president and vice president would be coming today, but they refused. As a result, Morne had the helicopters moved to the airport in Honduras as not to outshine the old Soviet egg beater.

The reception was as grand as the ship could muster. There was red carpet leading from the helipad down the steps and a crowd of a hundred onlookers dressed in their Sunday finest waiving small Nicaraguan flags clapped incessantly as the president and vice president exited the helicopter. El Presidente managed a small smile and a slight wave, while his wife glowed in appreciation of the supporters. Beto Duran did not like seeing three shiploads of Anglos docked on the coast of his country, but he knew he needed them. He had made deals with the Chinese and the Russians to develop the country only to have them take the money and fail to deliver. *The damn Chinese had taken more land than these gringos and he had little to show for it. They were the newest robber barons of the third world*, he thought. Certainly, his personal assets were greater due to the Chinese contributions, but there were no tangible results for the people. There certainly was no grand legacy project bearing his name as a testament to his stewardship of the people and the revolution.

Isabella, however, was more practical. She knew these people were bringing badly needed infrastructure to the country and it would bring the population into the twenty-first century. While she knew her husband wanted them gone, she knew they would never leave, and she did not want them to go. A deal could be struck with these people and honored. She was much younger than her husband and where he was looking at this project as his final monument to Sandinista rule, she was looking at it as a steppingstone. Afterall, she was the vice president. She had every intention of being elected president and walking among the other leaders of the world. The girl from the Managua barrio was not going to be denied the pinnacle of power.

"Welcome to the Santa Maria, EL Presidente," Morne said extending his hand.

"Gracias," he replied with his cold hooded eyes and a slight grin. He turned to Sam and extended his hand.

"Buenos Dias, Doctor Harrington," he said.

"Buenos Dias, El Presidente. May I present Ms. Katherine Visser."

Beto Duran took Katherine's hand and raised it to his mouth. The old revolutionary paused, smelling her sweet perfume as he stared into her blue eyes. With tenderness, he brought her fingers to his lips. Katherine, playing her part, blinked long as if entranced by his charm and flashed her million-dollar smile. Inside her stomach reeled from the kiss of the old lizard.

Morne greeted the vice president and passed her to Sam as he turned back to the president. Sam shook her hand by taking her fingers into his palm.

"Madam Vice President, may I present Ms. Katherine Visser," he said.

"Charmed," was all she said to Katherine.

"As am I, Vice President Duran," Katherine replied with as much sincerity as she could fake as they stared into each other's eyes.

Isabella gave her a knowing grin and took Sam by the arm to follow Morne and her husband, leaving Katherine to follow behind. Marcus Odendaal joined Katherine in the procession. She gave him a look letting him know her Austrian ire was enflamed. The big farmer just winked at her, and it tamped down the flames. She took him by the arm, and they followed. The remainder of the President's party followed them off the ship. There was a procession of trucks for the grand tour when they exited the ship. Each was idling with the air conditioning running inside. President Duran's chief of staff took the front seat as Morne and the President sat in the rear of the first truck. Sam and Isabella were in the back seat of the second truck with just the driver in the front. Katherine, Marcus, and Jayden took the third truck. Johannes and Ansel opted to skip the meeting as there was no point in overwhelming the Nicaraguans with too many ARC executives.

The tour went directly to the nuclear power plant under construction. As they climbed the road leading up the escarpment, they passed a large wooden sign that read *El Presidente Beto Duran plana de energía nuclear*. Morne noticed the smile on the President's lips. The sign had only been installed that morning, but it seemed to serve its purpose. Morne made small talk with the President as they drove. His chief of staff translated everything. When the trucks came to a stop, they were in the shadow of a mammoth nuclear reactor's cooling tower with its slightly exaggerated hourglass design.

"Magnífico," the president said as he stepped onto another red carpet that led into the inner sanctum of the power plant. Isabella was equally impressed. They saw the tower when they flew in, but it was so much bigger in person. Again, Isabella took Sam by the arm, and they followed behind the President and Morne as they began their tour of the site. Everywhere men and women were working diligently constructing the future of the country. It was a marvel to behold and even the president was overcome with the scope of the project and what it meant. After the tour of the nuclear plant, they went to the border with Honduras and looked at the new bridge being built between the two countries. Sam offered to show them the airport, but the President declined saying he could not enter Honduras without letting his friend President Orlando Rodriguez know he was coming. Sam found that humorous as Rodriguez visited two months ago and rode across the bridge to see the nuclear plant without a word. He wondered if the President was afraid the Americans might be waiting on the other side. The tour continued to where the town was beginning to be laid out. The roads were under construction and the 3-D concrete building printer was standing by. As soon as the various building foundations were laid, the 3-D printer would begin printing a building a day from structural hempcrete. They told the visitors this is where the power plant workers would live in the future. Morne explained how the buildings would be hurricane proof, rot proof and bug proof because of the characteristics of the hempcrete. As Ernesto Ruiz translated, Beto Duran realized the town would literally expand by the day like a virus replicating in a petri dish.

The tour finished back at the ships and continued with a briefing in the boardroom aboard the Santa Maria. Morne showed a map of the path of the towers and how things were progressing. He showed them a master blueprint for the town that was to be built for the workers. The main street was named after the President and the main cross street for Isabella. Marcus told them about building the food infrastructure to feed the workers and their families. The president was impressed, and he recognized they were doing a great job. But then, he knew that before he even saw the power plant. The cattle they passed were fat, their crops looked healthy and their workers on the ship were big and strong. Part of him hated them for how easy they made it look, but then he remembered they were investing the equivalent of Nicaragua's entire GDP on this one project. Anyone could be successful with that kind of money, he told himself. The President asked for an audience with just Sam and Morne. Everyone departed except for Isabella and Ernesto Ruiz.

"We have a problem that needs to be addressed," Ernesto translated for El Presidente.

"What is that?" Sam asked.

"The cartels have been inconvenienced by our project."

Sam looked at Isabella. She looked to her husband.

"I don't see how that is our problem." Morne chimed.

"They are a vital part of the economy of Nicaragua, Señor. We have to accommodate them," Ernesto repeated.

"What do they want?" Sam asked.

"They want to transport their merchandise through this area."

"No," Sam said.

"No? You dare say no the President?" The chief of staff asked without being prompted by El Presidente.

"We had a deal. This land belongs to ARC for us to establish a working power plant and keep the area secure. We cannot have outsiders transporting drugs and who knows what else through here. It will not be safe for our people or the power plant. We must decline I am afraid," Morne offered.

"This is not a request. You will allow them to traverse this area and cross into Honduras," Ernesto translated.

"I'm afraid we cannot do that, Sir." Sam said looking at the old rebel rather than his proxy.

Duran listened to his translator and then spoke.

"I will make it safe for you," the president said.

"How?" Asked Morne.

"I will have the army escort them through this area. The army cannot cross the bridge into Honduras however, so you will have to manage them on the other side."

"I don't like this," Sam said glancing at Isabella, but she offered no sympathy. She and the President discussed the plan before they arrived. She had pled ARC's case to no avail and ultimately it was her that offered the compromise of the army escorting the drug smugglers.

"You don't have to like it, but you will accommodate this request. The President says he will be more than happy to station the army here permanently if you are concerned about your safety," Ernesto replied.

"No. We will accommodate your request," Morne said.

CHAPTER III

After living in the warm embrace of tropical Nicaragua, the biting chill of a wintery Washington D.C. was unpleasant for Sam and Dan. The damp cold seeped into their bones as the wind scoured any exposed skin even on the shortest of walks. They were in Crystal City to meet a CIA friend of Dan's who'd transitioned to the DEA.

"What do you say, Boogie Man?" Jay Nobel said as he stuck out his hand.

"I say it is good to see a brother again," Dan said as he grabbed Jay's hand and pulled him close. "I'd like to introduce you to Sam Harrington."

"Nice to meet you, Sam. Any friend of Dan's lacks the ability to steer clear of the morally bankrupt, so I think you and I will get along fine."

Sam could not help but laugh and shook the man's hand. They grabbed a booth out of the way in the restaurant they were meeting in for some privacy.

"So, you got problems with the cartels down in Nicaragua, eh?" Jay asked.

"We do, and they are about to get worse. We need some intel on these guys," Sam said.

Jay pulled some papers out of his jacket pocket and tossed them on the table.

"You guys are dealing with the Azteca cartel, one of the biggest cocaine cartels in Latin America. The fact you have not had a more serious encounter this far is amazing. The CIA has a source in the Presidential offices. Duran told Gabriel Perez, AKA El Tigre, to leave you guys alone and to only transport his goods through the west. And, we have been making hay with that information ever since. We doubled down on the western side of Central America, and we have been hitting these guys hard. We've intercepted a half dozen planes, twice as many boats and a bunch of vehicles. Hell, we even captured a homemade submarine they were using."

"They must be hurting," Dan said.

"They are. We've taken millions of dollars worth of product from them."

"Why do they call him El Tigre?" Sam asked.

"Guy loves tigers. He even has a few at his main house."

"Where's that?" Dan asked.

"In the southern part of Nicaragua in the Ungoverned Zone. It is a great big hacienda sitting in a remote valley. There are no roads. The only way in is by air."

"Sounds like Afghanistan," Dan replied.

"I think that is where he got the idea. Nobody is going to approach his house, at least not in a vehicle. It is either a two-day hump through some tough terrain to get in there, or you have to drop in from the sky. Which is pretty smart, because the Nicaraguans can't mount an aerial assault and neither can his competitors. But it does mean if someone is going to come take you out, it is probably Dev Gru and at that point you are just screwed."

Dan chuckled. Dev Gru, short for Development Group, was the new identity Seal Team Six was wearing. It was an observation of the intel community that if you wanted intelligence gathered, especially if you wanted a target alive, you sent in the Army's Delta Force. If you didn't really care if anyone lived, you sent in the SEALs. That reputation is why the Jedi of Dev Gru got the Bin Laden assignment and Delta got Al Bahgdadi of ISIS.

"What else is in that valley?" Sam asked.

"I put some aerials in your stack of papers. One of their biggest cocaine labs is at that location. It sits right on the runway, not far from the hacienda. There is also some housing on site for factory workers and for his guards."

"On a scale of one to ten, how dangerous is this guy?" Dan asked.

"Thirty-five," Jay said. "The guy is a complete psychopath. We've been told by more than one of his couriers we caught that he feeds disloyal workers to his tigers. Maybe it is a legend, but they all believe it. He's not Pablo Escabar, but he wants to be. He just hasn't had to be, yet. He has President Duran in his pocket, so he has state-level protection at least until Duran dies. No need to kill cops when they don't even bother to harass you or your couriers. He has made an example of some of the gang members in Central America who tried to screw him, and he has killed a few journalists. One guy went missing and when somebody checked his house, all they found were his hands sitting on his computer's keyboard like they were typing. On the screen it just said *I never should have written anything bad about El Tigre.*"

"Great." Sam said.

"Even his insiders fear him. It is rumored if you screw up, he either feeds you to one of his tigers or marks you in some way to let the world know he owns you."

"How much manpower does he have?" Dan asked.

"As much as he needs for ten dollars a day, and he is a billionaire," Jay replied.

Sam's Citation X touched down gently on Katherine's new runway and turned towards the staging area where the planes were kept while the hangers and the terminal were being built. Katherine was waiting outside her pickup. Her blonde hair was in a ponytail, and she was wearing skin tight riding pants, knee high riding boots and a white cotton blouse unbuttoned enough to send Sam the message that she missed him. Sam's smile mirrored hers as he descended the steps. Her message was received and understood.

"You look amazing," he said before he kissed her.

"You look good yourself," she replied batting her eyes as they broke.

"I'm sorry I'm late. Had to drop Dan in Managua."

"No problem. Why?" She asked.

"He had some… unfinished business…at the bank."

"I see. And does this business have a name?"

"I'm sure she does. Probably a very pretty name by the looks of her."

He tossed his bag into the back of her truck. A longer reunion would have to wait. They would give the pilots a lift to the Santa Maria and then he had to meet with Morne to debrief what he found out in D.C.

The Board of Directors sat around the long table in the executive meeting room. Admiral Sharpe was in attendance. He and Dan were not officially members of the board, but their opinions were highly valued. Morne invited Admiral Sharpe to attend even though Dan was in Managua on what Sam said was a business matter. Tradition shifted since the Santa Maria arrived in Central America and Morne no longer sat at the head of the table, but rather he and Sam sat next to each other in the middle. Sam reported what he and Dan discovered in their conversations with Jay Nobel. There were grim faces all around. Nobody wanted to deal with the cartel, but at the same time, few were really afraid of Gabriel Perez while sitting on the Santa Maria. Afterall, they had a hundred trained mercenaries and over two thousand fit male construction workers all of whom were required to participate in rudimentary military training and drilled twice a month. The Israelis had a vested stake in the operation and Mossad's liaison to ARC supplied several shipping containers full of weapons for the defense of the project. Everyone at the table was convinced they could handle anything the cartels could throw at them militarily.

"So, what do we do about the drug shipments?" Ansel Van Dyk asked.

"We let them go through."

Sam's lips drew tight and a frown formed on his face.

"If we don't let them through, we will have the Nicaraguan army in here. We will also have to fight the cartel. While I don't like it either, we must play the part of the willing participant for now," Morne said as he turned sideways to look at Sam.

"I understand it is the only option, but it's a weak move. Capitulating to either Duran or Perez is a losing deal. They won't be happy for long. They will want to test and see how far they can go."

Big Marcus Odendaal nodded in agreement.

"Quite Right," Admiral Sharpe added.

"We are going to play the hand we have been dealt and buy ourselves time to finish our construction. Then, we will make our stand. With more men and more leverage."

"How do we deal with the fact the army cannot cross the bridge? We can't ask the Honduran army to escort drug dealers," Sam pushed back.

"We will leave that to Dan and his men," Morne said.

Ariela Sade took a taxi from work to the Intercontinental Hotel where Dan was staying. She saw Dan leaning against a pillar in the lobby as soon as she entered. He was the epitome of cool. Handsome in a rugged way, his smile did a poor job of concealing the air of danger ever present in his aura. Still, it was a nice smile, she decided.

"Buenos noches, Dan."

"Hello to you, too. I thought we might have a drink at the bar and then the concierge has a car to take us to a nice restaurant."

The bar was pleasant and Ariela ordered a martini while Dan had a whiskey.

"Are you from Managua?" Dan asked.

"Si. I was raised here. My father was a professor at the University. He passed away, but I still have my mother and sister."

"Are you close?"

"Si. My mother is a saint. My sister is another matter. She is rebellious, but she has a good heart."

"Where is the fun in not being a little rebellious?"

"I am afraid she will get herself in trouble. She likes to associate with dangerous men."

"And you don't?" He said with a cocked eyebrow.

"I…admit there is sometimes an attraction, but a woman must be careful."

She turned her head ever so slightly and made direct eye contact.

"How careful?"

"Very careful. She mustn't let her heart over-rule her head."

She tapped her index finger on his chin then gave him a small kiss.

Dinner was romantic in a quiet corner of a small restaurant with tender steaks and excellent wine. When they returned to the Intercontinental, Dan asked her if she would like to see his room, but she declined. She told him if he would stay another day, she would like to see him again tomorrow. He ended up staying three more days and each night he took Ariela somewhere different. They learned much about each other and on the third night he found out what kind of lover she was, and it energized him like few had before. As for her, she found him insatiable, giving at times and demanding at others. They were a matched set and they fed off each other. On the third day, he was sorry to be leaving her and she was sad to see him go, but they vowed this was not a one-time thing. It was too good, and an absence was only going to make it more intense when they reunited.

Coming down the dirt road towards the ARC lands was a convoy. In the front was a Jeep flagged with the Nicaraguan colors and the eagle pennant of a colonel. The colonel rode shotgun in the Jeep with a machine gunner behind him. Following the Jeep were three covered trucks and bringing up the rear was a truck full of Nicaraguan soldiers.

As they approached, Johannes nudged Sam in the ribs.

"Look, they've got a Dushka! That brings back some memories, eh?"

"Not good ones," Sam replied as he felt the scar on his bicep start to involuntarily throb at the sight of the DShK machine gun.

The colonel told his driver to stop. He was in full regalia with medals and merits from the revolution and other awards from the army. He approached Sam, Johannes and Dan with an air of dignity. He stood at attention but did not offer a hand.

"Estoy Coronel Alejandro Vasquez."

"Pleasure to meet you, Colonel. Sam Harrington, Johannes Kohlar and Dan Weston,"

"The pleasure is mine, Doctor Harrington," he responded in English.

"We appreciate you being here, Colonel. If the convoy would just follow these two pickups, our other trucks will follow behind. When we get to the bridge, you and your men follow me in the maroon pickup. The other trucks will follow the white pickup over the bridge into Honduras. We have a rest area designed where you can wait for the convoy to return and escort it back through ARC property."

As Sam was explaining, a man exited one of the drug runner's trucks and approached from behind the colonel.

"Who are you?" Dan asked as he stepped forward and put himself between the man and Sam.

"Me? Who am I?"

Dan said nothing.

"I am the one in charge of those trucks, and I want to hear the plan."

"The plan is you stay in line. When we get to the bridge, you follow that white pickup and if you vary from the plan, there is going to be a problem. Comprende?" Dan said with a voice as sharp as a razor.

"All is understood," the colonel answered for him.

Johannes led in his white pickup with Sam following. The colonel and the rest of the convoy passed Dan. Dan had four big trucks full of armed men on the side of the road. He got into the first one and they brought up the rear. Dan picked the radio up off the dash and keyed it. Suddenly a sleek Eurocopter appeared overhead. It flew circles around the convoy looking mostly behind, but also ahead as they traversed the outer limits of ARC territory. The admiral was on standby with a quick reaction force in case anything went wrong, but the show of force was enough to send the appropriate message to the drug smugglers and the military.

Everything went smoothly and at the bridge the two army vehicles peeled out of the convoy as the drug smugglers crossed the bridge behind Johannes. The drug smugglers were escorted into Honduras past the edge of the ARC owned properties and allowed to proceed on their way.

Sam led the two army vehicles down to an area of the beach that overlooked the mouth of the Coco River. ARC arranged for two open wall tents to be erected with seating and refreshments laid out for the military personnel. Here they would wait for a few hours until the smugglers returned from exchanging their drugs for cash. A truck full of cash would be a tempting target for bandits, gangs, or even an enterprising army officer, but the colonel knew where his bread was buttered. Sure, he would take a couple of stacks of US dollars for his trouble, but El Presidente personally selected him for this mission. He was a loyal man, and he would do his duty to see the cartel trucks back safely into Nicaragua. If this initial run was a success, he would probably appoint an equally loyal major to handle these duties. If he was offered more than a couple of stacks, he might keep the detail for himself.

Chapter IV

The setting sun saying its last goodbyes over the western horizon concluded a stressful day. The cartel smuggling operation cost ARC a precious day's construction. Morne shut down operations and devised a surreptitious route to keep the smugglers away from the reactor and more importantly away from the cruise ships. Now that the event was over, the third shift was going to work. He was reading through his notes and rubbing his forehead as Sam approached.

"It went well".

"Yes. Thanks to you, Johannes and Dan."

"You know we just opened pandora's box."

"What choice did we have?"

Sam's phone buzzed with a text. It was from the tool manager. He dialed back.

"Doctor Harrington, I was out fetching a part and some men, boys really, came along and gave Patson some trouble. I got back before it got too out of hand, but I am afraid things escalated."

"What do you mean?"

"This one boy, Adolf, is a troublemaker. He is always giving Patson a hard time and Patson has always handled himself well, but …"

"But what?"

"The boy did not want the shoddy tools, and he reached across the counter and grabbed Patson. Patson took ahold of his shirt and then grabbed him by his big nose with a pair of pliers."

Sam was listening as his grin began to creep up the corners of his mouth.

"Is that it?"

"No, Sir. The boy challenged Patson to the ring. Patson accepted."

"I see. How old is this young man?"

"Maybe nineteen, but he is tall and strong."

"Text me this Adolf's full name. I will see Patson when he gets off work. Make sure you provide him proper guidance for the workplace."

Patson softly opened the door to Sam's lodgings. Sam was seated in a plush chair reading his e-mails on his tablet.

"I hear you got into some trouble today."

"Yes, Sir," Patson replied as he began to tell the tale.

"He challenged you to a fight in the ring on Sunday?"

"Yes, Sir. And I accepted."

"Do you want me to put an end to it?"

"No, Sir. I will fight him."

"I understand he is bigger and older than you."

"He is, but he has a weakness."

"What is that?"

"His big nose will still be very sore on Sunday," Patson said with a toothy smile.

Sam could not help but smile back.

"Dan is waiting for you in the gymnasium. Go now."

Patson watched in awe as he approached the corner of the gym where Dan was assaulting the heavy bag. He had never seen someone land so many punches in such a fast manner. Dan stopped as he sensed Patson nearing. Patson also stopped because when Dan turned, his face was not the face of the man he knew. His jaw was tight, his mouth formed an evil frown and his eyes burrowed holes into Patson as beads of sweat dripped from his temples.

Dan took Patson over to a table. He taped his hands and wrists and put gloves on him. They walked to the middle of the gym floor.

"Show me what you got."

Patson threw a jab, which Dan sidestepped. Left hook, right cross, left hook. All swishes. Then Dan punched Patson in the face hard enough to get his attention. Patson retaliated. Right hook, left jab, right jab. All fast, but all misses. Again, Dan struck him. A punch to the face followed by punches to the ribs and stomach, but this time Patson struck a solid blow to Dan's face.

"Better. Get your head in the fight."

After the sparring match, Dan sat down with Patson.

I can't make you any stronger in the next few days, but we can improve your technique. Besides, all of that rugby has made you strong enough. You are fast and you have good stamina. Most people can't survive a one-minute fight to save their own lives. You are going to have to go six minutes over three rounds. To do that, you must move quickly and land punches. Hard punches and lots of them, but you can't let the bigger man tie you up, he will wear you down with body blows."

"I will do what you say."

"I know you will. The other thing we must do is find the demon inside you and release it."

"There is a demon inside me?"

"Every man has a demon inside, and you are a man now."

Patson knew it was true. He'd seen Dan's demon when he walked in. He hoped to never be on the wrong side of it.

Dan's phone buzzed as Patson left. It was an incoming video chat from Ariela. He accepted and her pretty face with her pouty lips filled the screen.

"Hola, Dan," she said with a smile that instantly brought one to Dan's face.

"Hola, Sweetheart. How are you?"

"I am good, but I miss you."

"I miss you too. What is going on in Managua?"

"Just work and all of the nonsense. More protests today. The policia shot some demonstrators, which just made things worse. I am worried about my sister, Zanita. She is caught up in it all and hanging out with the wrong people."

"Are you safe?"

"Jes. I am safe. Pull the phone back let me see you."

Dan extended the phone to arms-length. Ariela could see his taught muscles expanded and bulging from the workout. His shirt was sweated through and his hair was wet.

"Sorry, I've been working out. Giving a lesson so to speak."

"You look sexy. So tough and rugged," she said as she bit her lip. "Do you think you can come to Managua soon?"

"Patson has gotten himself into a scrape and is going to box on Sunday, so not this week."

"Patson is the boy, no? I know you are fond of him."

"I am and I can't leave, but what if you came here?"

"How?"

"I'll have a helicopter pick you up and fly you out. When can you get off work?"

The wait staff finished clearing the table in Katherine's dining room and placed a serving of lemon iced cake with fresh berries in front of each person. It was an intimate affair with just two couples, Katherine and Sam accompanied by Dan and Ariela. Sam's attention turned to Dan as the women chatted. Polar opposites in appearance and life experience, they none the less seemed to be getting along famously. Where Katherine was blonde, blue eyed and fair skinned with fine features, Ariela sported long flowing black hair, tan skin, pouty lips, and high cheek bones. Both came from middle income families in their respective countries, and both used their brains and looks to advance themselves. Katherine came from a world of greater opportunity and thus was far more experienced and vastly wealthy. She was also more than a decade older, but they seemed to be well paired.

"How is Patson going to do tomorrow?" Sam asked Dan discreetly.

"We'll see."

"I have some advice for you to pass along to him."

"You are his adopted daddy, why don't you tell him?"

"Better this comes from you. Adolph drops his left hand when he fights. Also, his ribs will be a little sore tomorrow on the left side."

"What?"

"Let's just say there may have been an altercation this afternoon between Adolph and someone who wanted to get off the third shift."

The two men grinned at each other.

"You were never going to let this be a fair fight, were you?"

"It would be one thing if this was a ranked sporting event, but this Adolph is older, bigger and a bully. I'm going to give Patson every edge I can. Is he ready?"

"We will see tomorrow. He is strong, but what's more he is fast and coordinated. He can take a punch, but I too checked out the opponent and he could do some damage. Maybe more than Patson can stand."

By order of the company, there was no work on Sunday. Most attended church services in the mornings followed by lunch and sporting events in the afternoon. Typically, the events were rugby or cricket followed by boxing in the evenings. Boxing was big amongst the male population. Betting, although officially frowned upon, was everyone's chance to participate. In the afternoon, Morne and his wife along with Johannes and Anna accompanied Sam and Katherine and Dan and Ariela to the cricket match. It was the Niña team verses the Pinta team. Morne and Johannes explained the rules to the non-South Africans as they looked on in bewilderment but were very pleased when they got excited with the crowd when the ball was hit.

After dinner, Morne collected Anna, Katherine and Ariela and escorted them to the boxing matches. Anna and Katherine did not usually attend the matches, but since Patson was fighting, they felt they should. Anna was his adopted mother, and she was worried sick about the fight. Katherine considered herself also an adopted mother of sorts and she too was worried. Sam, Dan and Johannes were with Patson. All three were wound tight in anticipation of the upcoming fight. Patson was remarkably calm. The match was set as the third fight of the night. They kept Patson behind the scenes to avoid distractions. Johannes kept checking the fights and when it was time, informed everyone.

Sam walked out first, serious, and steely-eyed. If anyone was going to harass Patson, they were going to have to get through him. Patson walked behind followed by Johannes and Dan. Sam was surprised by the cheers as Patson was made visible to the crowd. Patson was more so as he and Sam entered the ring. Many spectators were chanting his name.

Adolph approached from the other side with a companion. He was wearing shorts and a sweatshirt. His gloves were under his arm and Sam noticed his hands were not taped. Then he noticed the man's next to him were.

Sam approached and Patson followed.

"Why are your hands not taped?"

"I'm feeling a little under the weather, Boss. I am using my right to name a proxy for the fight."

"Nonsense. You forfeit if you do not fight."

"No Sir. I have the right. I am using it."

The crowd heard the statement and booed. Sam looked at Adolph's friend. He was bigger and stronger than Adolph. He was six inches taller than Patson and his muscles were hard and well developed. Patson was a big boy, but this was a man. A hard man.

"Patson is not going to fight this man. You forfeit if you don't fight," Sam declared over the noise of the crowd.

"I will fight him," Patson declared.

Sam turned towards his adopted son as the crowd went wild.

"I don't like this."

"It will be OK, Father."

Sam turned back to Adolph and his proxy.

"Win, lose or draw, your problems with Patson stop today."

"Yes, Sir," the bully smiled.

Anna and Katherine held onto each other as the bell rang. Sam, Johannes and Dan were barking commands to Patson. The bigger man approached and Patson met him mid-ring. The man threw jabs, but Patson backed away first right and then left. The big man advanced with more punches that did not connect. Patson knew the man was trying to drive him into the corner, against the ropes where he could not escape an endless array of body blows. Another unsuccessful jab and a wild swing were thrown at Patson before he lashed out with a haymaker upside the big man's head then retreated behind the man. The crowd went wild.

The man spun around and threw a combination, but Patson danced fluidly away. The man advanced. Another miss, and Patson landed a hard right into the man's eye and floated out of reach. The man spun towards him again and lashed out. Patson threw a left, but the man had learned. He rushed forward and landed a body blow to Patson which sent him reeling backwards. The man followed. He landed a blow to the head, the left ribs and the right ribs. Patson snuck in an upper cut but could not get free before more punches rained down on him. Protecting his face and ribs as best he could, he hunkered down for more punishment as he tried to move to the side. He escaped, but he was hurting. He'd been hit in fights before and taken some bad shots in rugby, but nothing like the blows delivered by this man. The noise of the crowd was a nonsensical storm, but over it he could hear Dan's instructions. "Hit and run. Hit and run."

He went back at the bigger man and landed a right to the eye and an upper cut. He managed to evade the counterattack. He went back in for another attack on the man's left eye but got caught by a blow to the shoulder on his way out. The bell rang and they retreated to their corners.

"How are you, Son?"

"He is strong. I can't tell if I am even hurting him."

Dan got up in the boy's face.

"You are hurting him, but you must keep moving. He will tire out. Hit and move, Hit and move. You aren't going to knock him out. You gotta win on the decision."

The bell sounded and Johannes put Patson's mouthpiece back in. The second round started like the first. For the first half-minute, Patson landed some hits, and the bigger man missed a lot, but it was mostly a ploy. The bigger man was watching and waiting for his chance and when Patson moved in to take an opportunistic shot, he saw it. He ducked his head, got low and started chopping away at Patson's ribs. Heavy blow after heavy blow landed. Patson was sliding towards the ropes as the bigger man just kept pounding him. When Patson tried to strike back, he left himself unprotected and the man focused his strength on the undefended ribs. Patson could hear Sam, Dan and Johannes screaming instructions, but he could not make out the words over the pain. He was doing his best to keep his gloves up and protect himself, but he was sinking. Then the man caught him in the head with an elbow, the oldest and dirtiest trick in boxing. He saw stars behind his eyes and felt the grip of desperation tightening in his bowels. A heavy unprotected blow dropped him to his knees.

The big man backed off as the referee came between them. Patson was on all fours. The referee was counting. He raised his head and looked towards his corner. He did not look at his two adopted fathers, but looked at Dan whose face sported the sinister frown he saw in the gym. Something inside him felt like an electric jolt to his heart. Ignoring the pain, he jumped to his feet, slid past the referee, and punched the bigger man in the face. He hit him hard three times before the man realized what was happening. The man's natural instinct was to protect himself, but as he did, Patson savaged his head. He swung a powerful arm at Patson, who ducked under it and landed two blows into his ribs. He rushed forward, but Patson would not let himself be pushed into the ropes again. He moved quickly and landed two more headshots. The crowd was in a frenzy as the bell rang.

As Patson approached his corner, he wore a face none of the three men had ever seen before, but all recognized from combat. In the stands, Katherine and Anna were aghast at the punishment the boy had taken. Every hollow thud of the big man's gloves landing upon Patson's body reverberated through their hearts. Ariela was impressed with the boy and how Dan coached him. She was as excited as the crowd. Johannes gave Patson a little water while Dan whispered something in his ear. When the bell rang, Patson looked at Sam who simply stared him in the eyes and nodded as he swelled with pride for the boy. Win or lose, this was a big moment in Patson's life.

The final round started with the big man hitting Patson so hard, he lost his footing and went down. *"Best to let the boy know who is in charge here,"* he thought as he sucked as much air though his mouth as he could. The referee never made it to Patson before he was back up and coming at his opponent. Two more heavy punches were thrown, and both avoided. Patson lashed back. He struck the man over and over, landing punches and moving back out of range. The man had slowed. He tried to press his weight advantage, but Patson was too quick. He was a construction worker, not a professional fighter and the first three punches were most of what he had left. Patson was used to running for an hour on the rugby field back home. He moved quickly and worked to find the openings. He took a few glancing shots, but nothing like the first punch of the round. Then, he opened the man's left eye. Patson saw the red on his glove when he drew it back. The crowd saw it too and grew louder. The rules were that the ref could not stop the fight unless the fighter or his corner asked him. The bigger man waived off his corner.

He would not lose to this boy. Patson knew the man must protect his eye and leave other parts open. He took his shots where he could get them. The man was exhausted, but also angry at being cut. Like the bull who has been lanced through the lungs and was now taunted by the matador, he charged powerfully and without grace. The demon inside Patson repeatedly punished him for the recklessness. Finally, the bell sounded, and the crowd clapped for the brilliant fight fought.

The fighters returned to their corners. The man had his eye looked at while they waited on a decision. The referee called the fighters to the middle of the ring. Adolph accompanied his proxy. Sam, Johannes, and Dan accompanied Patson.

"In a two-one split decision, the fight goes to..." and the referee picked up the bigger man's arm. Patson had not been able to swing the votes after being knocked down twice. The crowd turned rowdy expressing their displeasure at the decision. Patson turned towards his entourage. He was about to say something when he felt his hand being grabbed. He turned back and it was Adolph lifting his arm in a symbol of victory. His opponent came over and lifted Patson's other arm. The crowd went wild.

CHAPTER V

The helicopter deposited Ariela at the Managua airport early Monday morning. Her weekend trip was wonderful and last night the passion with Dan lasted until early this morning. Dan showed her the three luxury ships, took her to the nuclear power plant and showed her the beautiful new bridge crossing the Coco river. Everyone was kind and accepting of her and she was shown every courtesy. She was convinced it was not just because she was with Dan, but rather the people were simply genuine and courteous to everyone.

She took a taxi home to get changed and drop off her bag before work. She was startled when she entered her apartment. Her sister was there with a man. A young man, but an outlaw at first appearance no less. Ariela hauled her younger sister into the bedroom and closed the door.

"Why do you have a man in my apartment? He looks like a criminal."

"According to the government anyone who opposes the Durans is a criminal."

"He is going to get you into trouble."

"He has protection."

"What does that mean?"

"Nevermind."

"You need to avoid him. I don't want to see him here again. I gave you a key so you could stay here if needed, not for you to bring someone like him here."

"I know, but your apartment is so nice, and we needed a place to be alone."

Ariela just sighed in frustration. Zanita was young and had her whole life ahead of her, but she had an unhealthy attraction for bad boys, and Ariela was afraid it was going to lead her to ruin. Zanita had no problem attracting men. She was pretty. Not as glamorous as Ariela, but pretty enough to open doors and do well if she applied herself.

"Where were you all weekend? With your boss, the banker?"

"No. I was with someone else."

"Really? Who?"

Ariela filled her baby sister in on the wonderful weekend she had with Dan while she quickly dressed and fixed her hair. Her sister listened wide-eyed like she did when they were children and Ariela would tell her about the world her older sister was allowed to explore.

"Get him out of here," Ariela said as she ran for the door.

Zanita and her boyfriend did not leave that morning. They lounged around until it was time to go to the bar. The Azteca bar was where they spent many evenings. It was a money laundering business for the Azteca Cartel and it was a fun place. A place to watch and be seen. The two most popular patrons were Carmen Aguilera and Vera Conde. Everyone there knew them, and they were the life of the party. They had big Instagram followings not only in Managua, but around the world. Every night they would be in the bar posting selfies and pictures in their low-cut shirts and pants so tight they appeared to be painted on. They were Zanita's heroes and she wanted to be just like them, but she also knew she needed to watch herself. They were the alpha females and would not take lightly to being challenged. They posted pictures of themselves holding pistols and straddling AK-47s. Carmen had an elaborate Aztec pyramid tattooed on her back with the name of the Azteca Cartel circling it. Vera had tattoos as well and loved to wear as little as possible to show them off. They had no problem stating they were part of the Azteca Cartel and bragging online about the cartel's accomplishments, real or embellished.

CHAPTER VI

S am's view this week was the ocean and he was watching the sun rise over the Gulf of Mexico with a hot cup of coffee. Looking east always made him think of Patson, who was back in boarding school in South Africa now. He missed him and wondered what he was up to today. There was a tone from his phone and his tablet lit up. It was a message from Dan. *Video Call with DEA 08:00* was all it said. Sam dreaded the thought of talking to the Drug Enforcement Agency of the United States. For three months ARC had allowed the transit of cocaine and God only knew what else through its territory. If the DEA was calling, it meant they knew what was happening.

Sam was in the conference room with Morne when Dan entered. They knew he was coming because they heard his whistling as he approached.

"You seem to be in fine spirits this morning," Morne said.

"I guess I am," he replied.

"Would that have anything to do with the fact Ariela is visiting this coming weekend?"

"I believe there is a direct correlation, Doctor Harrington."

"She is a lovely girl. Far too lovely for the likes of you," Morne piled on.

"Clearly something must be wrong with the poor woman if she is associating with a reprobate like Mr. Weston here," Sam added.

Dan offered each gentlemen a middle finger and then started logging into the video call. Internally he admitted he was happy Ariela was coming as he punched buttons. She had become a regular feature around ARC on the weekends and neither Sam nor Morne said a single word about Dan's use of the helicopter to bring her back and forth even though sometimes she was the only passenger. She and Katherine became fast friends and were a wicked team when it came to cards as couples or in the ladies only games. As a couple, Dan and Ariela accepted each other for who they were. Dan carried the baggage every warrior carries, and he had more than his share because he emersed himself in a violent world first for his country and later for money. Ariela carried the baggage of being a beautiful woman in a miserable country and all that women, beautiful or not, had to put up with to get ahead in such places.

When the call was over, the three men just looked at each other. They had just been put on notice by the United States Government. The DEA showed them video footage of one of the drug convoys being escorted through ARC territory. It had been taken by a Global Hawk, a drone the size of a 737 deployed by the DEA. Sam laid their cards on the table. He explained to the agents how they were essentially being blackmailed by the Nicaraguan government to allow passage of the convoy. The agents showed no sympathy. These were major drug shipments. They threatened all three with charges and reminded Sam and Dan they were American citizens subject to the full extent of American law. They threatened to have ARC's nuclear materials export permits reviewed, and in such, negated. Morne appealed to them to understand the predicament ARC was in working with an outlaw regime and being threatened by not only the regime, but the cartels. Again, they got no sympathy from the DEA agents, but they did get an agreement for another meeting.

Morne called a meeting of the Board of Directors that afternoon. He explained the situation to a grim-faced group.

"What power does the United States Government really have over us?" Marcus Odendaal asked.

"They can pull our nuclear export license for one and they could add us to the list of sanctioned enterprises in Nicaragua. The President of the United States has already named Nicaragua one of the axis' of evil along with Cuba, China, Iran and Russia. Sanctions would severely hamper anyone wanting to do business with us. It would be a devastating blow."

"And, any US Citizens can be charged under US law, so that is myself, Dan and some of the workers," Sam said as Katherine put her hand on his. "Worst case, they could do something drastic like use military action against us. That would be equivalent of when Reagan took out Noriega in Panama. It would be an invasion of a sovereign nation and it would involve US special forces. They would obviously be looking to round up the people in this room they know about, mainly Morne, myself, and Dan for extradition back to the United States."

"So, what do we do?" Ansel Van Dyk asked.

"We must determine how to manage the three big threats, the US, the Nicaraguans and the Cartels. We can't make everyone happy," Morne responded.

"Who is the biggest threat?" Jayden Hocks asked.

"I believe it is the Americans," Morne said. "If they sanction us, we will be unable to continue building the power plant and everything is lost. The Nicaraguans need us. If we fail, they fail. The cartels are the wildcards."

"What can we do?" Katherine queried.

"Dan and I are going to fly to D.C. and meet with the DEA," Sam said.

"Are you afraid you will be arrested?" Ansel asked.

"Not unless we really screw up."

Johannes pulled over on the side of the road in Honduras to allow the drug laden trucks to pass. The escort would end here. The lead cartel truck pulled up next to Johannes. The ruffian who led these convoy's name was Enrique. He looked at Johannes but did not say a word. Johannes stared back. Neither man showed weakness. Finally, Enrique motioned for the driver to continue. The cartel trucks passed, and Johannes turned around the ARC escort. They would set up on the road a hundred meters back and wait for the cartel trucks to return in four or five hours. The ARC helicopter stayed above the cartel trucks until they were a half hour down the road before it turned back to refuel. It would gas up and return to its overwatch in four hours.

Enrique was in a fine mood. Within two hours they would rendezvous with the Honduran gang they were to meet and transfer the product for cash. Millions of US dollars to be precise. They had done this trip now more than a dozen times and it had always gone like clockwork, but this was the largest load they had done to date. He had to add two additional trucks to carry the larger consignment of drugs. El Tigre trusted him to bring the load through and return with the money. El

Tigre also insisted on adding additional armed men. Men he knew were of the highest loyalty factor. Enrique was not insulted. The haul was enormous and the cash on the other end was enough to tempt any person. He also knew there was nowhere on Earth he could hide if he stole the money. El Tigre would have him tracked down, brought back, and fed to one of his tigers. A distant thumping roused him from his thoughts. He assumed it was the ARC helicopter returning. *"That is strange,"* he thought. It never followed them this far into Honduras. Also, the sound was different. He leaned out the window. He saw not the sleek ARC Eurocopter, but a US Blackhawk complete with door gunner.

"Más rapido!"

He screamed at the driver as the road took a bend, but the driver slammed on the breaks. Ahead of them the road was blocked by a troop transport and several cars. There were armed federal police spread out across the road. As the truck came to a halt, the jungle on both sides erupted with armed police emerging from the vegetation. The DEA and the Honduran Federal Police had set a trap. Enrique cursed the ARC people as he slammed his fists into the dash of the vehicle. He knew they sold him out. Then he thought of that damn tiger, the man-eater in the pit.

The cherry blossoms were bursting from the trees like pink cotton candy as the black Suburban passed carrying Sam and Dan towards their clandestine meeting. Dan's DEA buddy Jay Nobel brokered a meeting with a more senior agent on Dan's behalf. The meeting was to take place at the Old Ebbitt Grill. It was one of Sam's favorites. The bar was classic, the food was excellent and any place with African taxidermy over the bar was home for him. They found the DEA agents in the back in a booth.

"Good to see you again, buddy," Dan said to Jay.

"You too, this is Agent Hopkins."

They all shook hands as the waitress appeared and disappeared with drink orders. They exchanged small talk until she returned and then Sam laid everything out for the DEA.

"We are disgusted by the Nicaraguans forcing us to allow drug shipments to traverse the area they granted us, but they basically put a gun to our heads. They went back on their word they would keep the cartels out of our area."

"You made a deal with a bunch of commies, and you are surprised they went back on their word?"

"We are not naïve, Agent Hopkins. We thought we had this under control, but they basically gave us no choice."

"How so?"

"They said they would station the army on our lands if we did not agree and that the shipments would still continue."

"I see."

"We are essentially caught in the middle between the US, the Nicaraguans, and the cartels."

"That is unfortunate. What do you propose as a solution?"

"I think we would like to hear your thoughts first."

"My thoughts are this. You are US citizens assisting one of the most notorious drug cartels in the world smuggle truckloads of cocaine through Central America. Cocaine the Mexicans cut with Chinese fentanyl, which has caused the overdose deaths of over a hundred thousand US citizens in the last twelve months."

Dan looked at Jay with a steely glance. He looked away, disgusted by his superior's accusation.

"We don't want to be in this position. Do you have a suggestion how we get out of it?"

"Cooperate."

"How?"

"First, you tell us anytime there is a scheduled shipment. Second, you give us access to your airport for our helos and fixed wings and third, you give us access to your docks if the Coast Guard or Navy have need."

"There was a shipment earlier today. We will let you know when the next one is scheduled. Probably in two weeks. You can refuel at the airport as it is in Honduras. You can even use it to launch operations, but only if they are in Honduras. You cannot do anything in Nicaragua. We will take a ship into our docks only if it is in distress. But we have a small tanker and we will refuel the Coast Guard or Navy in International waters if they buy the fuel."

"If you allow us to install a radar sight at the airport to look into the ocean for boats and subs, you have a deal, Dr. Harrington. Jay, show them the video."

Sam nodded in agreement as Jay Nobel pulled out his tablet. He started a video showing areal footage of the cartel trucks being taken down on the road in Honduras.

"It is good you were forthcoming about the shipment today. That was an hour ago. We took down a massive shipment that came through your area. We have Federal Police in the trucks now completing the delivery to see if we can seize the cash at the meet point as well. It is already a great day for the DEA gentlemen, it may be our best in years before it is over."

Sam's blood ran cold watching the video. The cartels might blame ARC for the capture of their merchandise.

"Call Johannes," Sam told Dan with an icy tone.

Dan left the table to walk outside.

"We will have the legal agreement drafted for your execution," Hopkins said.

"We can't have something that falls under the Freedom of Information Act. The Nicaraguans will get a hold of it in a heartbeat. We will sign a sealed immunity agreement for all US citizens working for ARC in exchange for what you are asking."

"Done."

"One last thing. The deal has to include citizenship for my adopted son, he is South African."

"Easy. This administration is all about giving citizenship to anyone who wants it. I don't even have to say pretty please. Anything else?"

"If this starts to go bad, we may need some back up."

"Always willing to help out law abiding citizens in a foreign land."

Enrique's toes gripped the edge of the tiger pit. Below him a massive male tiger paced back and forth staring up at him with striped face and golden eyes. It roared loud enough to send the birds from their perches in the trees. Enrique felt the rumble in his chest. Somewhere in the deep recesses of his primal brain, the sound registered. The tiger took a deep breath through his nose taking in the scent of the man. He smelled no urine, but he did sense fear. He continued his pacing keeping his eyes on the man perched precariously above. Enrique could not back away because of the gold-plated Desert Eagle pressed to the back of his skull.

"Have you seen what El Diablo does to men who fail me?" Gabriel Perez asked.

It was a rhetorical question. Perez had good tigers his guards paraded around the house and even patrolled the property with, but this was the bad tiger. The man eater who could never be trusted outside its cage.

"You have failed me in grand fashion, Enrique. I think the tiger will be fed today."

"El jefe, Por Favor. We have been together for so long. There was nothing I could do. We were completely outgunned by the DEA and their Honduran lap dogs."

"You should have fought them anyway."

"It would have been pointless."

Enrique felt the Desert Eagle pushing him towards losing his balance on the edge. The great striped cat saw the movement and moved into position to receive his prize. Enrique saw the wetness of the cat's mouth as it panted softly and stared up at him. It roared again while locking eyes with him.

"Did you really pay to get me released just to feed me to this beast?"

The Desert Eagle pushed him farther. He was on the balls of his feet. His core was tight and pushing back against the steel digging into his skull. The tiger panted faster and seemed to be coiling to jump up and pull him into the pit. Suddenly, the gun was gone, and he fell backwards. He stumbled to catch his feet, but Perez knocked them out from underneath him and he landed on his back on the cement. He was now staring up at the barrel of the Desert Eagle. He could hear the tiger roaring with anger at being teased and denied live prey.

"I did not want you to die in a prison in Honduras. You are right, we have been through too much together, but you will not fail me again. Do you understand?"

"Si, El jefe. With my life, I swear this."

"On your life it is then. You will get the tattoo, no?"

"Si. Anything to show my loyalty."

Chapter VII

S am and Johannes pulled up to one of the two hangers ARC built on the side of the runway in Honduras. They were there to see Annon's latest idea, and they were extremely curious. Sam was a pilot himself and had a solid friendship with Annon. Annon was the bush pilot that flew him in and out of Mozambique on multiple safari trips. Annon was a happy Afrikaner with fair hair and a powerful build. He was always delighted to see Sam and he was eager to show off his new toys.

"Hello, Sam. How are you going?"

"What is that?" Johannes asked.

"It's a gyro-copter. Isn't she a beaut!"

"It looks like a little helicopter. Did you build it in the garage?"

"Same principle, a rotary wing, eh, but much safer."

"No way that thing is safer."

"Ah, but it is. The only power is the fan pushing the craft forward. Lift is obtained by the rotary blade turning around strictly from forward momentum."

"No way."

"Ja. If it loses power, it still has lift due to forward momentum. We turn the motors off all the time in practice. I can land on that runway with no power at all. But the best part is we can keep them in the air for around ten dollars per hour.

"Let's go for a ride," Sam said.

Sam was seated in tandem behind Annon. Johannes was in the other craft behind its pilot with a death grip on the bars in front of him. The fan prop behind Sam was roaring as the little two-stroke motor revved high enough to move the craft forward. The blades of the rotary wing above started to spin faster and faster as they moved down the runway. They felt themselves being pulled up as the blades bit into the air and gained lift. They turned south and crossed the Coco River. Sam looked down at the bridge under construction and the old dragon paralleling it.

The gyro-copters flew in formation past the nuclear reactor and Sam could see the workers below stopping to stare up at them. These were amazing little craft. He could instantly see the possibilities. They followed the dirt roads away from the reactor and as they approached the end of ARC territory they encountered the first roadblock. Dan sealed the colony to outside traffic when the DEA took down El Tigre's big shipment. The roadblock was a pickup truck with three armed mercenaries, but behind the truck twenty-five meters was a flatbed truck with a squad weapon mounted. In front of the pickup were claymore mines, courtesy of Razi and the Israeli Government. They were strapped to the trees pointed towards the road. They were at a level to take out anyone in the bed of a stake truck, the kind used by the cartels. Dan had a quick reaction force ready to respond to any encounter and he had sentinels camouflaged in the vegetation further out to warn of approaching vehicles. Now with the gyro-copters, ARC could push aerial surveillance even further out without using the bigger, faster and much more expensive Eurocopters.

Sam pulled out his phone and texted Katherine. He told her to go up onto the main deck of the Santa Maria. She and Anna did so and heard the high-pitched whine of the gyro-copter motors. The aircraft buzzed by the ship and Sam waived to her. She waived back with a big smile on her face. Johannes held on, deciding his pilot was having far too much fun for his liking, but he did see Anna waiving at him. He managed a quick waive back. Everyone on the ship was staring and waving at the little aircraft as they circled the ships and put on a show. True to Annon's word, when they approached the airport and lined up on the runway, he and the other pilot cut the engines. What was a noisy world became instantly silent. Both craft softly descended to Earth and touched down as easily as if they were seagulls.

The cartel convoy noisily rumbled along one of the dirt roads leading to ARC territory following their military escort. This was their first shipment since the DEA incident. Gabriel Perez communicated his displeasure and suspicions to President Duran. Duran assured him the gringos had nothing to do with the DEA intercepting him in Honduras and to try again when he was ready. The trucks crawled up hilly tracks and rode the low gears down the opposite side to save the brakes. Enrique, who now sported an orange and black tiger tattoo on the right side of his face and neck paid the army major running the escort three-thousand US dollars and the agreed upon inspection of the cartel trucks was all but forgotten. Enrique added two more covered trucks to this convoy. One truck contained additional armed men and the other contained something special for the DEA if they showed up.

Enrique thoughtfully stroked the new tattoo on his face. The bandages recently came off and it was tender. He was thankful his boss didn't feed him to El Diablo for failing. He was also thankful he paid off the Hondurans to let him escape custody. Honduran prison was no place for a man not associated with a gang. In Honduras, the prisons were built and then handed over to the gangs to run. The federal police surrounded the prison and kept anyone from escaping. Inside it was *Lord of the Flies* on steroids. If you were not in the gang running the prison, it was a death sentence. An ugly, twisted, and sadistic death. He was sure the men captured with him were probably dead by now. He tried not to think about it and focus on what was ahead. He heard something and looked out the window. A tiny helicopter, more of a flying motorcycle, was passing overhead. He keyed his walkie talkie and told his people to ignore it. The DEA would not be flying over Nicaragua in such a contraption. It must be the gringos of ARC.

El Tigre asked him if he thought the African gringos gave them up to the DEA. He was honest in that he did not know, but he also said he was suspicious and did not feel like they could trust these people. The convoy rolled by one of Dan's scouts concealed in the vegetation who radioed their position back to ARC. When the convoy approached the entrance to ARC lands, Enrique was surprised to see the welcoming committee.

There was a bulldozer blocking the road and one of the ARC Eurocopters circling overhead. Two stake bed trucks were facing the other way and in the beds were squad level machine guns pointed at the convoy. Spread out were over fifty armed and tough looking men. The major called for a stop of the convoy, then his vehicle moved forward and stopped short of the bulldozer. Dan greeted him as he exited.

"Hola, Major," Dan said from behind his Oakleys with a Cuban Montecristo clenched between his teeth.

They knew each other from the previous escort missions. The major replaced the colonel starting with the second run. Dan pulled a fresh Cuban cigar from his pocket. The end was already punched. The Major put it into his mouth and Dan produced his butane torch.

"Why the big production?"

"Things did not go as planned last time. The convoy was supposed to come back within six hours. They never returned. We never heard anything. I get a text from you yesterday saying the next convoy would be here today, but no details."

"It was just a change of plans. They did not tell me either. Remember, I waited a whole day for them, but everything is fine now."

"We need to search those trucks."

"I have already done so. Everything is fine."

"Then you won't mind if I take a look."

"I am afraid I cannot allow that. It would be seen as disrespectful given I am their escort."

"You are only their escort to the border."

"I am afraid it is impossible. Please let us just go and everything will be fine."

"I guess we have enough men to keep them under control, but you tell them to watch themselves while in ARC territory. Will they be coming back this way?"

"Yes. They will be coming back in four to six hours after they cross the bridge. I am to wait on them like usual."

"Good. We have your usual hospitality spot set up on the beach."

Dan was in the back of the convoy riding shotgun in a pickup. He dialed his DEA contact in Washington.

"Hello Boogie Man," Agent Nobel answered.

"Your boys ready?"

"Yep. We'll hit them around the same spot."

"I've got some new intel for you. They have added two trucks. Both covered. The major was very insistent I not look in them. You boys need to be prepared for something unusual."

"Like what?"

"Don't know. More guns, bigger guns, something."
"Copy."

Enrique hoped this was going to be an easy run, but he prepared as best he could and worked out a plan in his mind to be successful no matter what. Once they crossed the border and the ARC helicopter left them, he called a halt. Rudimentary as it was, this was the only passable road. If there was a trap up ahead and ARC was involved, the DEA would be expecting him on a time schedule. Part of his plan was to use a scout. After an hour, he sent a lone truck ahead. It was empty, but the driver had a radio. After thirty minutes, Enrique started the rest of the convoy following. He called the first truck, and they reported back there were no issues. A small wave of optimism rose in Enrique's heart. It lasted but a few seconds before his ear detected a disturbance. It was the telltale thumping of a Blackhawk's rotors.

DEA Special Agent Richard Anderson got a message from his superiors to watch for something unexpected. He hid is team and the accompanying Honduran Federal Police in the jungle with spotters on the road. He allowed the single scout truck to pass unmolested. It would be stopped as soon as the main convoy was overtaken. Now that it was out of sight, he summoned his vehicles and men from the dirt track where he hid them. They were spread across the dirt road behind the cover of a bend as a roadblock to stop the convoy headed their way. He was in touch with the Blackhawk staying out of site. He also had a comm link to the drone driver sitting at Nellis Air Force Base in Las Vegas operating the Globalhawk high overhead. He was feeding GPS location and speed of the convoy to Anderson and the Blackhawk pilot.

Anderson gave the order for the Blackhawk to show itself as the convoy approached the bend ahead of the roadblock. With the order, the pilot dropped the nose of the helicopter and picked up speed. Soon he could see the convoy ahead. He told his door gunner to be ready. The plan was to come to a hover behind the convoy and bare their teeth to the frightened drug runners below as the trucks rounded the bend. As the helo closed, the pilot saw the canvass coming off the rear truck. He was trying to make sense of what he was seeing as 12.7mm rounds from a Russian Kord machine gun started punching rounds through the Blackhawk.

"Gun, Gun, Gun," was the radio transmission Agent Anderson heard over the thumping of a heavy machine gun around the bend.

Enrique saw the roadblock up ahead as his truck started into the bend. He radioed the alert. His men cut the chords holding the tarp on the rear truck so the Russian gun could be operated without interference. Two men in the back of his truck cut a hole for themselves through the tarp behind the cab of his truck. They emerged atop the cab armed with RPGs, rocket propelled grenades. Each took aim at a Federal Police truck and let their grenades fly. They struck both vehicles exploding them into huge fireballs killing the officers standing near them. Enrique's driver accelerated and rammed a path through the flaming wreckage. Like angered porcupines, Enrique's trucks sprouted assault weapons from all sides and his men opened fire on the Federal Police. The fire from the trucks was withering against the police trying to take cover behind trees. Enrique saw a corpse on the side of the road wearing body armor that said DEA on the back. He ordered the driver to stop. Bullets from the Federal Police were sporadic as his men continued to shoot it out. He detached the Velcro flaps on the sides of the body armor and pulled it over Agent Anderson's head which sported a hole through the eye socket. He would wear this when he entered El Tigre's hacienda in the jungle, a trophy from his success.

The Blackhawk circled ahead of the convoy at treetop level. The door gunner was pounding the cartel trucks with his machine gun. The RPG team both fired at the helo, but the pilot was an experienced war vet. He yanked the collective and rose above their trajectories to avoid them, but then he was high enough to be targeted by the gun at the back of the convoy. Rounds stared striking the helo again and he was getting all kinds of alarms. He banked right to get ahead of the gun but leveled out to give his door gunner another chance for some payback. The gunner opened up on the rear truck, but the pilot could not hold the bird steady for long as the 12.7mm rounds caught up to them. They were in trouble, and he had to find a safe place to set down. He was trailing smoke and knew it was bad. He gained altitude and headed for ARC territory hoping to make the airport.

Enrique could hardly wait for the propellers of the King Air to stop spinning before he exited the rear door. He knew he was safe here in the valley of the tiger. The DEA could not get to him. The only way in was the airstrip which was barely long enough to accommodate small cargo planes and the airspace was protected by the Nicaraguan government. The US Government would have to perpetrate an act of war on Nicaragua to try and take him into custody. Once off the plane, it was a short walk to the hacienda, El Tigre's sanctuary.

Enrique entered the front gates and was greeted by security. There were two armed guards, one of which was a cat handler. They were happy to see him. Enrique was not happy to see the tiger laying on the ground controlled by the thinnest of leashes. He liked tigers before Gabriel threatened to throw him into El Diablo's pit. Now he was wary, and looking into this cat's yellow eyes brought the memory of El Diablo back in vivid color. He broke the connection by looking away. The two guards were feeling his body armor and asking how he obtained it with a sense of awe. He was someone they respected before he got the tattoo on his face. Now with the tiger's image on his right cheek baring its fangs and its body and tail wrapping around his neck, his stature was elevated even higher in their minds. The fact he wore captured DEA body armor was nearly unbelievable to them. He passed them with a quick two-sentence explanation and went to find the boss. When Gabriel Perez saw him, he was taken aback.

"Enrique, mi hermano! Tell me of your adventures and successes," he declared unable to hide his excitement in seeing his face-tattooed loyalist wearing his captured symbol of American oppression.

"It was a glorious battle, El Jefe. We killed the Yankees and their lap dogs. We even shot down their helicopter. You were right, though. The ARC gringos betrayed us."

"How do you know?"

"The major escorting us called and told me he saw a smoking American military helicopter make an emergency landing at the ARC airport."

Gabriel clenched his fists and looked over at the decorative ceramic skull of Santa Muerte, the death saint, on his desk.

"No more convoys," El Tigre said as he stared into the empty eye sockets of the painted skull the drug cartels and gangs worshiped as a false god.

Chapter VIII

Aapo stepped lightly on the thin trail. His bare footsteps were silent, but he could not have heard them anyway over the ungraceful clods behind him tripping on every stick, slipping on every muddy patch, and dragging their noisy burros behind them. Aapo was an indigenous warrior from the tribe that inhabited the rainforest bordering Nicaragua and Honduras. His people had lived there since before recorded time and he wore nothing except his loincloth with his haunches showing, his quiver holding his bow and arrows and a necklace strung together with alternating jaguar claws and hog tusks. For the most part, his people shunned outsiders, but sometimes they would meet them and trade on the outskirts of the forest. Sometimes the temptation to interact more was too great. It was that way for Aapo. He knew it was risky to consort with the people from the outside world, but he was a curious soul, and he loved the things he could trade for, or steal from, the outsiders. He acquired a few things over time, but his most precious item was a slim jade-handle knife he kept in a hidden pocket in his loincloth.

He enjoyed the outsider's tobacco. It was much finer than the tobacco the women of his village grew, and it came in the little white tubes with the brown ends. He would tear the brown ends off before smoking. While he enjoyed their tobacco, he really loved their white powder. They would only give him a tiny bit, but oh how it made him feel good when they did. He could run all day through the jungle when given just a touch and when given a little more, he could commune with the ancestors better than the medicine man.

Aapo agreed to escort these people through the rainforest and across the river. He met them south of where the farmers used to be before the pale people came and he led them on a surreptitious path into the rainforest. There were six men who carried rifles. He'd seen what those could do to a tree and did not want to anger those men. There were twelve men carrying backpacks of different colors and twelve donkeys laden down with heavy burlap sacks. Aapo did not know what was in the packs and sacks, but it must be important because they gave him a whole pack of the little white tobacco tubes to start the journey and promised him a carton of what they call cigarillos when they got across the river.

Aapo was forced to stop frequently for the people to rest. He would smoke one of his cigarillos while he watched them sit and drink from their canteens. Occasionally, one would share their water with him, or something they were eating. He liked to eat their food. Often it was something he had never tasted before. On this break he was looking up at the half-moon. This was the second time he escorted these people through these lands. He listened to them speaking to each other. He understood a few things, but not enough to follow the conversation. The armed men were complaining about the smuggling routes becoming increasingly hazardous as the DEA wanted payback for the killing of Agent Anderson. The Americanos shifted their seemingly endless resources to the area. The US Navy was all over the Gulf and the Pacific, the DEA was on the ground and in the air, and since ARC betrayed them, there was no vehicle route to the east. Through the rainforest was the best option.

They had been walking for hours. Aapo stayed ahead of them to find the trail and better listen to the land. He could see well tonight by the moon. Suddenly out in the darkness, his nose detected something out of place. He stopped and looked about. The footsteps behind him were closing. His eyes followed the path of the odor he detected. He could almost make out a shape that seemed to be out of place. Then a baritone voice cut through the darkness.

"Para ahí, pon las manos en el aire! Stop right there, put your hands in the air!"

Aapo started running as the men behind him started firing blindly into the darkness. His feet carried him through unknown footings with grace and their thick leathery pads kept him from feeling any pain. He heard muffled sounds and the rifles ceased firing as the cartel gunmen were head-shot by bullets fired from suppressed weapons. He ran fast, trying to disappear into the forest when suddenly he was knocked to the ground. A man, really a giant compared to Aapo, clotheslined him from behind a tree. He sat atop Aapo and bent his arms behind him. He secured his wrists with zip ties. The man marched him back to where the party was hunkered down. The men carrying the backpacks were stripped of their possessions and were zip tied as well. The men with the rifles all lay dead. Aapo suddenly wanted nothing to do with the outsiders anymore. If he ever got free, he vowed to his ancestors he would never seek them out again.

Sam returned from Katherine's quarters as he did most mornings and took his shower. He sat on his balcony looking out to sea and wondered what Patson was doing today in South Africa. He heard a ding as he took his first sip of coffee. A message from Dan appeared on his phone. *URGENT, JAIL* was all it said. Sam called Dan and was told to come see for himself. He called Johannes and asked him to meet him at his truck. They took the turn off the main road and went deep off the beaten path to the sea container with the windows cut into it. Outside there were a dozen backpacks and a pile of burlap sacks. Stacked on top were a half dozen AK-47s and two handguns.

Sam looked at the container and saw the faces pressed against the expanded metal grates. They looked scared and desperate and he hated it. None of them said anything, they just waited for their fate. Maybe they knew ARC never hurt any of the curriers before, but the curriers never fired on ARC before either. Dan explained to Sam and Johannes.

"We had the gyro-copters up last night. We equipped the pilot and a spotter with night vision and FLIR infra-red. We saw the column from a distance with the FLIR. We put three teams in the field ahead of them and they walked right into the middle of our positions. We told them to put their hands up and they started shooting. We took out the shooters, secured the rest per our procedures."

"We are going to need some new procedures, I suspect," Sam said.

As he stopped speaking there was a tribal chant coming from the jail, yet when the three men turned to look, the faces in the windows were silent.

"What is that?" Johannes asked.

"I think it is their guide. Some kind of Indian."

"Open the door. Line them up," Sam ordered.

They opened the door to the container. The porters filed out singly and were made to stand against the container. They all looked at the ground and hoped this was not a firing squad. The chanting continued from inside the container. Sam peered in. Aapo was facing the back wall rhythmically swaying and chanting. Through the beams of filtered light Sam could see his body glowed with a sheen of sweat. Aapo had taken his concealed jade knife and scratched an image into the paint on the back wall of the container. Sam imagined him praying to it for his release and salvation. As Sam's eyes adjusted to the darkness, the image revealed itself to be a crude elephant.

Sam got Aapo's attention and motioned for him to follow. Cautiously, Aapo followed Sam to his pickup where Sam climbed aboard the lowered the tailgate. Aapo followed Sam into the bed of the truck and Sam asked Johannes to drive them to the food production facility. Aapo seemed to sense Sam was a friend, although he was leery of everyone after last night. He held onto the roll bar on the pickup. He had never ridden in a vehicle and the speed was exhilarating. He followed Sam into the facility with Johannes bringing up the rear. He was amazed at the vegetables he saw growing in the air and the system that sprayed water onto their roots as they hung there. Sam pulled a ripe tomato from one of the plants and gave it to Aapo. He bit into it and smiled. Sam took him to a room with a big window looking outside and asked him to sit. The concept of a chair was foreign to him, so Johannes showed him how to use it before he and Sam went outside.

"Was that a drawing of an elephant?"

Johannes was one of the few that knew Sam's secret. He released some of the great beasts into the wilds of Nicaragua as penance for killing an African rouge years ago.

"Yeah."

"And I guess this fellow believes your elephants are some kind of gods."

"Kinda looks that way."

"What do you want to do with him?"

"I am concerned. If he is an indigenous person to the rainforest, then he has been in long term contact with these people who at best have shoddy vaccinations. I think we need to vaccinate him and let him go. If he caught a disease or something from those folks, he could take it back to his whole tribe. It could be the story of the American Indian all over again."

"I can get the doc. How long should we keep him?"

"We'll let the doctor tell us."

Aapo stayed a week in his new environment. He was Sam's charge, but Dan came to visit each day. He was fascinated by the little Indian. He brought him cigarettes and they compared tattoos. Aapo's were tribal and on display all the time as they circled his naked biceps and his back. The first time Dan removed his shirt and showed Aapo the magnificently colored tattoos that ran from his wrists all the way up to both shoulders, Aapo was amazed. He stared at the tattoos carefully and ran his fingers over them talking in his native language that Dan could not understand.

Sam made sure he was well fed, and they took walks together around the area. The language barrier was enormous, but they communicated in the most basic of ways. They would draw the elephants in the dirt with a stick and when Sam drew five, Aapo added two more. Sam realized the bull must have bred two of the cows right after they landed. Sam pointed to the tusk on the elephant in the dirt, then he pointed to the ivory cross around his neck. Aapo placed his small tan fingers on the white ivory and understood. Sam was a man of powerful magic.

Sam brought in the ship's doctor, and he gave him a shot of antibiotics and vaccinated him for the most basic and dangerous of diseases. Sam introduced Katherine to him, and he was fascinated by her blonde hair and blue eyes. He had seen neither before. He wondered if she was a powerful witch. It was another sign of Sam's magic to have such a woman as his own.

On the seventh day of his quarantine, Sam and Johannes collected him and took him down to the docks around dawn when they were least populated. Aapo was astonished at the size of the ocean liners docked in the bay. It was a world he could never have imagined. Sam motioned towards one of the patrol boats and they boarded. Sam cast off the line and headed towards the mouth of the Coco River. He drove the boat far up the river and deep into the rainforest. When Aapo motioned towards the bank, Sam pulled the boat up to it and tied off. Once on dry land, Sam handed Aapo his quiver and his jade knife. He also handed him the carton of cigarettes from the smuggler's packs. Sam pointed to Aapo and then to himself. Then to the spot they are standing and made an arch with his hand in the sky three times. Aapo nodded, smiled, and said something Sam could not understand. He was saying he understood they would meet again someday at this spot. Sam pushed off, noted the GPS coordinates, and gave Aapo a blast from the boat's air horn as a sendoff.

Chapter IX

Ariela exited the elevator of her apartment building and began the walk down the hall. She was stressed. Every aspect of her life was complicated it seemed. Work was getting difficult as of late. She felt bad stringing her boss along. She had been his mistress for some time now and they were friends as well as lovers, but she realized she had fallen hard for Dan. She could not see being physical with the banker going forward, but she also knew he could and would fire her if she cut him off completely. She was hopeful she and Dan would come to some kind of a permanent arrangement, hopefully one where she could move to the ARC colony and be with him full time. The complication was her sister. Ariela held little sway over Zanita anymore it seemed, but still she tried to look out for her. She thought if she left Managua, Zanita would completely run wild. Already, the country seemed to be tearing itself apart. The protests were raucous and seemed to be escalating despite the brutal retaliation of the hit squads that no doubt were funded by the Durans. The clergy was involved trying to mediate a peaceful resolution between the parties, but it was hard to know who was genuine in the negotiations. Even the church was suspect these days.

She turned the key and found the door unlocked. *Zanita must have let herself in, or more likely forgot to lock the door when she left*, she figured.

"Zanita," she called out as she crossed the threshold.

There was no response, but there was a nice aroma of cooked meat in the apartment. She dropped her purse and keys on the table by the door and called again.

"Zanita."

Zanita was in the kitchen with her headphones on cooking. Ariela tapped her on the shoulder and scared her half to death.

"What are you doing here?"

"A little sister can't cook dinner?"

"You've never done it before."

"Well, the time felt right. Now sit down, the baho is ready."

Ariela allowed Zanita to serve her. The steamed beef and plantains under the banana leaves smelled wonderful. Zanita must have been cooking for hours. Ariela suggested a bottle of wine from the three she had in the kitchen and Zanita eagerly agreed. The sisters caught up on everything going on in their lives. Zanita was extremely interested in Ariela's new love and all things surrounding ARC. She was very inquisitive about life in the ARC community, the power plant and all of the amazing things Ariela encountered. She was really interested in the luxury ships in which the ARC people lived. They sounded like paradise, and she laughed when she heard they were named the Niña, the Pinta and Santa Maria. It was right out of their history books with Christopher Columbus. Ariela took this unexpected opportunity to ask about what was going on in her life. She was more than concerned when Zanita talked about the men, boys really, she had been hanging around. Ariela knew there was much she was hiding but held off the lecture she wanted to give, hoping this meeting would become a regular thing. If her and Dan became a permanent thing, maybe it would serve as a lesson for her baby sister. Maybe she could even get her a job at the bank if she settled down a bit, maybe even her own job if the timing was right.

CHAPTER X

D an called Special Agent Nobel from his quarters aboard the Santa Maria. He had just finished breakfast in the galley and was stretched out on a sun lounger on his balcony. His view this week was the escarpment with the power plant.

"How are things in paradise?"

"It's all mai tais and piña colatas, you know with the exception of the drug cartels and commies."

"We've been hammering the cartel shipments since Anderson's death."

"That may explain why we encountered a dozen porters escorted by six gun thugs and an Indian trying to make their way through our territory."

"Feather Indian or Dot Indian?"

"Lives in the rainforest in a hut, Indian. I've never seen anything like him. He was a cool dude. Loin cloth and the whole bit."

"Amazing."

"Anyway, the smugglers decided to shoot it out. We took out their shooters and captured the rest. We made them watch while we burned their cocaine. We hauled them to the edge of the territory and set them out afoot with a bottle of water and a Hershey bar."

"What did you do with Indigenous Nicaraguan?"

"Sam took him up the river and let him go. I don't think we will see him again. Can't imagine he enjoyed the whole experience. Do you have any intel to share with us?"

"Only that we have moved Enrique Sanchez up on our most wanted list and stepped up the resources assigned to intercepting narcotics coming out of Nicaragua. We can't stop all of it, but we are making more busts than before. The Navy captured a submarine full of coke last week. Made the news up here."

"OK, keep me informed. I have a feeling this thing is escalating on us."

Dan was trying to get Ariela off his mind. He and Sam just left her office with a half a million dollars in cash and he needed to be on top of his game. *Why did she have to look so damn hot*, he thought as he exited the bank ahead of Sam. Julio pulled up and he and Sam made a quick entry into the rear of the pickup. As Dan closed his door, a bullet burst through the front windshield killing Julio's front seat protection detail. A second bullet hit Julio before he could step on the gas. Dan and Sam got as low as they could in the medium sized pick up, but realized it was no protection. High caliber rifle bullets continued to slam into the truck showering them with pieces of tempered glass as the bullets punched through the windshield and into the bodies of the men in the front seat. Sam opened his door and slid out to keep the truck between himself and the shooter. Dan crawled out headfirst through Sam's door. People were screaming and running away from the truck. Dan had his 1911 out. Sam had the money. Dan wanted the AK in the front passenger seat but couldn't get to it.

"Sniper, semi-auto," Dan yelled.

"No kidding. Bank?"

"Wait," Dan replied. He reached under the backseat as bullets continued to strike the truck. He was reaching for his bag of goodies when he heard Julio groan. When he crouched back down behind the truck, Sam was peaking over the bed.

"Down the street, third floor."

"Julio is alive."

"OK. What's the plan, Boogie man?"

"Pop smoke, grab Julio, head for the bank."

Dan threw a smoke grenade in front of the truck. A massive cloud of white smoke began forming. The fire hitting the truck intensified as well as spread out into the surrounding concrete. Dan stayed low and opened the driver's door. He pulled Julio out and he and Sam got under each arm. The shooter guessed they would be heading to the bank, and fired random shots into the smoke. They ran as best they could toward the bank with bullets whizzing by them. As they got close to the door,

Ariela jerked it open, and they crashed through onto the tile as the gunfire outside continued.

Sam sat in Isabella De La Corte Duran's office. The $500,000 sat on her desk in a tan duffle bag with Julio's blood stains on it. She showed concern for Sam's safety, but assumed since he was not hurt, the bloodstains were from his driver, thus not worth mentioning.

"This attack was from the cartel. Retaliation for the drug seizure from the DEA and us taking out six of their gunmen who opened fire on our people."

"You do not know that for sure. You must admit, a gringo in Managua is a target. A gringo with $500,000 US dollars is a big target. It could have been any number of criminal elements wanting to rob you."

"Why can't we just wire you the money?"

"The United States has wrongfully branded our democratically elected government an outlaw regime. As such, our international banking options are limited. You have seen the violent, lawless protests in our streets. We need cash to pay for law enforcement activities to protect the people."

She said it in such a benevolent way one would think she was talking about funding a girl scout troop instead of the roving gangs of head smashers employed to break the back of the resistance.

"My gut says it was the cartel. We need you to have a word with them. We know about the shootout with the DEA. Tell them we had nothing to do with the seizures. No more convoys through our area and no more smugglers trying to cross on foot."

"My husband may feel differently."

"I'll let you handle your husband. We've closed all the roads coming into the territory we control. The cartel is not going to get through."

Sam got up to leave. The vice president did not rise.

"Doctor Harrington, do not let our friendship give you false expectations about how you can act in my presence and what you may ask of me."

"Madam Vice President, I've had an employee killed today and another hangs on by a thread all in an attempt to kill me while I bring you your money. If ever there was a day I was going to take liberties, it's today."

Admiral Sharpe's quarters were the appropriate place for the retelling of the firefight in Managua earlier in the day. The Admiral served a fine scotch to the group designated as the warrior's council seated around his manly furnishings. Morne, Marcus and Johannes sat and listened to Sam and Dan's account of their narrow escape. They were angry someone tried to kill their friends and each of them wished they had been there to assist. Julio was in a Managua hospital. Sam made sure the doctors understood the bill would be taken care of and he made a sizeable down payment while there. The prognosis was good.

"We have news for you as well, gentlemen. While you were gone, the cartels probed our defenses," Johannes said.

"What do you mean?"

"They sent three different convoys, each with two trucks down three different roads. We stopped them at checkpoints, but we are pretty certain it was a defensive probe."

"How do you know they were cartel trucks?" Dan asked, perturbed, he had not been alerted by his people already.

"All three were different, but all three were the same. Three different trucks with vegetables in the back. We've never had someone trying to sell vegetables before, much less three in the same day. Our men found each of them had a camera and a GPS unit," Johannes replied.

"We have to tighten up security," Sam said flatly.

"We are pretty safe here, but the tower crews are vulnerable. Certainly, in Nicaragua, but also potentially in Honduras," Johannes said.

"We are going to need more security personnel," Dan said.

"Should we draft from the construction crews?" Marcus asked.

"We can't afford to slow down construction and we need more professionally trained men. I'd say at least two hundred. What do you think Morne?" Sam asked.

"Agreed."

"Billeting will be an issue, but we will find a way," the admiral added.

"Then it is settled. We send some of our security men from here to the tower sites and we will augment here with any construction workers with combat experience until we can hire more soldiers," Morne said.

The hot water felt good cascading over Sam's body as he adjusted the shower nozzle and let the water wash the day from him. He swayed a bit from the fatigue and the scotch. He heard his front door close. Katherine called his name with her Austrian accented English. He yelled back that he was in the shower, and he would be out in a minute.

"I cannot wait a whole minute," she said as she entered his bathroom and began stripping off clothes. Sam smiled. She was a beautiful, graceful woman, but her disrobing was more spastic and frantic than sexy. He had to give it to her though, she was fast, and she looked great. She jerked open the shower door and rushed in pressing her naked body against his while kissing him. They stayed like that for more than a minute before she pushed back.

"I heard you were almost killed."

"It wasn't that bad."

"I heard there was shooting."

"A little bit, but it wasn't that close."

"You are lying, Mister," she said accentuating each individual word. "If I ask Anna, is she going to tell me the same story Johannes will have told her? Will Ariela?"

"Fine. I will tell you everything…after."

Afterwards, they lay in each other's arms in the bed. Katherine's wet hair was cold against Sam's chest, but her body was warm and tender.

"I feel terrible for Julio and the other man, but I am so happy you and Dan are alright."

"If Dan wasn't such a prepared boy scout, I don't know that we would have gotten out of it. The smoke grenades saved the day."

"And Ariela saw the whole thing?"

"I don't know how much she saw, but she opened the back door for us."

"The poor girl. She must be traumatized. Has Dan checked on her?"

"He called her while I was in with Isabella. Didn't say much about it."

"You should send the helicopter for Ariela, and we should do something nice. Maybe have a dinner with everyone invited. Make her the guest of honor, show her we appreciate her, and she is part of the family."

Javier Cordova's helicopter landed in a clearing near Henry Claassen's trailer. He was re-assigned to the Managua tower set from the inbound Honduran leg. It was an emergency transfer and he stepped off the helicopter with nothing but his duffle. It seems the board at ARC was expecting some trouble and they wanted him there to organize and run the protection detail in coordination with the Nicaraguan army. Two squads of mercenaries, eighteen men total, were dispatched from ARC territory to the Nicaraguan tower project. They landed right after Javier and outnumbered the assigned Nicaraguan soldiers nearly two to one.

Javier got up to speed with Henry and sought out the Nicaraguan Lieutenant. He did not wear his BDU blouse this time. Showing up in Nicaragua in a US military uniform was beyond inappropriate, but the Nicaraguan lieutenant sensed his military background in his demeaner, and he liked the fact he was a Latino. He did not care for the overly muscled white men Henry brought in, but he could respect Javier, especially if the big South Africans answered to him. As they felt each other out, Javier was honest with the Lieutenant about his service background. The Lieutenant was impressed.

"What kind of problems have you had to date, Lieutenant?"

"Just petty crime, Major."

"We have reason to believe one of the cartels may see this tower operation as a soft target and take the opportunity to attack."

"The cartels know the army is protecting this vital piece of infrastructure. I do not think they will bother us. The cartels operate with honor unlike the gangs."

"I don't share your optimism."

"What would you suggest then?"

"We work cooperatively. You manage the day-to-day interactions with the community following the construction and you establish a roadblock one kilometer down the main road to check for contraband and any possible weapons. My people will do long range reconnaissance, overwatch and protection for the ARC workers, We will also be a quick reaction squad if anything goes wrong."

"I don't think you have enough men for all of that."

"I agree and I can see you have an eye for military detail. I am going to take your suggestion and bring in a dozen more men. I am sure you will also agree we don't have the available vehicles we need either. I am going to buy six Toyota pickups from Managua and bring them in. One will be your command vehicle so you and I can stay in touch with our men easier. Any particular color you like?"

"I like the patriotic blue of the Nicaraguan flag," the lieutenant said knowing it was a very nice gift for his cooperation.

Vice President Isabella De La Corte Duran knocked lightly on her husband's bedroom door. It was late and she was just getting home from an event as her husband, the old warrior and President was crawling into bed. He was still a capable man, but the virility of his youth was noticeably absent.

"Darling, may I have a moment."

"Of course, My Sweet. Come."

"Did you hear about the attack on the ARC people today?"

"I did. I am glad they were not hurt."

"They seem to think Gabriel was responsible."

"Hard to say. Lots of criminal elements at large these days."

"True, but can you send Gabriel a message asking him not to cause trouble with the ARC people."

"I can, but Perez and his cartel funded our revolution, the government, and our family for decades. Can we turn our backs on them now that things are difficult for them?"

"That is true, and I value your loyalty, but we are doing what we have always done, which is give them a safe place to produce their crops without fear of persecution. It has always been their responsibility to transport their goods to their markets. Look at the innovations they made in airplanes, the speed boats and even submarines. ARC is our future. It is the future of Nicaragua and Central America. It is your legacy and nothing should threaten it."

The old Sandinista stared at his wife's pleasing face through cloudy eyes.

"I will send Gabriel a message tomorrow," he replied as he dismissed her from his bedroom with a kiss on the cheek.

CHAPTER XI

The Eurocopter sat down gently on the Santa Maria's landing pad. Attendants rushed forward but did not open the doors until the rotors completely stopped spinning. Opening them earlier would have turned Ariela Sade's long black hair into a whirling mess of tangles. As the blades stopped spinning, Katherine emerged from the door of the nearest room and welcomed Ariela to the ship. She took the day off from her duties to spend with Ariela while Dan was off working various security issues related to their new heightened preparedness. Katherine and Morne's wife planned a party for that evening in Ariela's honor with more than a hundred people invited, but she was glad to have her new friend to herself for a while.

Katherine had Ariela's bags taken to her quarters. She told Ariela she had a whole day planned for them, but she had to check on something at the airport before they got started. Overseeing so many projects meant there never was a day completely free of responsibility. She and Ariela took her pickup across the dragon to the airport. Katherine showed Ariela the different projects underway. Ariela never knew a woman with so much responsibility. Nicaragua was still a macho culture in many respects. Katherine stopped in front of the terminal under construction, and they walked through the humidity to the planning office. Each of the men working inside, including Katherine's number two, stopped cold when the two entered. They were used to seeing their boss and respectfully tried to ignore her beauty, but they had never laid eyes on Ariela. In the limited world they inhabited, she was a dark-haired vision. She shattered the falsehood that was the gender-neutral workplace the civilized world worked so hard to create. The men stared at Ariela, then it was if they suddenly saw their boss for the first time. They were the antithesis of each other. Katherine while in her early forties was blonde and fair with crystal blue eyes. Ariela's hair was as black and shiny as onyx with darker skin and deep brown eyes.

Katherine asked her head foreman to update her on the problem they were trying to solve and he failed to respond. She snapped her fingers and called his name. It broke the spell, and he stammered while looking about for his papers trying to recapture some semblance of professionalism. The other men in the office suddenly realized they too had been entranced and scurried back to work. Katherine and Ariela glanced at each other. Ariela winked.

Katherine slipped her four-wheel drive champagne colored pickup down a small muddy track through the dense vegetation. The jungle reached out with its tender leaves to caress the truck as it passed. Their destination was a secluded beach spot. As far as Katherine knew she and Sam were the only two humans to have ever sat on this tiny beach, now she was sharing it with her new friend. She had a cooler packed in the back seat and arranged for them to have a private, girls only, picknick on the beach with white wine and delicacies from her private stores.

"This is my secret spot. I thought you might like it as much as I do," Katherine said as she spread the blanket on the sand under a palm. Ariela complimented her on it and sat down to enjoy the experience. Katherine presented a cold bottle of Riesling along with olives, fruits, cheeses, and cured meats.

"Is it difficult?" Ariela asked.

"What?"

"Everything. To live here, to have so much responsibility, to be the only woman on the board of directors?"

"There are always difficulties. But, if you love what you are doing, you don't seem to mind as much."

"You handle everything so well."

"I have my moments. I can tell you this, I will have a time getting those foremen back in line now that you made your appearance."

"That was not all me."

"It was. They never acted that way before."

"I think they just don't let you see. It was obvious they are all taken with you. You have them twisted around your finger."

"More likely they live in fear."

"I will concede respect, but do not discount yourself."

"You are a good friend," Katherine said with a self-deprecating smile as she handed Ariela the tray of crackers.

"What is South Africa like?"

"It is a country in transition. I don't know what it will become, but I know the change is painful."

"What was it like before the revolution?"

"If you were white, it was good. If you were black, it was not. And if you were Indian or Asian, you were caught somewhere in the middle. But it was the only first world nation on the continent before the revolution as you call it. Now, it lies in tatters, and it is failing everyone."

"We were taught in school the revolution was a great victory for communism and the people. An end to imperial rule and racism."

"The Communist certainly played a role in supporting the resistance and armed revolutionaries, but South Africa is not Communist. It is a democracy with a capitalist economic system. A system distorted by the new ruling class of politicians. Four of every ten working people are unemployed. Inflation is rising, infrastructure is crumbling, and property values are plummeting due to the social justice reforms attempted by the ANC. It is a ticking time bomb that will become the greatest humanitarian crisis of this century."

"I had no idea. Is that why you all left?"

"Yes. Before we left, each of us was under surveillance by the State. The intelligence services sent men to attack me and find out what I knew. I'd be dead if it were not for the actions of a brave young man."

"Ay, Dios."

"Let's not talk of such things on a beautiful day. Tell me about you and Dan."

"After you tell me about you and Sam."

They both laughed and Katherine swallowed her bite of cheese.

"Tell you about my cowboy?"

"He is an American cowboy, isn't he?"

"He is. I mean he is so much more, but he has the heart of a cowboy."

"I think Dan is a cowboy, too."

"He certainly has a wild streak, but I think he is more of a pirate than a cowboy."

"Yes, I think you are right. He has a dark side to him. A part of him he keeps locked away. Pirate is probably a better description, but a fair and just pirate."

"A privateer as it were. Let's toast to your privateer and my cowboy then," Katherine said with a raise of her glass.

The two chitchatted while they snacked, drank wine, enjoyed the salt breeze, and watched the birds. They exchanged their life stories in greater detail than they had with any other women in a long time. Ariela was fascinated with Katherine talking about modeling on the runways in Europe and raising a family in South Africa. Katherine assured her the modeling was overblown and not that big of a life event, but still it sounded glamourous. Ariela, who learned long ago to be guarded about revealing too much about herself, lowered her defenses and talked about growing up in Managua and her position at the bank. She confided in Katherine the nature of her relationship with the bank manager. She felt no shame in her disclosure and Katherine's reassurance that girls must do what they have to do to get by showed there was no judgement. Still, Katherine wished Ariela had been born into a society where she had more opportunities. She was not just beautiful; she was smart and clearly resourceful. She could have gone far in America or Europe or nearly anywhere other than Nicaragua. But there was ample time for her to find her path. She was still young, full of potential, and she had new friends.

Sam stopped by Dan's quarters and rapped on the door. Dan jerked it open and stepped back. He was fumbling with a black bow tie in the mirror. Sam stepped up to assist as it was obvious, he was never going to get it tied.

"Whose idea was it to wear tuxes?" Dan mumbled as Sam's big fingers delicately twisted and turned the black ribbon to and fro.

"I suspect it was Katherine's. You know how women love an excuse to dress up."

"You look like a waiter."

"Be still."

"I haven't even seen Ariela," Dan mumbled with his neck stretched high.

"Katherine kept her all to herself today."

"Feels like a wedding."

"You ready to marry this girl?" Sam said in a fatherly tone as he spun Dan around in the mirror to look at himself.

91

"Ready for the honeymoon, does that count?"
"Come on, we're going to be late."

The entering guests were overwhelmed by the grandeur of the transformed ballroom. It was *Alice in Wonderland* meets Dr. Suess, all directed by James Cameron. There were six ice sculptures including ones with champagne flowing through them and others with vodka. The chef had buffet stations around the room with such an assortment of teasing and tantalizing tastes, it would take someone most of the night to sample them all. The band consisted of ARC musicians, who started early and were prepared to play all night. There were over a thousand white roses intermingled with the native flowers of Nicaragua covering the tables and extending down from the ceiling on vines acquired from the natural environment. The lighting was never direct, only small lights interwoven into the flowers and bounced off mirrored balls and colored back-grounds. Katherine and Morne's wife spared little expense. Katherine coordinated with a party planner in Dallas and flew her, a master cake baker, a semi-famous chef, an ice sculptor, and all of the things needed to be brought from the US in on Sam's Citation X. Dan's tuxedo was even in one of the shipments. Everyone with a management position in ARC was invited to attend with their spouse or guest. Most wore suits and evening dresses, but the Board of Directors was strictly black tie and evening gowns.

The liquor flowed freely, and the party was in high gear when the band suddenly struck up a royal sounding tune overwritten with heavy trumpets. Two spotlights converged on the stage. Admiral Sharpe in his Royal Navy mess dress complete with a chest full of medals and brandishing his saber was the center of attention. He said nothing but bowed and turned to the side with a silent, but powerful introduction of his white gloved hand. Katherine emerged from behind the curtain with the feminine grace she was known for in a wispy black gown whose top was lace and silver sequins. Everyone was taken with her beauty and the applause began, but she quickly stepped aside and motioned with her hands to Ariela who seemed to materialize from the ether in the darkness behind the lights. She emerged in a form fitted black sequin dress with red roses cascading from her breasts across her stomach and down the left side. She walked forward like a catwalk model as instructed by her new mentor. Her long black hair was fashionably styled atop her head and her eyes sparkled like Katherine's posh diamond necklace that hung weightily around her long slender neck. Her smile was so appreciative and genuine, the applause grew to a thunderous level. The admiral took each lady under a wing and descended the steps to present them into the arms of Sam and Dan. As he did, the band started a waltz, and the two couples danced a short one to the delight of the crowd. When it was over, both men kissed Ariela on the cheek and presented her again to the room of admirers. They all knew the story of how she flung open the bank door amidst a hail of gunfire to get Sam and Dan to safety and again, the applause was overwhelming. The rest of the board of directors joined in for another waltz and then the party was back into full form with the band going all out to get the party goers on the dance floor.

Most everyone at the party approached Ariela at some point and thanked her for her heroism. The feelings were genuine, and the emotions ran true. She knew these were the nicest people she would ever meet, and this party would be a highlight for the rest of her life. The evening was capped by a massive fireworks display at midnight that everyone in the ARC colony was able to enjoy as the night was filled with brilliant colors and lights along with the accompanying thunderous claps.

Ariela's dress hung on a hook attached to the bathroom door. Dan's tuxedo lay in a pile nearby. The moon was up late, and its blue beams flooded the room. Dan noticed how they reflected off the diamonds still around Ariela's neck as she lay in his arms running her foot up and down his leg.

"You looked so beautiful when you appeared on stage. That dress was stunning."

"Thank you. Katherine showed me six dresses, each more beautiful than the last, and told me to pick the one I wanted to wear. I could see the tickets attached and jokingly asked her if I got to keep the dress afterwards. She told me no. Then she said you get to keep all of them. I told her it was too generous and not necessary, I could have brought a dress with me or borrowed one from her, but she insisted. She said besides, one of her dresses would have never fit in the boobs, or how did she say it… posterior."

"That is a true statement," Dan said as he ran his hand over her shapely hip. He pulled her close and they kissed. When they parted, they stared into each other's eyes. Dan parted his lips to form the word "I" and as he did, realizing what he was going to say, Ariela kissed him quickly. There was no need to say it. They both felt it.

Chapter XII

J avier Cordova was sleeping fitfully. He lay under just a sheet and his mosquito netting. A cold shower before bed helped, but little could keep the Nicaragua temperatures at bay for long. He awoke sweaty as he heard the footsteps running in his direction. He was already slipping his pants on by the time the sergeant announced himself.

"Multiple trucks headed this way, Major."

"Threat assessment?"

"Unknown. Three non-military trucks with high wooden sides inbound from the south is all the scout reported, Sir."

"Flip on the jammer. Alert our people. Then alert the Nicaraguans."

Javier deployed long range scouts hidden down the roads leading to the camp and work sites. They were Javier's advanced warning system and even the Nicaraguan soldiers did not know their locations.

The sergeant flipped the switch on the electronic jammer Javier mounted atop the construction trailer. No one in the camp was going to be able to make a phone call to alert anyone of their sudden activity. The armed protection force had ten minutes to be mobile. Javier met the Nicaraguan lieutenant at the command trailer.

"We have three unknown trucks coming from the south. Just like we planned, we need you and your men to make the roadblock. We will back you up," he said in Spanish.

"Si," the lieutenant said as the started issuing orders to his troops. His sergeant was getting their military vehicle started while the rest piled into the back. Thirteen minutes after Javier heard the footsteps approaching, everyone was moving southbound.

As his body jostled in the front seat of the lead truck riding the swells and dips of the uneven dirt road, Enrique's mind remained still and focused on what lay ahead. He was looking forward to getting some payback on ARC. His gut told him ARC betrayed him to the DEA. He shot his way out of that trap and wore a dead ATF agent's body armor now as a symbol of the victory. His three trucks were rapidly approaching the ARC tower construction camp. He planted a spy in the camp followers to give him information on how things worked and what security measures were in place. He knew they added more armed personnel after the DEA trap, another sign of their guilt in his mind. He did not necessarily want to kill the Nicaraguan soldiers and hoped they would stand down and not fight. He needed them to tell the story. The story of how El Tigre's men showed them mercy while they killed the ARC security forces, raided the payroll trailer, and distributed the money to the workers.

His spy told him the Nicaraguan forces operated the checkpoints on the road and that the ARC personnel were usually asleep during the night with only a handful of men on sentry duty. He picked the early hours of the morning for his attack, the time when they would be most vulnerable. When he estimated he was a half hour away from the camp, he called a halt. He told his men to dismount. They had been in the trucks for a couple of hours, and he knew they would all be asleep. He told his men to eat something and drink water. They passed around spicy empanadas and bottles of water as they gathered in a circle. He produced a quart sized plastic bag with cocaine in it. He dipped the end of his long tanto knife into it and went around the circle offering it to each man. In the red glow of the taillights, he spoke to them as they sniffed the cocaine from the blade as if paying homage to the shiny steel they knew would draw gringo blood that night.

"Tonight, we get revenge for our friends. We get revenge for ourselves. And we get revenge for El Tigre. These African gringos betrayed us to the Americans and the Honduran Nacional de la policía. If our friends are still alive, they sit in a Honduran prison tortured by the devils that join the gangs. They have most likely all been murdered. and their bodies left to rot in the sun outside the prison. These gringos did that to our friends! These gringos tried to do it to us! If we had not been prepared and had the blessing of Santa Muerte, we too would have been killed, or in prison, which is the same thing. Tonight, we are going to drive in there and kill every last gringo we can find. Do not kill the people following the camp. They must tell our story. They must tell how El Tigre took vengeance upon those that betrayed him and how he was generous to those who did not. Allow the army soldiers to flee into the jungle. We do not want to kill the soldiers, but if they fight, kill them like dogs."

"Venganza! Venganza! Venganza!"

With vengeance still ringing in their ears and the cocaine sharpening their senses, they all inserted magazines into their weapons and fed live rounds into the breaches. Enrique looked up and saw the man on the machine gun charge the breach. It was the same gun they used to shoot down the Blackhawk. Now he would turn it on the canvas tents of the sleeping gringos.

Soon the headlights of the lead truck reflected off the army vehicle ahead. The vehicle's high beams came on instantly blinding Enrique and his driver. Enrique's driver flashed his high beams back and the soldiers dropped their lights to low. The convoy stopped well short of the army truck. Enrique could see two soldiers standing there with AK-47s. He told his driver he would talk to them. The driver passed the word back via his walkie talkie. Enrique stepped out with the bag of cocaine in his left hand and one-hundred US dollars in the other. His pistol was clearly visible in his waistband.

He approached the wary sentries with his trademark swagger and asked if they would accept a small gift in appreciation of their service to the country. The sentry on the right was friendly and willingly accepted the cash. The one on the left was jittery.

"What is in your trucks?"

Enrique stepped close to him and offered the cocaine up to the guard. The tiger on Enrique's face seemed to come to life in the headlights as he told them he was transporting cocaína. The soldier retreated slightly. Enrique acted offended and put his hand on his pistol. He saw the other soldier glance behind their vehicle. *It was a trap!*

"Arremetida! Attack!" Enrique yelled as he shot the soldier in front of him in the belly and the one holding the cash in the head. He retreated towards the trucks as the drivers accelerated towards him. The lead truck crashed into the army vehicle pushing it to the side as the other trucks followed. Kalashnikovs spat flames and roared from the sides of the cartel trucks into the darkness, but the darkness roared back.

The Nicaraguan Lieutenant agreed with Javier's plan. He assigned two of his men to the checkpoint. Their job was to stop the convoy and inspect it. If it was simply three trucks going to market, then it would pass, but if it were a threat, they were to play the complicit buffoons and it would be dealt with quickly.

Javier watched the exchange through his night vision goggles. He could tell this man was trouble. He carried himself with confidence. He was muscular with hugely over-developed biceps and moved with an athletic grace. The DEA body armor raised a question, but the tiger tattoo on his face left no doubt which side of the law he was on. Javier pressed his throat mic and told everyone to be ready. It went bad in a split second. The first gunshot was bright and loud, the second was nearly instantaneous as the shooter was quick. Javier's men heard the man yelling attack and running away. Javier ordered his men to open fire, but it was superfluous. The trucks erupted with automatic weapons fire with men shooting over the wooden sides of the trucks. The third truck's wooden sides dropped, and a machine gun started pouring deadly fire into the darkness. The ARC troops responded in kind. The outcome was preordained. Two squad-level weapons poured hundreds of rounds into the trucks as easily as a gardener using a water hose. The stream of tracer bullets flowed from the windshields along the doors and splintered the wooden barricades and the bones of the men hiding behind them. The ARC troops with assault rifles took careful aim at the heads appearing over the wood sides and unlike their opponents in the trucks blindly firing into the darkness, they could see their targets clearly through their night vision systems. Javier Cordova himself fired the shots that killed the machine gunner and the big fun fell silent. It was over before it began. The trucks were stitched with bullet holes. The level of fire was such there were no survivors. None except Enrique who, shielded by the trucks from most of the incoming rounds, managed to slip into a ditch and crawl away leaving his DEA body armor behind because of the weight.

One of the sleek ARC Eurocopters settled down to earth near the sight of the battle at first light. Sam, Dan, Morne and Marcus disembarked to inspect the savagery. Fifty cartel henchmen lay in the road lined up neatly facing the same direction. Many of them were headshot, but they also had other bullet wounds. An AK-47 lay on each of their chests. It was a hell of a picture and a powerful message to anyone thinking about messing with ARC.

The smell of blood and spent cordite took the visitors back to their past. They were all combat vets from the bush wars although Sam saw combat in other places as well and Dan had been in more hot spots than he could remember. This scene was a reminder of their past, but it was also a harbinger of the future. They all realized at some point they were going to have to fight again for ARC.

They congratulated Javier on the victory and were very pleased there were no ARC casualties. They expressed their gratitude to the Nicaraguan lieutenant who admitted it would have gone very differently without the ARC forces. Javier and Henry Claassen gave a briefing to the four on how it all went down. Javier produced the DEA body armor found not far from the trucks.

"I guess we know who this belongs to."

"Ja, as if there was any question," Marcus chimed in.

"This Enrique has more lives than a cat," Dan added.

Sam stepped up on the truck with the machine gun. Using his phone, he took a picture of the long row of dead men. Morne circled a meeting with Marcus, Javier, Henry and the Nicaraguan Lieutenant.

"Henry, are those trucks drivable?"

"No windscreens, but they will run."

"Lieutenant, if we load the bodies into those trucks, can your men take them back to Managua? It would be right for our people to do so and we want to make sure they get a proper burial."

"Si. But I will have to go with them."

Morne could see the man's apprehension. He knew he was worried about his own people as well as the cartel.

"When Sam and I meet with president and vice president Duran, and if any military officers come to investigate, we will let them know ARC was simply supporting you and your men. You are the real heroes of the day. You kept our workers safe from the criminals."

Morne said this in a voice loud enough to be heard by everyone around. Javier stated it again in Spanish to make sure the Nicaraguan forces understood as did the workers.

The Eurocopter landed Sam, Dan, and Morne at the Managua airport. One of Julio's nephews was waiting on them with two escort vehicles. It was a relatively quick trip to the Presidential Palace where Sam and Morne attended an impromptu meeting with the vice president. Isabella's chief of staff cleared her schedule when Sam called with news of the attack. She stared impassively at the photo on Sam's phone of the fifty dead narco-soldiers laying across the road.

"And how many men did you lose?"

"None. But you lost two good soldiers."

"Such is the price in dealing with criminal elements. These look like gang members to me."

"Isabella, with all due respect, you know these are not gang members. These are cartel soldiers sent to kill our people working on the towers."

"Ja. We all know these men were sent by Azteca Cartel. It is an escalation after a failed assassination attempt on Sam and the DEA intercepts of their drugs in Honduras."

"And what do you know of the DEA intercepts in Honduras? Did you tell the DEA when the trucks were coming?"

"No," Morne lied.

"Then tell me why a DEA helicopter landed on your runway in Honduras?"

"Because it had been shot full of holes and our runway was the closest safe landing. When they declared an air emergency and sat down, what were we to do?"

"Gabriel Perez believes you are complicit."

"I don't much care what he believes," Sam stated.

"We simply want to build the power plant and towers in peace and bring electricity to the people, Madam Vice President," Morne added.

"As I see it, there are two options. The government can send more troops to the tower site and the power plant, which I suspect you will not like, or perhaps my husband can get Perez to stand down. We will have to entice him. Most likely with money, so I will need assistance from you."

"We are not going to pay ransom to keep the cartel away and I believe we have shown we don't need more troops," Morne said.

"Do you really think a man known as El Tigre is just going to stop now that you have slaughtered fifty of his men? He will come at you harder. We need to offer him a million dollars a month and hope along a stern warning from El Presidente will be enough to dissuade him from further violence."

"We are not going to pay a million dollars a month," Morne countered.

"You will have to pay it. You will make it a donation to the Ministry of Agriculture, and they will give a grant to one of El Tigre's companies. It will be clean money for him."

"You are not following me, Isabella. There should be no payment. The government must put their foot down on the cartel. They must come under control. They are threatening the future of the country."

"Every day is a fight for the future of our country. We have protests and uprisings, no doubt influenced by the Americanos," she said with a slight look of distain in Sam's direction. "We have gangs attacking protesters. The media worldwide spreads the lies coming from the law breakers. The church is involving themselves in matters of State, and now, we have the cartels, who have always been on the side of the government, putting us in a bad position with your project."

"So, it would seem we are the only law-abiding people in the groups you just mentioned."

"Are you? Are you so law abiding? You just showed me a picture of fifty Nicaraguans you killed."

"That was self-defense."

"Was it? Why do you have so many armed men? Should we start looking into that?"

"Isabella, our agreement with your husband and the government was that we could bring in our own security to protect our investment. That is all we have done, but we may have to increase our security if the government cannot control the cartels," Sam interjected.

"Enough discussion! I will ask my husband to speak with Señor Perez. I will tell you where to wire the money. It is that, or we send troops to take control of things and make sure you are protected. Please travel safely. My office will be in touch," the vice president said dismissingly.

Morne spoke to himself in Afrikaans as he and Sam walked to the vehicles. His tone was terse and angry.

"If you want me to join in the discussion, you've got to switch to English."

"She is a fool. Does she really think a drug lord worth a billion dollars is going to be swayed by a million dollars per month?"

"It is probably just her extortion scam to take more money from us. If he can't get his product to market, he is losing more than a million dollars a month."

"Ja. I think you might be right. She admitted they are desperate to tamp down the protests. She needs our cash to fund the counter protests and the head crackers."

"Or to run. She may be setting up an escape plan for herself."

"She is pragmatic, but I think she is too ambitious. I think she will go down with the ship versus running."

President Beto Duran's chief of staff, Ernesto Ruiz entered the presidential office with dignified haste.

"El Presidente, tengo al señor Gabriel Pérez esperó en su teléfono satelital por usted."

The aging Sandinista sighed, looked at his desk phone and pushed the button with the red light next to it. His chief of staff sat down to listen to the conversation over the speakerphone. Duran was feeling tired today and was not looking forward to the confrontation he knew was about to happen, but his wife made it very clear in bed last night he must bring Perez under control. El Tigre threatened their plans with his foolish attack on the towers and he must stop the nonsense now. They had enough problems quelling a new wave of protests. The interference of the Catholic church as a self-proclaimed intermediary between the people and the government was making things harder. They didn't have time for El Tigre and his vendetta.

"Hola, mi amigo. How is your fine son doing?" President Duran asked.

"Leon is doing very well. He is very smart and an accomplished soccer player. Thank you for asking. How are your grandchildren and our esteemed first lady and vice president?

"They are well. It is me who has the troubles."

"How may I ease your troubles, El Presidente?"

"You must stop this vendetta you have with ARC. They must be allowed to finish their project and bring electricity to the people. The people need to see progress. Surely you have seen the news and understand the problems we are facing in the streets."

"I have seen it and I am ready to assist, but you gave these gringos control over the eastern border crossings. I am forced to use the West and the damn Hondurans are working with the Americanos to seize as much of my product as possible. The Americanos have me bottled up on the sea and in the air. I need that Eastern route open to trucks. I tried to send couriers with burros overland through the east and the gringos killed the guards. They lined them up and executed them in front of the porters to send me a message. Now, they have killed fifty of my men. I cannot let all of this go unpunished."

"You are not the law. I am the law. If there is punishment to be dealt out, the government will do it."

"You are the law of paper and television. I am the law of the jungle."

"Gabriel. We have known each other a long time. I am telling you to stop."

"Who are you to tell me? I am the one losing money every day. I am the one who must show the world you cannot kill fifty of El Tigre's soldiers and get away with it. I am the one who helped bring you back to power and pays your monthly stipend!"

"I do not want to see us come to bad blood over these gringos. The country needs them. Isabella and I need them."

"So, there we have it. The gringos are more important than me. After all these years working together, you and your bitch are ready to take another path."

"You will not disrespect the vice president," Duran said picking the title he wanted to use for this argument. El Tigre noticed. He could have said Isabella, or my wife, or the first lady. If he picked one of those, there would be little room for compromise.

103

"I will disrespect anyone who turns their back on a relationship built on my sweat, my blood and my money."

"We are headed down a bad path. Neither of us profit from a war, but I am willing to accommodate you if that is what you want," the President said coldly.

"A war with me is unwinnable. I can make what Pablo Escobar did to Columbia look like a sweet Sunday afternoon. You want car bombs, assassinations of public officials and a complete collapse of the Nicaraguan economy, push me."

"You say that because you think I will have to use the army to fight you. I will just pick up the phone and tell the Americanos to come get you. I have a US Senator in my pocket. The US military will just appear in the darkness, and you will never be heard from again. And if you are not afraid of that, remember this. My government is the only thing keeping their drones from circling you. Without that protection, they only have to push a button to kill you."

"Hijo de puta!"

"That is no way to address your president. Now, tell me again about your troubles moving your product north."

The conversation lasted another twenty minutes. When it was over, Gabriel sat by himself. Maybe there was hope in what the President was offering. He would have to see. His life had been a series of obstacles and he overcame most all of them to this point. This was just another problem to be solved. As a boy, it seemed he had to fight every day against the bigger boys, but fighting made him tough. Fighting made him clever. Soon, he learned to use his mind more than his muscles. He formed alliances with other boys. He made sure when he fought, he had the upper hand. He made an example of the boys he bested, then he offered them a place in his alliance. When he was recruited by the cartel, he worked his way up by taking on the riskiest tasks and being dependable.

There had been two leaders, partners from long ago. One had an unfortunate accident, and Gabriel informed the other partner he would suffer the same fate unless he allowed him to assume the mantel of drug lord and pay him an annual stipend to disappear. Gabriel still remembered watching the realization in the man's eyes as he saw the devil before him. He was a dangerous man in his own right, but he knew his time was up when Gabriel made the offer. He also knew Gabriel would keep his word, and Gabriel had never missed a payment in all these years.

Sam's mobile phone lit up. Isabella's private number appeared on the screen.

"Give me some good news, Isabella."

"I have excellent news for you, Sam," Isabellas said with the slightest bit of flirtation in her voice. "El Presidente came to an understanding with Gabriel Perez. El Presidente is going to use government transportation to move the commodities and in return Señor Perez will cease his vendetta against ARC."

"That's it? We kill fifty of his men and he walks away?"

"There is one more thing. El Presidente has stipulated ARC must pay for the expense of the endeavors, but that is only estimated at one-hundred thousand dollars per month."

"Morne said we were not going to pay."

"Señor Delport said you would not pay El Tigre. He did not say you would not reimburse the government. Besides, El Presidente is demanding it and I fear what he will do if you decline," she said with a melodic tone.

Sam agreed and hung up the phone. On the other side of the country, Isabella De La Corte Duran, First Lady, and Vice President of Nicaragua smiled as she examined the new polish on her perfectly manicured fingernails. She just increased her annual earnings by $1.2 million per year. If her husband ever found out, she would have to share it, but that was not a big concern.

Two weeks later, Dan was standing on his balcony looking out to sea when his mobile phone dinged softly with a number he did not recognize. There was an audio file on his encrypted app with a text that just said *from a friend*. He was hesitant to open the file, but figured it was worth the risk. The file was two men arguing in Spanish. Although he had no idea what they were saying, the tone was clear. He heard gringos mentioned amongst the yelling, so he assumed it was about ARC.

The ARC board gathered in their meeting room aboard the Santa Maria and listened to the argument between the Nicaraguan President

Beto Duran and the biggest drug lord in Central America. They had a staff member translate everything into English so they could follow along.

"It appears we are off the hook with this tiger fellow, eh?" Ansel Van Dyk proffered.

"I'm not so sure," Sam replied.

"You heard him agree to the deal with the President. He leaves us alone and in return the Nicaraguan military flies his drugs across the border into Honduras, El Salvador, and Belize," Jayden replied.

"I heard him accept the help of the military in moving his product. If the translation is correct, he never commits to letting us off the hook."

"The translation is correct and I believe so are you. It is implied, but the words never come out of his mouth," Morne added.

"Do we believe this gives us some bit of a reprieve?" Johannes asked.

"Surely it must," Katherine added.

"I don't want to bet the lives of our people on this guy's word," Sam said.

"Ja. We cannot trust him or the president," Marcus added with his deep baritone voice.

"Don't overlook the obvious," Dan said. "This came from someone in the US who likes us. Probably Jay Nobel. That means the DEA knows the Nicaraguan military is about to start transporting narcotics via planes into the neighboring countries. The Nicaraguans will be sneaky, but at some point, they will get caught by the DEA and then it is going to go public. Ronald Reagan had a field day showing pictures of the Nicaraguans helping the cartels back in the 1980s. It was big news and there were sanctions and all kinds of things. I guess these guys don't learn from their own history."

"Dan is right. This will only be temporary. The US will shut this thing down and the Tiger is going to want his eastern routes back and that means coming through us," Sam said.

CHAPTER XIII

S am and Katherine waited outside immigration in Terminal D of the Dallas/Fort Worth International Airport in Irving, Texas. A month passed since the audio recording was forwarded to Dan and Sam and Katherine were taking a hiatus from the colony by spending some time at Sam's ranch. Katherine waived and got Patson's attention as he exited with his backpack and suitcase. He hugged them both and Sam took his luggage from him.

"Are you tired from your trip?" Katherine asked as they climbed into Sam's maroon Ram pickup.

"No Ma'am. I'm excited to be here."

"We are going to stay at the ranch a week and then fly down to the ships," Sam said.

"Excellent. I am excited to see my friends again."

"I am sure they are excited to see you again too. Have you been studying the things I asked?"

"Yes Sir. I am scoring very well on the practice tests."

"I'm sure you are."

Sam arranged for Patson to get ahold of the PSAT study materials and he hired a tutor to help him virtually via web meetings. This test would not get him into a US college yet, but it would get him noticed and let Sam know where the boy really stood academically. The test was being given at the local high school this week and Sam arranged for Patson to participate. It helped that he was able to take his semester exams early and leave for the winter break before the end of term.

"The exams are in five days. That should get you past the worst of the jet lag and enable you to study some more. Katherine wants to take you shopping for a new suit."

"Do I need to wear a suit to take the test?"

"No. but every man needs a suit and you look like you have grown three inches, so Katherine is going to take you to get one while I am in a meeting."

Sam attended a board meeting at MADEC, the company he built up to be a public utility and leader in oil exploration. He had been the CEO until he got involved with ARC and was attacked in the press by the greenies for wanting to put a nuclear reactor near the Nicaraguan rainforest. He was demonized as a fracker armed with a nuke whose ambition would destroy a world heritage site. They called him a murderer because he was an outdoorsman in the same vein as Audobon and Roosevelt. He was the polar opposite of their lies, but they controlled the press. When Middle America Drilling and Electric Company's stock fell eight percent, the board asked for his resignation. It was a close vote and nasty discussion. The chairman of the board was the force behind the decision and in a surprise turn of events, the board jettisoned him as well and then asked Sam to return as the chairman of the board. They saved face in the press by firing Sam and the chairman, then quietly installed Sam as the chairman a few months later so as not to lose the top talent. The chief operating officer drew his line in the sand like Travis at the Alamo. He told them if they fired Sam, he was gone too, but Sam talked him out of that stance. MADEC was as much his baby as Sam's and now he was the new CEO.

Since Sam was tied up with the board meeting, Katherine took Patson to Brooks Brothers and bought him a beautiful dark blue suit and all the necessary accessories. They had lunch at a nice restaurant and avoided anything to do with Tex-Mex or barbeque. Since she and Sam arrived a week earlier, he had force fed her as much as she could take because he missed it so much. He told her as soon as things were more settled in Nicaragua, they needed to open a Tex-Mex restaurant as he was sure it would be the most popular place in town. She laughed and said it would never turn a profit as he would surely bankrupt it with his own eating.

Sam escorted Patson to the local high school and introduced him to the principal who would look after him. The principal was a kind woman and showed him to a classroom for the testing. Patson sat in the back and focused hard on the test. Even though the test did not mean a lot, he wanted to impress his adopted father. Tempting as it was to check out a few of the pretty girls in the class, he kept his head down. When Sam picked him up, he asked how he thought he did. Patson's reply was that he might have missed a couple. The reality was he scored in the top two percent. Colleges and Universities in the US were about to notice the orphan adopted by Sam Harrington from the African bush.

The next morning, Patson rose early and donned his new suit Katherine bought him earlier in the week. He only knew Sam and Katherine were taking him somewhere. He walked into the kitchen to see Sam and Katherine dressed in fine suits themselves. Katherine's was Chanel and Sam's was a custom job from a small shop in Fort Worth that was cut to accommodate his Lucchese boots. Sam drove them downtown to the federal building in Fort Worth. They parked in the garage and walked the tree lined streets with a seemingly endless parade of large pickup trucks passing as they did. Patson was curious when inside the great building they stopped in front of a door simply marked immigration. He started to put the pieces together as Sam turned to him.

"Patson, would you like to be a citizen of the United States?"

"Are you serious?"

"We didn't get dressed up for nothing, Son."

"Do I have to take a test?"

"It's all been arranged. I will require you to learn what you need to about America, but you don't have to take a test today."

"It's like a dream."

"So, that is a yes?"

"Oh Yes! Thank you."

"What about you?" Sam asked as he turned to Katherine.

"What?"

"Part of my deal with the DEA. If you want it, that is,"

Sam's eyes twinkled as he held the letter in front of Katherine. He watched her calculate a million possibilities in a fraction of a second.

"Who doesn't want to be an American?" She replied as she hugged him and then kissed him on the mouth. For a woman who was persecuted and driven from her home two years ago, it was a powerful moment.

They walked through the door and Sam handed two sets of papers to the bureaucrat behind the desk who in turn asked them to enter another door and take a seat. As they entered, they saw a room full of people. A lot were Hispanic, refugees from the failed economies of Central and South America, but there were Asians, African, Scandinavians and Italians all in the same room. When the federal judge arrived, she stated this was her favorite part of the job. In unison, they said the pledge of allegiance and took an oath. Sam's heart was full as he mouthed the words they recited. Despite the self-loathing lies and corruption of the truth the media continued to fill the airwaves and internet with, America was still the shining light in the world and people from all over the planet were willing to risk everything for a chance to be an American. That universal truth was what made the whole thing work and Sam knew if the country could root out the power hungry and corrupt, it would stand forever. But if it couldn't, he was building a place down in the jungle that would.

CHAPTER XIV

Sam's Citation X touched down on Katherine's runway in Honduras, which he described as smooth as a baby's bottom. Johannes and Anna were at the hanger and Patson beamed when he saw them. They all had lunch and Patson filled them in on becoming an American and informed them Katherine was also an American now. His enthusiasm was contagious, and everyone was happy to hear of his schooling and adventures. Sam gave him the day off and then put him back to work in the tool shed helping his former mentor. The reunion was sweet and genuine between the old man and Patson. The first man in line at the tool shed that morning was the big man Patson fought in the ring along with Adolph who put him up to it. They were grinning and happy to see him again. They agreed to eat lunch together even though it was their off time as both men were still working third shift.

After a couple of weeks at work, Sam caught Patson at breakfast and asked him to request a couple of days off for a little adventure. They boarded one of the patrol boats and Sam pointed it towards Honduras. They cruised under the dragon and marveled at the new bridge above them. They motored up the Coco River with Patson sitting in the front watching for submerged obstacles that would tear out the bottom of the boat or rip the lower unit off the motor. Sam navigated to the spot where his GPS indicated he dropped Aapo and he sounded the air horn three times. He drove thirty minutes further upriver and sounded the horn again, doing so at ten minute intervals as the river floated the boat back to the GPS coordinates. He nosed the boat up to the bank and Patson tied it off to a tree. He tossed Paston some mosquito repellant and they rigged two fishing poles.

"Now we wait," Sam said as they put their bobbers in the water.

Aapo appeared a few hours later quietly standing at the edge of the fire in his bare feet and loincloth. Sam smiled and he smiled back. Patson looked up from the fire. He never heard Aapo approach. Aapo pointed to his ear and then at the boat, then pointed to his nose and to the fire. They all grinned in understanding. The three sat around the fire and exchanged thoughts as best they could. Aapo was fascinated with the looks of the boy and could tell he was subservient to Sam. He was honey colored like Aapo's own people but had slightly slanted eyes and the curliest hair of any person he ever encountered. He wondered if Sam and the colorless woman with the sky eyes conjoined to make him. If so, there was powerful magic at play. The boy seemed friendly and he could not help himself from touching his curly hair. When the fish was gone, Sam drew an elephant in the dirt with a stick and pointed to the forest. Aapo nodded in understanding. Sam stood and kicked dirt over the fire, while Patson retrieved a Sam's day pack as well as his own. He held up a finger to ask Aapo to wait before going to the back of the boat and pulling up a full stringer of fish. Aapo was delighted with the bounty the boy gifted him.

Sam and Patson followed Aapo deep into the forest. It was not the impassable vegetation of the coast, but a massive rainforest of towering trees with diverse ecosystems at different altitudes. They walked for hours at a leisurely pace Aapo seemed capable of keeping up all day. Suddenly the forest parted and they entered a clearing with primitive huts suspended upon stilts many feet up in the air. Sam and Patson felt they had somehow passed back in time to the stone age. Aapo called out and his tribesmen gathered. They were wide eyed and amazed. They assumed Sam was the big white man from Aapo's stories, but they did not know what to think of Patson. The chief, who was also the tribe's shaman, pressed forward to look at the two.

"Who are these outsiders? Why have you brought them?"

"The old one is Sam. He is a friend. The young one is Patson. He is the son of Sam and also a friend."

He held up the stringer of fish for everyone to see.

Sam and Patson recognized their names, but could not comprehend the rest of the discussion, and discussion there was. The medicine man with his jaguar pelt cloak carried on and chided Aapo for bringing the strangers to their home. He already carried the stigma of being a rogue and travelling too far. Now he was bringing danger to the tribe. Several of the men agreed with the chief. The chief's eldest wife was not convinced though. She approached the two men. She stretched high to reach the top of Sam's head and stroked his hair. Then she reached over and lightly ran her fingers over Patson's. Patson smiled and she laughed. She scolded the men for thinking these people were dangerous. Sam fished out a pack of cigarettes from his bag and opened it. They all watched excitedly. He gave Patson his lighter and started handing cigarettes to everyone, men and women. Patson went around lighting their cigarettes and they were all amazed at the flame extended and extinguished by the disposable lighter. When everyone was drawing on their cigarettes, Sam handed the lighter to the chief and bowed slightly. Then he showed him how to use it until he could do it on his own. The chief declared they were to be friends of the tribe and motioned for them to follow. The chief showed them around with the whole tribe following. They had no idea what he was saying but smiled and nodded as if they did. There was a central fire circle in the shade of an enormous mahogany tree. Two staves with forked tops were driven into the ground outside of the fire and a spit spanned between them with some sort of animal roasting over the coals. It had been gutted and skinned, making it difficult to tell what it was. As Sam looked more closely, he saw the large front teeth extending from the drawn-up lips behind the vapers of smoke. He smiled and looked at Patson.

"Capibara."

"What is a capibara?"

"Giant hamster."

Patson started to recoil but remembered his manners. The chief motioned for them to sit, and the men did. The women milled around chatting with each other. They presented the men with a sour alcoholic drink from clay pots. Sam was given the honor of being first and then Patson. Sam smiled while his stomach decided if it would betray him. To Patson, it was a vague reminder of his home long ago and he smiled. He took a second big gulp and Sam issued a soft warning behind a smile for him to slow down.

Aapo gave an order to both of his wives and they began butchering the capibara and gave generous portions to Sam and Patson on broad leaves. They both admitted the rich lean meat was delicious with its smokey flavor. They both had seconds and ate some potato like roots that had been grilled over the fire until the sugars inside caramelized and were tasty and sweet.

The sun set behind the trees and dusk fell over the forest. With bellies full of rodent and fish, everyone lounged around the fire. Sam cleared the floor with his boot to form a dirt pad. He drew a crude elephant in the dirt. Aapo got everyone's attention and pointed to the elephant and gave a great dissertation about how Sam was linked to the elephant gods. He pointed to Sam's ivory cross and then to his own teeth and then to the elephant. The discussion became lively. The white man was powerful enough to wear the tooth of a god around his neck. They heard Aapo's stories from his earlier encounters, but now they could see it for themselves. Sam could not follow the discussion that lasted well over an hour. Finally, Aapo brought it to a close. He stood and began to sing a long slow tribal song. He was proud of his strong voice and Sam and Patson were surprised by the powerful notes coming out of such a small man. When he finished his solo, the rest of the tribe joined in and from time to time one of the men would take the lead and sing louder in his own solo while the others chanted along. When they finished, Aapo turned to Sam and prodded him. Sam smiled. He was no singer. He turned to Patson and said you are up, Son.

Patson stood and gathered himself. He began to sing an African tribal chant from his childhood, a sweet lullaby.

"Sleep now, little warrior…

It is your time to dream and grow strong…

The problems of today are not yours…

It is your time to dream and grow strong…

The cattle wait for your care…

Our people wait for your spear…

Sleep now, little warrior…"

The men and women joined him in the rhythm slapping their bellies and thighs to the beat of his song. He repeated the lyrics a few times and they were joyous when he concluded. Then they turned back to Sam. Sam waived his hands indicating he would not be taking part, but they goaded and insisted until he had an idea. He opened his pack and produced his phone. They were shocked when it lit up and he manipulated it. He entered his music app and scrolled through the different artists. He paused on Robert Earl Keen, Jr, but decided the Texas crooner might not be the best way to introduce the tribe to western music. He picked a haunting melody and introduced them to Adele. They sat silent and listened to the singer hit notes they had never heard a human make. Sam's power with the group continued to grow as he commanded such a seemingly magical device. He took Aapo's picture and showed them all the glowing image on the phone. This caused great discussion and they wondered how Aapo was now contained in the device and still sitting next to them. To calm everyone down, he took a picture of Patson and a selfie to show them there was nothing nefarious with the device. They seemed content with the outcome, although Sam wondered if they thought he had taken their souls. Late into the night, Aapo led Sam and Patson aloft to his hut with his two wives and their three children. Everyone slept on the floor. For Sam, it was a bit uncomfortable, but for Patson, it reminded him of the worker's quarters at Werner Von Schultz's safari camp where he slept as a child. He dozed soundly to the noises of the night.

Aapo led the way through the rainforest. It had been roughly seven years since Sam tracked an elephant. It was on the other side of the globe during the darkest point of his life. He was out of head with grief over the loss of his wife and got pushed into a mission to save a village from a rogue. It ultimately cost him a small fortune and part of his soul, but he killed the bull elephant in the last months of its life. It was an incredible beast whose ivory would have shattered the record books. Sam identified with the elephant and finding only more pain and disappointment in its death, he destroyed the ivory out of spite. The experience could have been the tipping point for a life wasted from that point forward, but salvation came to him in three things; a Spanish priest working the wild bushveld of Africa, the ghost of his wife Sarah appearing to him during a lightning storm, and the man-child walking behind him right now. Those three things coalesced at the same time to save him. He still supported the priest financially in shepherding his flock, and he last saw his wife's ghost the day he released these elephants they were tracking, but his greatest joy was helping an orphan with no chance become the strong brilliant young man he loved.

115

Aapo stopped and pointed at the ground. Sam saw the giant track on the forest floor. Then he saw the next and the next. As he oriented with them, he saw the direction they were headed through the forest. It was an easy track to follow, and he instinctively checked the direction of the wind. Once an elephant hunter, always an elephant hunter. The breeze was good, and they took up the pursuit.

Aapo was incredibly adroit in his environment, but he was no elephant expert. Sam politely took the lead after a bit and slowed the pace. Sam knew if they spooked them, the herd would run for half a day. After a half hour, they all heard a branch snap ahead. Sam wore a big smile as he turned and looked at Aapo. His mood was infectious and Aapo smiled back. Slowly, Sam led them forward continually checking the wind every ten steps or so. They kept moving forward until something out of the ordinary moved. They all saw it at the same time. An elephant stood a mere thirty feet way. It was pulling a branch off a tree and feeding it into its triangular shaped mouth. It was a young cow. Sam looked around and spotted another up ahead. He motioned for the group to get low and crawl behind him. He led them to a big tree with some clear area in front of it. They saw two more cows and finally spotted the bull. He was healthy and his tusks were large. He was eating a tree the size of a wooden fence post. As he fed himself the last of it, he started a guttural singing, and it was contagious within the group. Soon the whole herd was singing together in contentment.

The three men lay under the low bushes taking it all in. Sam was watching a cow walking towards the bull when he noticed a disturbance behind her. He was puzzled until he saw the grey baby bounding behind her reaching for her tail with his trunk. There was a disturbance behind it, and another baby came running after its playmate and grabbed his tail. Sam was overcome with joy. The bull must have mounted the females soon after they arrived. *Gestation on an elephant is twenty-two months; he must have worked quickly,* Sam thought. The third female he released sauntered by springing with a calf inside her. Finally, the younger bull passed by bringing up the rear as was his duty. Sam's elephants had grown from five to seven and would soon be eight. He motioned for Patson and Aapo to move backwards and as he started to follow, he thought he saw a white dress slip behind a tree.

Chapter XV

Ariela ripped the black hood off her head. She was lying on a hard bed in a room painted sunflower yellow. It was a large bedroom with two beds, a desk, a sitting area, and a bathroom. Her mouth held an acrid taste and was so dry she had difficulty swallowing. She rose wobbly onto her feet. Her high heels were still on. She opened the drapes and saw bars over the windows. The view beyond was beautiful jungle. She rounded the bed and almost tripped over her suitcase. It had been rifled. She went to the heavy wooden door. It had a lock and handle like a hotel door and was locked from outside. She jerked and pulled but found no give to it. She opened the window and heard roaring of water. She went into the bathroom and looked in the mirror. She knew she was trapped and felt nauseous. She gripped the sides of porcelain sink to steady herself as she stared into her own eyes trying to remember what happened.

She remembered landing in the helicopter and moving through the FBO to a waiting taxi. She gave the driver her address and he drove two blocks before stopping. A man entered the backseat and as she tried to get away another entered the other side. She struggled as they put the hood over her head. and she felt the sting in her arm. They must have drugged her. Where she was now was anyone's guess. Panic started to rise in her, but she tamped it down. She thought of Dan and that he would surely come to rescue her. She just needed to stay alive until he could find her.

There was a soft knock on the door. Adrenalin flooded Ariela's bloodstream making her vision sharper and her hearing better. Her breathing quickened and a tiny ray of hope entered her mind. A soft knock was a gesture of kindness.

The door opened as she rose from her seated position on the bed. Enrique entered and took stock of her for the first time. She'd fought like a jaguar when he tried to put the hood over her head, so he had never seen her fully before. Now, here she was wearing a beautiful designer dress with her hair done and her makeup perfect. Her eyelashes were long and her mascara dark creating a smoky look to her eyes. He was captivated by her.

An hour before, as Ariela stared into the mirror, she knew she had two weapons. Her mind and her body. She picked through the ruble of her suitcase and found one of the dresses Katherine gave her. She had been bringing them home in her suitcase one at a time over the last couple of months. She hung it in the shower and started working on her makeup and hair. She would use her mind to do battle with whoever was behind this, but her body would be the distraction.

She stared at Enrique sizing him up. He was a big man with a broad chest and powerful arms. The tiger tattooed on his face and neck made him seem sinister and he looked at her with eyes that seemed to be undressing her.

"May I help you?"

Enrique simply held out his hand in a gesture to join him. She approached without saying a word and put her fingers into his hand. He walked her out the door and down the hallway. She heard the bedroom door close and lock automatically with a click. He walked her into a courtyard where Gabriel Perez sat under an umbrella reading a stack of papers. Ariela took stock of the drug lord known as El Tigre. His silk shirt was unbuttoned nearly down to his linen trousers, and he wore expensive Italian loafers. He stood to greet her, and she saw the outline of his abs and how his shirt hung over his chest and stretched over his biceps. His hair was dark and thick with heavy matching eyebrows and a mustache so full it consumed his entire upper lip, but what she focused on was his crocodile smile and dark eyes. She saw him sizing her up and threw a touch more hip into her walk.

"Welcome to my hacienda, Señorita Sade."

"Gracias. I didn't have much of a choice."

"Please, let us not talk of such unpleasantness. Let me show you around."

Ariela walked with Gabriel. He took her outside the gate and showed her the majestic waterfall coming down from the cliffs above. He told her when the clouds settled low over the cliffs, it looked like the waterfall came from Heaven. He took her to the main courtyard. She marveled at the huge fountain against the eastern wall with a stone sculpture three meters high and three meters across of a tiger's head with water flowing from the tiger's mouth into a pool. Gabriel took Ariela by her slender arm and moved her to the western side of the courtyard. They passed between two tall stone monoliths with iron rings driven into them three meters above the ground. They equidistantly framed the opening of El Diablo's pit, of which Gabriel brought her to the edge. Ariela was mesmerized by the enormous copper striped cat staring up at her with great yellow eyes and a pink tongue lazily draped over its front teeth. Gabriel's grip on her arm was tight, an implied threat to set the mood for the next part of the tour. Ariela stared into the golden eyes of the cat as it rose and prowled towards the wall. She saw it lick its lips and take in a deep breath through its nose. It could smell her perfume. And her fear.

Gabriel escorted Ariela into his air-conditioned study and she gasped. Her sister Zanita was sitting at the table in the room. A boy a little younger than her stood next to her.

"Zanita! What are you doing here? Are you OK?"

"Your sister is fine. She was most helpful in fact, as I hope you will be. Please, meet my son, Leon."

"Mucho gusto, Señorita Sade."

Ariela did not return the greeting as she was focused on her sister's tear filled eyes and her bottom lip trembling in fear.

Zanita had been brought to the hacienda against her will two days earlier. She was hauled to the airport by her boyfriend along with Carmen and Vera, the Instagram girls from the bar. While she had not been mistreated, Carmen and Vera were slapped around a good bit before they were loaded into the back of the twin-engine plane that flew them to the hacienda. All three girls were terrified of what awaited them. When they landed, Carmen and Vera were dragged to another part of the house to see El Tigre. Zanita was locked in a bedroom. The Instagram girls' cries permeated the house for a time, then everything went silent. She was pretty sure she heard two gunshots outside the hacienda but couldn't be sure. When her boyfriend came and got her, they passed a window. She saw a worker with a wheelbarrow hauling the lifeless body of a girl across the yard. She saw a naked girl with an Aztec pyramid on her bare back lying face down on the stonework. She knew it was Carmen. The back of her head was missing. Her boyfriend brought her into Gabriel Perez's study and roughly sat her down. He told her to give El Tigre all of the information about ARC she gathered from her sister.

Gabriel walked behind his desk and sat in the luxurious leather chair. Behind him a large painting of a woman Ariela assumed was his mother hung behind him. The Santa Muerte death saint, the green skull that brought good fortune and money, was perched on the credenza behind him. Enrique moved closer to Ariela and herded her towards the desk. She stopped a few feet in front of it. Instinctively she looked for a weapon, but all that was on his desk was a power strip with five different satellite phones plugged into it. As if he could read her mind, Gabriel reached into his rear holster, removed his gold-plated Desert Eagle, and laid it on the desk.

"I have a problem you can help me with. Since your ARC friends killed fifty of my men, I have lost respect with the Mexican cartels that move my product into the United States. They are now slow to pay me and suddenly my shipments are the ones being seized at the US border. I need to send a message that there are consequences to crossing me. I need you to tell me about your African gringo friends building the power plant."

"I want assurances."

"What kind?"

"That my sister and I will not be harmed. That we will be protected while in your care and released as quickly as possible."

"I will give you what you ask, if you give me everything I want."

Gabriel questioned Ariela for an hour and a half. Her feet hurt from her high heels on the hard tile floor, so she shifted her weight from time to time to ease the discomfort. *Nothing she would not endure at a party, nothing she could not handle here,* she thought. He took copious notes on a yellow legal pad with a felt pen. He was polite but needled her for details about mundane things. She answered honestly because they did not seem to matter. She figured answering honestly would allow her to hide a lie amongst the truths when necessary. She would just have to remember the lies. He would be looking for inconsistencies.

Some things he seemed to know already, but she thought he might be guessing. Her brain was running multiple thought patterns as quickly as it could. What was he about to ask next and where would her answer lead? What had she told Zanita? What did he know and not know? What was she even saying right now?

Her first lie was about the ships. He asked a lot of questions about the ships. She lied about who lived on each ship. She told him she never knew the ships to leave the docks, even though every Thursday they went to sea and repositioned facing the opposite direction when they returned. She estimated the number of security personnel on each ship at a higher number than she knew. He asked if the ARC ships contained any children. She said they did. He asked on which ship the school was located. She lied saying she did not know. While this may have been another mundane question, she worried about it. She did not mislead him about the key personnel, even though she hated herself for it. She knew he might try to attack their families anywhere in the world if he wanted to, but she assumed he probably already knew about all of them.

After ninety minutes, he asked if she would like a glass of water. She did and Enrique fetched it while she relaxed. He sat it on the desk and walked back behind her. She was about to reach for the glass when Gabriel stopped her.

"That is a remarkable dress."

Enrique grabbed her from behind by the throat. He slid a knife under the halter around her neck and cut it away. The knife missed grabbing the gold chain that held the gold crucifix around her neck. Ariela clawed at the big hand choking her as she heard Zanita start screaming. The blade ran down her back and cut the rest of the dress away. Zanita's screaming was silenced by Leon's hand over her mouth. Enrique pushed Ariela, clad now only in her underwear, to her knees and pulled her head back by her hair to stare forward at El Tigre.

"Let us start again," he said as he calmly flipped the notepad back to the beginning.

A half hour later Ariela was struggling to focus. Enrique was not holding her by the hair anymore, but he ordered her to kneel upright with her arms behind her grasping the opposing elbow. It served to push her ample breasts, constrained by only a thin lacy black bra forward, which El Tigre seemed to enjoy as he leered at her between questions. If she tried to sit back on her feet, or let go of her elbows, Enrique would grab a wrist and raise her arm behind her back until she thought it must surely break. Pain radiated from her knees up through her spine. She kept trying to readjust, but there was no escape, and a thin sheen of sweat covered her body.

Gabriel pressed on with his questions and Ariela could not tell if it was her imagination, or if he was focusing on the ones she lied about. Zantia was taken from the room and brought back. She presumed to use the toilet or be fed. She herself had not eaten since she left the ship the night before, or was it two nights before? She couldn't be sure, but she felt weak. Time seemed to be frozen. She could not feel her knees now, but the pain in her back, neck and shoulders was ever present. From time to time, she would see sparkles in her vision she knew were not there. She tried to focus on answering the questions. She must repeat the same answers she gave before. She did not want to betray Dan and her new friends. She hoped she could hold out, but the pain was getting worse, and her mind was weakening. But she could see the legal pad and knew they were coming to the end of El Tigre's notes. She glanced down at the cross hanging from her neck and drew strength from the fact she knew they were almost done, and that Jesus would help her survive. She dug deep and used her reserves to push through. Her thighs and back were spasming keeping her upright and there was darkness at the edges of her vision, but she fought to hold on. As he finished the last question, Gabriel simply stared at her without saying a word. He flipped the pad back to the front and started again.

At some point, she gave up and collapsed onto her side. Enrique jerked off his leather belt and fed the end through the buckle to make a loop. He collared Ariela and pulled her upright on her knees. She hung limply by the belt. Gabriel opened his desk drawer and tossed Enrique a smelling salt. He crushed it with his free hand and held it under Ariela's nose. The ammonia ripped through her sinuses and she thrashed her head. She clawed at the belt around her neck until she could make enough room to breathe. Enrique would not let her fall again.

Gabriel began re-asking the questions. Ariela was unsteady on her knees and continually fighting Enrique to breath. She was red faced and the vein along her left temple bulged. She glanced over at Zanita, who had not spoken a word the entire time. Tears were streaming down her face. The questioning continued. When she became listless and did not answer, Enrique delighted in using the smelling salts. Gabriel would repeat the question and she would answer slower each time. She lost track of how long the questioning went on until finally, she blacked out to the point the smelling salts would not arouse her.

She awoke from the dark place with the ammonia of the smelling salts driving like nails through her brain. She recoiled and Gabriel sat her up on the floor. He gave her the drink of water.

"You are Ok. No damage done."

She sighed a small relief while she tried to assess the situation, but her mind was still too foggy.

"You told me the ships never leave port. Then you told me they always put to sea on Thursdays to drop their waste. Tell me the truth."

She smiled a crooked little smile at him. He smiled back and was startled when she spit in his face with the new moisture he had given her.

"Hand," was all El Tigre said as he rose wiping her spit from his cheek.

He pulled the belt tight and raised Ariela's head. She clawed at his muscular arms with less strength than she clawed at Enrique's before. Enrique walked over the table where Zanita sat and took Leon's belt from him. He wrapped it around Zanita's left arm and tightened it in a tourniquet until she squealed. Her squeals turned to horrified screams when Enrique pulled out his big knife.

"You said you would not hurt us," Ariela croaked.

"You have not told me everything. She will probably survive, but the hooks she uses for hands in the future will be a constant reminder you did not tell me everything."

Enrique placed the blade on Zanita's wrist and drew back to begin cutting through the joint. Zanita screamed while Leon held her down.

"Alto! Thursday. The ships put to sea on Thursdays," Ariela sobbed.

Enrique lightly pulled the knife across Zanita's wrist. The burr on the edge opened a thin slit of skin, just enough to burn and make Zanita squirm. He smiled at her. El Tigre released the tension on the belt and allowed Ariela to breathe.

"Which ship has the school on it? You said the Santa Maria, then you said the Niña, then you said the Pinta. Which is it?"

Ariela was sobbing at this point. Her insolent spitting made things worse. Her momentary victory had been erased quickly and she tried to take refuge inside herself. El Tigre pulled her upright by the belt and shoved the smelling salts under her nose. She fought against the belt, but he had her attention again.

"Cut the bitch's hand off."

"The Niña."

"At the back of the ship or the front?"

"The back."

"How far below deck?"

No answer.

"How far below deck?"

More smelling salts.

"How far down is the school?" He screamed in her face.

"Six or seven levels."

"Is the school on the right side or the left side?"

She did not answer. He pulled the belt tighter. Her face was red and the veins and arteries in her neck bulged. Her weary arms hung limply. She was giving into the darkness when she somehow found the strength to mutter…left. El Tigre dropped the belt and she collapsed into a pile on the floor, her long black hair cascading around her.

Ariela awoke. She was cold. The terracotta tile floor sucked the heat from her body as she lay there naked save her sweat soaked bra and panties. Her body was racked with residual pain. Her raw knees ached with the blood flow restored and her back was a series of knots connected to other knots. Her shoulders were weak and her neck was rubbed raw from the belt and scratched and cut where her own fingers dug into her flesh trying to create a gap. She raised her torso and focused ahead.

Leon was wrapping Zanita's wrist in a bandage. Gabriel was talking to Enrique when he noticed her attempting to rise.

"No need to get up, Señorita. I am through with the questions for now," he said as he walked over and stood in front of her. She looked up at him like a child playing on the floor and pushed herself up on a wobbly arm setting off a small electrical storm in her back.

"Then we have an arrangement," she said in a raspy voice she barely recognized as her own. "You will not harm us."

"I believe you answered my questions truthfully. I will not hold it against you that you lied about some things in the beginning. You are safe."

"And you will let us go?"

Gabriel did not respond. He simply snapped his fingers twice and Enrique hauled Ariela away.

Chapter XVI

Leon lay in his bed watching the ceiling fan turn. After the excitement of watching his father question Ariela, he'd gone down to the houses where the cocaine factory workers lived and coaxed one of their daughters into the jungle near the waterfall. He was charming and playful, working hard to get what he wanted. When she finally gave in, he took her over a small boulder overlooking the pool and when she complained he was being too rough, he was rougher. When he finished, she slapped him and walked home alone sniffling with tears in her eyes. He felt a little bit of shame and called after her saying he was sorry, even though he wasn't.

Momentarily satiated, he walked back to the hacienda. It was nearly bedtime, but he stopped by the kitchen and got a snack before retiring to his room. He thought about what he had witnessed today. It was exciting seeing Ariela nearly naked and on her knees. He liked the power his father held over her. It was intoxicating. Ariela was beautiful, but she was too old. She had to be thirty. Zanita was more his age. He felt powerful when he held his hand over her mouth while she was screaming. He thought she was pretty, and she seemed more compliant than her sister. She had been hanging around one of his father's men in Managua, but he was back in the city now. He heard his father promise Ariela they would be protected while in his care. He wondered if his father would be angry at him for spending time with Zanita. He decided he probably would given what he wanted to do with her. Still, he found her irresistible and decided the reward was worth the wrath of his father if he got caught, but he made himself a vow to be careful. He drifted off to sleep with visions of Zanita in his dreams.

The next morning, he was up early and in the kitchen when the cook prepared the breakfast for the two women. Leon volunteered to deliver it to them. He knocked on the door of the yellow bedroom, which was now a prison cell, then opened it. Zanita was there to meet him. He excused himself as he pushed past her to set the tray on the table. Ariela was in one bed and the other had not been slept in. It appeared the sisters slept together last night. Ariela rolled over and looked at him. Her neck was discolored from the belt and her exposed knee was red and raw.

"Puedo traerte algo?" He asked.

"Maybe some ointment for my sister's injuries," Zanita responded.

Leon nodded and returned a few minutes later with some first aid cream. She thanked him and smiled.

Leon was dutiful. He was there, breakfast, lunch, and dinner to deliver the meals to the women unless he was otherwise detained. He made sure his father saw him doing other things in the morning and afternoon. His father maintained certain chores he was required to do around the cocaine factory and the household property. He tried to act nonchalant about the women locked in the bedroom, but he thought about Zanita a lot. He thought about her when he first woke up and at night when he laid down.

Ariela and Zanita were living through their fifth night as captives in the Tiger's casa. They were becoming lethargic and stir crazy at the same time. The only people they ever saw were the ones that brought their food, which was mostly Leon. Ariela repeatedly demanded to see Gabriel, but she was always told the same thing. Apologetically, he was not available.

They did not cry anymore. They fought twice, once a slapping, hair pulling frenzy and once a war of words. Both times the older sister came out on top but felt no better for it. She was cruel for in those moments she hated Zanita for betraying her, but afterwards her heart softened, and regret set in until the pain and rage built back up and Zanita was the only one to take it out upon. For her part, Zanita tried to stand up for herself, but she knew she deserved everything Ariela said to her. She could not bring herself to beg for her sister's forgiveness, but she knew she was right and at night, when she was sure Ariela was asleep, she cried for being the fool. Ariela warned her about the men she hung around with, but she was drawn to the excitement. The bad boys did not obey the strict laws of the government. They flaunted them. She wanted to flaunt them and the rules of her home. The rules set by her parents and her older sister. Now she knew it was simply folly. She was a plaything for people more powerful and less caring than her. She would never be free. She might never see the outside world again. And if that was how it was meant to be, then she would do one last thing. Find a way to atone for her betrayal of her sister.

She was up early and slipped into the washroom. She quickly stripped off her clothes and showered. She used Ariela's razor to clean herself up and then applied lotion to herself so that her skin was as smooth and shiny as Venetian plaster. She added a dab of perfume and a bit of makeup as she looked at herself naked in the mirror. She was not her sister, but she was attractive enough to accomplish what she wanted. Afterall, she noticed how Leon looked at her and ignored her sister whenever he brought their meals. She quietly re-entered the bedroom and took to the closet. She found one of Ariela's dresses that was form fitting. Form fitting on Ariela, not on Zanita. But she rationalized she could make it work. She retreated to the bathroom and slipped it on, adjusted it as best she could and once satisfied set her mind to the task at hand. They needed an ally. They needed Leon.

Zanita knew she had but a few moments before he would arrive. She opened the window of the bathroom. Bars prevented her from escaping, but outside a sacuanjoche grew and its closest flower was just barely within reach. She stretched out and pulled at a leaf to bring it closer as the bars dug into her shoulder. She was barely able to pluck the flower. She stuck the fragrant blossom over her ear and marveled in the mirror at the spiraling pedals that started yellow at their base then swirled pink on one side and white on the other as they spread out. She decided it was adjusted perfectly just as there was a knock at the door. She swooped into the bedroom and presented herself in front of the door.

Leon was shocked. Zantia looked amazing. So amazing he did not know what to do. She took the lead.

"Please come in. You may set that over there on the desk," she said giving him instructions for the first time.

He complied.

"I want to thank you for being so nice to me and my sister. You have simply been wonderful, Leon."

"Gracias. I like bringing you things."

"I like you bringing things. You are so much more pleasant than the other people who bring the food. I think you and I could be good friends."

Leon looked at her. She was beautiful. He wanted her, but he also knew a game was being played.

"Do you think you can put a flower in your hair and fool me?"

"No. It's not like that. I just…"

"You just what?"

"I just wanted to say thank you. I know I may never leave this place. I just wanted a friend. Someone to go on a walk with or talk to other than my sister."

Leon took her in, then left without saying a word. Zanita crumpled onto the bed and started to cry. Ariela who had said nothing rushed to her side.

"I am so stupid. I thought I could get him to like me. I thought maybe I could…"

"You did good."

"No. I failed."

"You didn't. Trust me. You are under his skin."

Leon stood alone in the shadows watching El Diablo pace back and forth. The tiger's pen was an open pit, but below the surface, one side of the enclosure was thick plexiglass and could be accessed through the hacienda's basement. Leon liked to come down here and watch the tiger. The three-inch thick plexiglass was honeycombed with four-inch circles. It kept the tiger enclosed but allowed the sights, sounds and smells to flow freely from the cage into the basement. There was a recessed alcove where Leon could sit in the darkness and not be seen by anyone standing above in the courtyard. He would sneak down here when his father was going to throw someone in the pit. The view from up top was good, but down here, one could see the action as if one was the tiger himself. One time he even looked a man in the eyes as he flung himself against the glass. He thrust an arm through one of the holes and his face into another begging for mercy. Leon stepped into the light that day and the last thing the man saw was Leon staring back at him as the tiger landed on his back and bit through his skull. Now though, Leon's thoughts were on Zanita. He mulled the situation over and over as El Diablo paced. His father casually warned him yesterday to stay away from the girls, which made her even more desirable. Then there was the danger of Zanita herself. *Would she really try to trick him?* Most certainly, but he would be careful and keep her under control. He was confident he could do that.

Leon came back to the yellow bedroom that afternoon when he knew his father was taking a siesta. Zanita looked as beautiful as she had that morning and he had not been able to stop thinking about her.

"Would you like to take a walk?"

"Si."

He spirited her down the hall and down a back staircase to a side door. He opened it quietly and pushed her inside. The room was large and had been converted into what she first thought was horse stables, but quickly realized were full cages. She could smell the cats immediately. She stepped to the side and looked in the first cage to see a great tiger lying on a pile of straw. The cat acknowledged her but did not make a sound. It was magnificent with its copper coat and black stripes. Its huge yellow eyes seemed to glow in the dimness of the room. Leon led her to the next cage. This tiger was on its feet. She connected with this beast's eyes as well and it turned sideways and pressed itself up against the bars. With a slightly trembling hand, she reached out and tentatively touched it on the back. It made no reaction, so she began to pet it. It raised its head acknowledging that it felt good. She was moved that she could have a connection with such an animal. Leon let her pet the tiger for a minute, then led her outside through the shadows to a side gate in the wall and out into the rainforest beyond. He led the way down a path that ended at a spot overlooking the waterfall. It was the dry season and the water fell steadily down the waterfall and pooled below before starting its journey to the sea through the bottom of the valley. Small mists of water escaped its grasp and formed rainbows as it fell freely to the valley floor below. In the rainy season, the waterfall was an angry raging beast, but now it was a gentle lamb.

"It is so beautiful."

"I think it is the second most beautiful thing in the valley," Leon said exactly as he had practiced.

Zanita smiled and looked him in the eyes.

"Why did you ask me to come on a walk?"

"I like you."

"What do you like about me?"

"I like how your eyes lit up when you saw the beauty of the waterfall. I like how the light catches your hair. I like how smooth your skin is and how full your lips are."

"What else?"

"I like how brave you are and how smart you are."

"How am I brave?"

"You came out here with me."

"Are you dangerous?"

"No, but if my father finds out, he will be furious. That takes courage."

"I guess it does. Why do you think I am smart?"

"Because you are trying to trick me."

"What?"

"This morning was a blatant attempt to seduce me so I will help you and your sister escape."

"Leon Perez, you know nothing of women. I am not some silly village girl. I am a woman from Managua. If I like a man, I show him by looking my best. I don't play games. Besides, what could you do anyway? Can you fly a plane to get us out of here? I saw how your father treated you. You will do his bidding. You are loyal and will never cross him. I simply liked you and chose to show you. Please take me back to my room now!"

Zanita did not say anything more to Leon as he led her back into the house. She and Ariela did not speak for five minutes after the door closed and then only in whispers.

"Did you do as I suggested?"

"Yes. And I think it worked. He seemed very confused."

"Good. I am proud of you, baby sister."

The morning after his scolding by Zanita, Leon arrived with the girls' breakfast. There was a sacuanjoche flower in a small vase on the tray. As Leon placed the tray on the table, Zanita touched his hand.

"I am sorry for yesterday."

"I am sorry I said you were trying to trick me."

"Let's choose to forgive each other."

Zanita squeezed his hand lightly.

"Can we try another walk this afternoon?"

"Of Course."

As the door closed, Ariela winked at her younger sister.

The walks became a daily thing. On the second day Zanita asked Leon why Carmen and Vera had been killed. He said his father grew tired of them talking about cartel business on social media and bragging about activities the authorities and their competitors should not learn about. His father was an equal opportunity killer. Man, woman or even a child, he did not care. If someone crossed him or the business, they were dead. Zanita's blood ran cold when he told her this, thinking of the position she and Ariela were in. She admired the two Instagram girls and the images of their lifeless bodies in the courtyard being wheeled out in a wheelbarrow came flooding back. She wondered if there was a wheelbarrow waiting to take her corpse into the jungle.

On the third day, Zanita allowed Leon to kiss her. By day five, the passion was hot and by day seven, he was sneaking her into his bedroom at night and they were exploring each other as new lovers do. For her part, she was fiery and passionate, trying things the way he liked them and teaching him a thing or two. After each encounter, she felt more and more confident she was gaining control of the relationship. As for him, he was eager, but kept control, only showing her the side he wanted her to see. He kept the darker parts of himself from her so as not to scare her too soon. In his young existence, he'd witnessed much, and his father's psychopathic blood flowed through his veins. The simple girls of the cocaine factory workers were easy to manipulate. The young harlots of San José and Managua were street wise, but he was able to hide the darkest parts of himself from even them until the right time. A time when they could not escape, and they could not do anything but submit. Zanita was intelligent and thought she was more worldly than him. For now, he would play along like a normal man-child and let Zanita think she had the upper hand.

Chapter XVII

Patrick Callahan saw the airstrip ahead as the Cessna snaked its way through the green valley. The walls were high on each side and he could see the plane's shadow racing along the seemingly impenetrable vegetation below. The only break in the green was the stream flowing through the middle of the valley. He saw a beautiful pool a mile back where the stream dropped off a ledge and the waterfall carved the blue circle out over the millennia, but it was nothing compared to the one-hundred-foot waterfall he saw up ahead. The landing strip was cut to the left of the stream high enough up the bank to be out of the flood zone during the rainy season. He caught a glimpse of a great hacienda past the landing strip.

The hacienda was up a stone walkway. Pat carried his duffle over his shoulder following his pilot. He passed the main gate and a man with a tiger on a leash gave him pause. The tiger was beautiful, but scary at the same time with no bars between him and the great cat. The guttural purring of the cat seemed to reverberate in his chest. With the awe of the scene, his mind raced to take in the whole experience as it seemed completely unnatural. Still, it was not the strangest thing he ever encountered in his line of work. It wasn't even in the top ten, but it was startling to round a corner and come face to face with such a beast. He shrugged it off and continued towards the front doors convinced it was but another idiosyncrasy of the rich and evil.

Pat had talents and a lack of conscience that allowed him to use his skills in the service of less-than-lawful people and causes. Luckily for Pat, there seemed to be an ever-growing list of people around the world willing to pay handsomely for his expertise.

Pat was from Ireland, Belfast to be precise. He'd been brought up to hate the injustices of the British from an early age. He hated the Anglicans who looked down on the Catholics of Ireland and occupied their country with an iron hand. *How just was it that a man could not get a job in his own country because he was raised Catholic? How just was it that when good God-fearing men protested, they were shot down in the streets by the British police who claimed they were there to protect the populace? How was it possible to sit by and do nothing when the British Army rolled through the streets of Belfast in armored personnel carriers and machine gun bearing thugs raided the homes of good Irish families?* It wasn't and under a false flag, he joined the Royal British Navy when he turned seventeen. He enlisted to learn explosives. They'd been suspicious of him at first, but he played the part. He talked of how the IRA killed his family indiscriminately while trying to kill British soldiers. Without a family, he needed a future, and like so many desperate boys before him, he turned to the military for opportunity. He worked hard in training. He became professional and disciplined. He sang their songs and even attended the Anglican services. He fooled them all and was allowed to join the underwater demolition teams. He learned about diving, fighting, and blowing up things in the cold waters off England. Upon graduation, he got a weekend pass and caught a train to Glasgow where the IRA picked him up and brought him home to Ireland. British Intelligence would learn soon they trained a very formidable opponent. So talented was he, he still was on MI-5's most wanted list and MI-6 had authority to kill him if they ever encountered him outside the UK.

His skill served many masters in the past twenty years. Jews, Americans, Russians, Africans, and Muslims all went to meet their makers when the price was paid for his skills. Now it appeared someone in Nicaragua was to be added to the tally. He worked for whoever could afford his personal price, or whoever the Irish Republican Army ordered him to work for these days. This was an IRA job. Orders from Dublin were to visit Gabriel Perez, AKA El Tigre, and give him whatever support he required. In Pat's case, that meant something, or someone, was about to get blown up.

He was escorted into El Tigre's study. It was cool in the valley by the waterfall and the floor to ceiling doors were open to a Spanish tiled veranda with its view of the great waterfall. He took notice of the room. The furniture was heavy mahogany. There was a very solid table in the room and a desk. The tile floor was the same terracotta as the veranda.

Above the desk was a picture of a dark-haired woman he assumed must be a matriarch of the family. He saw the wooden mahogany cross on the wall and thought at least he was working with a Catholic. It was far preferable to selling his trade to the Muslims be it the Chechens, Palestinians, or Persians. Then he saw the Santa Muerte death saint statue with its green tattooed skull. He wondered what abomination this curse was upon the faith which he professed, but only tentatively believed.

Gabriel Perez made his appearance with Leon in tow. Enrique entered a moment later.

"Señor Callahan, it is a pleasure to make your acquaintance," Perez said with the same dead eyes Pat had seen time and time again from his employers.

"The pleasure is mine, eh. You have a very nice place here."

"Mucho Gracias. Is there something I can get you, a drink perhaps?"

"A good Irishman never refuses a drink. But, before we get to that, I need to see the payment."

Gabriel led Pat down the hall to a small gallery. Leon and Enrique followed. Pat was amazed. He was no art lover, but he knew the significance of what he was seeing. The *Sea of Galilee* was the only seascape Rembrandt ever painted. In one of the greatest art heists of all time, it was stolen from the Isabella Stewart Gardner Museum in Boston in 1990. Its value was in the millions of dollars and here it was hanging in a secluded house in the middle of the Nicaraguan jungle. It, plus $50,000 in walking around money for Pat, was the payment for the IRA's services. Pat approached the painting and stared closely at it. He was not an art expert, but it looked very old. It was either authentic, or a perfect forgery. He could see where it had been cut out of its frame when stolen from the gallery.

"I need to make a call."

He retrieved a satellite phone from his bag, went out on the patio and dialed a number in Dublin from memory. He held his bandana over the microphone in an attempt to disguise his voice. He knew the US NSA and the UK GCHQ would pick up the satellite transmission. He had to alter his voice patterns less the call be flagged, and MI-6 know where he was.

"Hello?"

He responded in Gaelic. "This is Gulliver. The payment is verified to the best of my ability."

"Proceed," was the response before the line went dead.

Pat walked back inside. "I'll take that drink now. What's the target?"

The Cessna landed in San José, Costa Rica. San José was a far bigger and better city than Managua and it was closer to El Tigre's compound. Pat Callahan needed to pick up a few things to complete his mission. Gabriel Perez sent Leon along to assist. Leon loved getting to the city, so he was more than happy to go, even if it meant being away from Zanita for the day.

Gabriel Perez's driver in San Jose picked them up at the airport. The first stop was a hardware store. Pat filled Leon's arms with tubes of waterproof silicone and waterproof adhesive. He sought out the strongest magnets as well as wire, electrical tape, cutters, and a soldering kit. He made Leon pay for it all. The car took them to a large camera shop and Leon bought waterproof camera cases the size of shoeboxes at Pat's request. Afterwards, Pat asked for a household goods store, and he had Leon purchase digital kitchen timers and batteries to power them. When it was time for a break from their errands, the driver drove to a retail area with restaurants and stores. The driver referred them to a nice restaurant. Pat, ever cautious, insisted on sitting in the back where he could see the front door.

"Let me see that knife you carry on your belt, boy."

Leon produced the six-inch long semi-circular blade from its sheath.

"That is a nasty looking blade. Looks like a raptor's claw. You have it sharp too. I'll have to be careful not to cut myself, eh."

"It is called a carambit."

"I know what it is called, boy. I like the ring for your first finger. Makes it like a pair of brass knuckles and this wicked blade is good for slashing. Really good if you can get it around a man's neck," Pat said as he held the knife up to his own neck.

"I want to go into a shop across the courtyard before we leave."

"What do you want to buy?"

"I don't know. A bracelet or a ring or something."

"For that lass I seen you sneaking around?"

"What?"

"I got a keen eye, boy. Didn't stay alive this long by not paying attention. I know you are sneaking that girl out of her room, and don't want anyone to know about it. What is her story?"

"Nothing."

"Nonsense. Tell me."

"She and her sister are guests of my father."

"What kind of guests?"

"I'm not sure how to say it."

"Prisoners?"

"In a way, but he promised to let them go and not to hurt them."

"What did they give him in return?"

"Ariela, Zanita's older sister, is friends with the people building the power plant. She told him all about them."

"So, she is the source of the information about their ships."

"Yes."

"Is this Ariela as pretty as your Zanita? Maybe you and I could go on a double date. It gets lonely at night by myself."

"I don't think my father would allow that. He made an agreement with her they would not be harmed. He told me to stay away from them, but…"

"But you can't help yourself can you, laddie. We've all been there. A forbidden lass is too much temptation for a young man. I've had my share that is for sure. I'll keep your secret. You buy her a nice piece of jewelry and tell her you love her, and she'll give it up to you."

Leon smiled back. The red headed Irishman didn't understand a thing. The bauble was not because he loved Zanita. It was to aid in his manipulations. It was time to let her think she was completely in control and up the stakes of their game. His dark side was gnawing to get out, but he would escalate things slowly. He wondered how much she would be willing to endure for the promise of freedom.

The car took them to the only PADI certified dive shop in Costa Rica. It was a top-notch store with the latest gear including technical diving equipment. Pat found a black wetsuit, black gloves, and a black hood. He picked out a pair of Scubapro black split fins. Being a technical diving shop, it carried the Draeger rebreather and several brands of underwater scooters. He chose the scooter with the longest battery range and a black rebreather. It was not the military version, the Mark V, which was a fully closed system, but those were only sold to NATO military members. This version was semi-closed so there would be bubbles, but not as many as a regular open circuit scuba regulator. He stumbled upon a new mask design. It was from DiveBecon and it allowed a diver to find their way back to the boat with a heads up display inside the mask that worked with a transmitter on the boat. He grabbed one of those as well. As Leon paid out thousands of US dollars for the equipment Pat went through his mental checklist. Except for the explosives and detonators, which El Tigre already possessed, he had what he needed.

The Cessna landed at dusk on the valley airstrip. They flew at top speed to make it before dark. There was no way to find or land on the strip after dark. The valley walls were steep and any attempt to land without sufficient light was a suicide mission. Leon instructed the men greeting the plane to carry the items purchased up to the hacienda's work room where Pat would assemble his explosives. He presented himself to his father and reported on the day's activities. His gift for Zanita was burning a hole in his pocket. His father could sense his anxiousness and asked what was wrong. He said nothing and asked to be excused. He left in the direction of the kitchen so as not to arouse suspicion.

His knock was light, but Zantia answered quickly. They smiled at each other and without saying a word, she closed the door quietly behind her as they slipped down the hallway. They worked their way past the tigers and outside the walls of the hacienda to the waterfall overlook. Leon unfurled a small blanket to sit on and ceremoniously presented the gold bracelet with little colored gemstones to Zantia. The bracelet glittered in the moonlight as she moved it back and forth to catch the light at the right angles. She handed it back to him and he fastened it to her wrist. They lay down on the blanket as lovers under the pale light with the roar of the waterfall behind them.

As they lay in their post lovemaking bliss, she asked him about Costa Rica. She had never been to a city as big as San José. She asked why he went and he told her it was to escort Pat Callahan around and help him buy the things he needed to sink one of the Gringo's ships. In his drowsy state he didn't realize what he said. She tactfully changed the subject asking about what he ate and what he liked best about the city.

When Leon brought her back to the room, she slipped in quietly and waited five minutes before she slipped into bed with Ariela. They spoke in hushed whispers.

"They intend to sink one of your friends' ships."

"How do you know?"

"Leon let it slip."

"We must warn them."

"Yes, but how?"

The sisters lay awake scheming about how to get out of the room. When they failed to come up with a perfect plan, they shoved a towel under the door, turned on the lights and started to tear apart the room looking for options. Ariela took the drawers out of the desk. They were empty, but when she peered inside, she saw a single sheet of paper stuck inside. She fished it out and held it up to Zanita.

"I have an idea!"

Leon lay in his bed. He was tired after the long day and relaxed after making love to Zanita. He replayed the evening in his mind. With stark fear, he suddenly remembered what he told her about Pat Callahan preparing to sink one of the ARC ships. The feeling of dread washed over his entire body. He felt hollow and his hand tingled, but he reassured himself she had no way of contacting the outside world and he pushed those feelings away. Then he grew angry. She had tricked him. Tricked him into telling her something important after sex. He would make her pay for that.

Chapter XVIII

D an's face was serious as he watched the Eurocopter descend from a cloudless sky through his Oakleys. Julio's nephew silently stood next to him. Javier Cordova exited the front seat of the helicopter with his sling bag.

"What's up, Boss?"

"I haven't heard from Ariela in over a week. We went to her place, and it does not appear she has been home. Her suitcase was not there. We also went to the bank. The President has some other girl taking her place and she told us Ariela hasn't been to work since she came back on the helicopter."

"Could she have taken off? Left the country?"

"Doubtful."

"You sure? Could there be another dude you don't know about?"

"I'm sure," Dan said with a cold tone and a mask of indifference that thinly hid his desire to punch Javier in the face. "We spoke to her neighbors. Nobody has seen her. We know our helo dropped her right here and she went through those doors at the FBO. The guy on duty that day is about to start work. Julio's nephew is inside making sure his co-worker doesn't call him and tip him off we are waiting."

Julio's nephew opened the tinted glass door and motioned them in. Dan led the way. He'd requested Javier come not only because he was a top-notch operator who spoke Spanish fluently, but also because he respected him as a battle-hardened officer who kept a cool head when things went bad. Dan was self-aware enough to know he needed a safety-catch for his impulsiveness. An impulsiveness than tended to punch or shoot first and ask questions later.

Javier and one of Julio's nephews grilled the counter man for twenty minutes. He remembered Ariela's last visit. He remembered her every visit. Gorgeous women did not get out of sleek Eurocopters every day in

Managua. He told them she went outside and got in a red taxi. Nothing special. Nothing out of the ordinary. Dan asked him to show them the security footage. He seemed hesitant, but one of the nephews simply started walking towards the office and he relented. Dan's heart leapt when he saw Ariela on camera. She did as the man said and exited the building into the back of a red taxi. Dan could see the name of the cab company on the door. He took out his phone and took a picture of the screen. As they left, one of the nephews saw a card for the taxi company taped to the counter.

Their Toyota pickup stopped down the street from the address on the card. It was like every other street in the barrio. Concrete block walls touching other concrete block walls with ownership differentiated by the varying pastel paints peeling from them. The universal soccer game was being held in the street by the boys living in this part of the barrio. The nephews led the way with Dan following and Javier checking their six as they approached the open double gate of the taxi location. A large tan rooster with a red comb and three-inch spurs stood sentry in the opening, but arrogantly gave way to the four men. Three tired taxis sat on thin tires with their hoods up while two mechanics worked in the Managua heat to resurrect them. If they could not, they would be scrapped for parts for the rest of the fleet.

"Donde esta el jefe?" A nephew asked the first mechanic, who never looked up from this wrench tightening, just motioned towards the building with his head. Dan jerked open the door and made eye contact with the boss sitting behind the desk filling out paperwork. The man was clearly startled by the big American. Dan seemed to cover the space of the room in two strides. He leaned over the desk up close to the man's face.

"I'm Dan Weston, and you are going to tell me what I want to know," he said in English.

Julio's nephew took over asking about a fare at the airport at the time the helicopter landed. The man searched through is paper log to the time and date of the incident.

"Lo siento, no tengo ningún registro de eso," the man replied.

"Check again," Dan demanded deducing what was said and stabbing his middle finger into the ledger.

The man looked again at the paper and shook his head.

"Get a list of every driver and their personal information, then get a list of every driver that was working that day," Dan said as he walked outside with Javier in tow. He pulled out his phone and headed toward the mechanics. He pulled up the picture from the security camera screen. The driver could not be made out, but the cab could, and he was betting these guys knew every car intimately.

Javier knew instinctively what Dan was going to do and got ahead of him telling him to slow down as he passed. He produced two fine Cuban cigars from his sling bag and asked the mechanics to look at the picture and tell him who the driver was. They could not tell the driver for sure, but they said the cab was not owned by the shop. It was owned by an independent who contracted with the shop. They gave him the name of the independent owner. Javier shook their hands and walked back into the office leaving Dan to watch the rooster strutting around the yard. Javier and the nephews came busting out the door a couple of minutes later.

"We have the owner's address. He is not working today."

The Toyota stopped a hundred feet from the gate of the owner's house as they had done previously. Javier and one of the nephews made their way to the gate while Dan and the other nephew cut through the alley to intercept anyone trying to go over the back wall. The nephew banged on the gate and hollered a greeting into the barrio house. A man, they presumed to be the owner, opened the gate slightly and queried who they were. After an exchange, he humbly invited them inside. There was no sign of the taxi in the yard. Javier whistled and Dan and the nephew joined them. The man told them when he was not driving the taxi, he would loan it to a cousin. He scratched his head thinking about the day in question but finally remembered he was not driving that day. He used his mobile phone to call his cousin. He asked him to come by the house. There were some men who wanted to talk to him. The foursome could hear the cousin becoming agitated on the other end of the phone. The taxi owner told him to get over there immediately. These men would not hurt him, and he wanted to know what was going on. The cousin arrived within twenty minutes.

"I was leaving early in the morning to drive the taxi and there were three men waiting. They told me they were going to borrow my taxi and to give them the keys. I told them it was not mine to give. One had a pistola in his belt and he handed me four-thousand Córdobas. He told me they would be back in a few hours. I did not know what to do, and I was afraid, so I took the money. They brought the car back three hours later as promised, and they gave me another one-thousand Córdobas telling me to forget all about it."

"Who were these men?" Javier asked.

"I don't know. I think they were cartel."

"Not a gang, but cartel?"

"Si. I was very afraid."

"What else can you tell us about the men?"

"One of them had a tattoo on his face and neck, a tiger."

Dan walked onto the dusty barrio street while Jaiver needled the man for details. His mouth was dry, and his guts felt like they were infested with worms. He dialed Sam from his mobile.

"Any luck?"

"Yeah, bad. Very bad."

Chapter XIX

Gabriel went to his son's room early the next morning after the boy's return from San José. He did not knock, but peaked in. Even though Leon was essentially grown, he looked at his boy sleeping in his bed and thought of when he was a child. He seemed so peaceful under the blanket.

"Leon, wake up. I need you to take Señor Callahan down to the submarines. Assist him with anything he needs today."

"Si Padre."

Leon and Pat boarded the Bell Ranger helicopter belonging to Gabriel Perez. The submarine manufacturing area was nearby on the coast. When they arrived, Pat saw men putting the finishing touches on a submarine. They worked under the cover of the trees hiding from the American spy satellites they knew passed overhead with their high-powered cameras and sensors. The workers dammed off a slew from the river and built the boat in the newly dry land out of thick fiberglass. When it was time to float it, they would simply open the dam and let the water rush in. Pat crawled all around the boat looking at its components. It was about fifteen meters long with a diesel engine that drove a screw prop threaded through the hull. It had tanks of compressed air to control its depth. It had a hatch on the top where he could enter and exit, and they could open it to take in fresh air. It had a compass as well as GPS for navigating the open oceans. Inside the hull he could see the fiberglass ribs that gave it rigidity. It was more a semi-submersible than a U-boat, as it would not completely submerge, but the cartels used these homemade submarines to move billions of dollars of drugs into the United States. It was crude, but if they were able to cross the Caribbean from Nicaragua to Puerto Rico with these craft, he should be able to use this one to get near the ARC ships.

Back at the hacienda, Leon helped Pat with the construction of his limpet mines. Each waterproof camera box was packed tightly with plastic explosives with just enough room for a timer to send an electrical charge to the detonator. On the bottom of the box, they applied a thick layer of marine adhesive and attached the magnets. They glued the fishing weights to the sides below where the lids closed. If a magnet failed, Pat needed the whole box to sink rather than float to the surface.

"Why do you call them limpet mines?"

"Aye. It is an old term for a mine you attach to a ship's hull. A limpet is a fish with a sucker-like mouth. They attach to other fish and cut a chunk out and eat it."

"These are not big explosives. How will you damage a big ship with these?"

"It all has to do with the compressibility of water. You can't compress very liquid much. Since the energy cannot be dispersed into the water, it must go elsewhere. That means the ship takes all the force. I intend to lay these alongside her keel. I'll unzip her like you taking the dress off that fine lassie you been sneaking around with."

CHAPTER XX

The Board of Directors listened intently as Dan stood before them. As he described what he found in Managua, the tension in the room was palpable. When he was finished, no one spoke. They all turned to Morne and Sam seated at the center of the table.

"Dan, I think I speak for all of us when I say how sorry we are this happened. We are all very fond of Ariela. Could I ask you to wait outside while we discuss this for a moment, then I am sure we will want your input and consensus."

As the door closed, Morne turned to Sam.

"What are your thoughts?"

"First, she has been missing for over a week. Is she alive or dead? Second, why did they grab her?"

"Intelligence," Marcus Odendaal said.

"Why do you say that?" Ansel queried.

"If they grabbed one of us, it could be for revenge or to send a message. They grabbed one of our people's local girlfriends. That is not much of a message for a drug lord to send to us. If we had her body and could see where she had been tortured or mutilated, that would be a clear message. They are sweating her for information."

"I concur," Jayden said. "Since we increased our security, our helicopters have intercepted and diverted an increased number of aircraft away from the area. Our patrol boats have done the same. It could be the cartel is trying to get intel on how to attack us. The internet maps don't give you much on our location right now as they are over a year out of date and the Admiral put the fleet to sea when we knew the satellite was coming over to take pictures."

"So is she alive or dead is the question," Ansel added.

"Let's table that for a moment," Morne said. The next question we must address is what information can be gotten from her. Katherine, you probably know her the best of anyone here."

"She knows the inter-workings of our daily lives, and maybe some things that are...takties," she finished in Afrikaans.

"Tactical," Morne translated.

"Thank You. Yes, tactical. She probably knows how many men Dan has and how our security works. The big thing she knows is where everything is located."

"The obvious target is the power plant," Marcus said.

"Or the ships," Sam added.

"They already tried the transmission lines and failed. That was our softest target," Johannes said.

"Our security is already in a heightened state. But it seems to me, immediately, we need to go into a hardened defensive posture. Does everyone agree?" Morne asked.

Everyone nodded their approval.

"Right. Then after this meeting, we will bring in Dan and Admiral Sharpe to execute and adapt our defensive posture. Now, let's address the issue of Ariela. Are we all of the same mind we should try and get her back?"

Everyone nodded, but Marcus spoke up.

"As long as getting her back does not mean we sacrifice something critical."

"Marcus! We must get her back. She is a friend and what kind of message does it send to anyone who would befriend us if we do not try," Katherine scolded.

"I am only saying, we cannot be foolish. We must keep our heads."

"You are both right. Katherine, we are going to do whatever it takes to find her and get her back. Marcus, there is no single person, the group seated here included, that is so important we risk the new home of the Afrikaner people. We will keep our heads. Sam what are your thoughts on finding Ariela?"

"Dan has the old Contra network combing the city for any scuttlebutt or clues to her whereabouts. The simplest thing we can do is call Isabella or the president and ask them to intervene. If that works, this is over today or tomorrow."

"And if it doesn't?" Katherine asked.

"Then we must find her, and that is not going to be easy. We are going to need help. If the Contras can't get a lead, we need to approach the DEA and the CIA. I suggest we do that as soon as we know Isabella has failed."

The military men convened is the admiral's stateroom. Sam's call to the vice president's office asking for help with Ariela was met with incredulities, but a promise to help. A map of ARC's operation was spread on the table. The Admiral turned up the lights so everyone could see the map clearly.

"We must decide how we are most vulnerable. An attack could come by land, air, or sea. It could also be biological or chemical," Sam started.

"Agreed. We have control of our food and water. I feel safe in that respect," Morne said.

"So, land. Dan, push your sentries out down every road and donkey trail. Twenty-four hours a day. We need eyes on any path coming this way. I can totally see them sending a hundred men down a goat trail to attack us."

"Copy."

"Also, let's make use of those gyrocopters. Keep one in the air all the time watching the roads. Make sure they have night vision."

"Copy."

"Sea. Admiral, what do you suggest?"

"We need two additional patrol boats."

"I can help with that," Johannes chimed in.

"Good. I believe we should place a shore battery on each side of the harbor covering the two entrances."

"What do you need?" Dan asked.

"A fifty if I can get them or at least a M-249 on each side should do."

"Copy."

"I will put a patrol boat outside the reef, another five-hundred meters out and the last two one-thousand meters out. Also, I want to fill the shore tanks with diesel and the terminal tanks with avgas, then get the tanker out of the harbor. We can send it to the States to get the patrol boats. Be back in a few days."

"I have a friend that owns a couple of Russian transport planes. I can have him pick up the boats and get them down here faster," Dan said.

"Then I will move the tanker into the mouth of the Coco to get it out of the harbor."

"What about an air attack?" Sam asked.

"We can arm the helicopters," Johannes said. "That will work for another helicopter, or maybe a Cessna."

"But, not a jet," Morne added.

"No, but what kind of attack is going to come from a jet?"

"Nine-eleven was a jet-based attack," Morne said.

"You think Tony the Tiger has a jumbo jet?" Sam asked.

"I think he has more money than Bin Laden did," Morne said without laughing at Sam's joke.

"Maybe, but so far we haven't seen any suicide bombers."

"What if it is not an airliner? What if it is a Lear filled with explosives?" Johannes asked.

"Admiral?" Morne queried.

"That would sink one of the ships if it hit the side."

"It also could damage the reactor," Marcus added.

"I believe we should prepare for the worst," Morne said.

"If we need that kind of capability, call your buddy Razi in Israel. We don't have the ability to intercept a jet. We are going to need some kind of surface to air weaponry," Sam said.

"If we are calling Razi, I have a few more things I would like to put on the shopping list including the admiral's fifties," Dan added.

Two hours later, Sam poked his head into the war room. Maps hung on the walls. White boards were covered in names and assignments. A bank of radios sat charging on a table under the windows looking out to the ocean. Dan was instructing one of his leaders where to place the advanced sentries along different roads. Sam caught his attention and backed out of the room.

"Isabella had the President call Perez. He denies knowing anything about Ariela's disappearance."

"Liar! We have video of her getting into the cab taken from the rightful driver by a guy with a tiger tattooed on his face."

"Agreed. Time to ask for a favor. Call your DEA buddy Jay Nobel."

CHAPTER XXI

The ARC Eurocopter descended out of the darkness onto the landing pad at the US Embassy in Honduras. A DEA agent was waiting, as were a half dozen armed Marines. DEA Special Agent Jay Nobel insisted on Dan coming to a SCIF, a Sensitive Compartmented Information Facility. The nearest one was the US Embassy in Nicaragua, but he and Sam could ill afford to be seen walking in there. This was the next closest and the DEA was even kind enough to allow them to land at the embassy, a rare treat for a civilian aircraft.

Earlier in the day, Special Agent Nobel sent a dozen pictures to Dan's phone. All were leaders of the Azteca cartel. Dan sent them to Javier, who took them to the taxi driving cousin. He verified pictures of two of the three men who took his taxi. The picture of Enrique was before the tiger tattoo was inked on his face, but there was no mistaking him.

"We got verification some of the pictures you sent match the guys we believe abducted our person. We know one of them. He uses the name Enrique," Dan said as he and Sam looked at the picture of Jay Nobel on the screen. Their friend was seventeen-hundred miles away in Springfield, Virginia on a secure video link.

"That is Enrique Sanchez. He is Gabriel Perez's chief lieutenant. If he was there, it is certain El Tigre is involved. He would not be free lancing."

"Agreed. We have been strategizing on what to do from this point forward," Dan said.

"No ransom demands?"

"Nothing."

"How long has she been gone?"

"Eleven or twelve days."

"That is not good," the agent sighed thinking of all the horrors he'd seen the cartels inflict on innocent people. "You need to do a swap."

"What do you mean?" Sam asked.

"They took one of yours, you take one of theirs. Then you trade."

"I like that. How do we pull it off?" Dan said enthusiastically.

"We have a list of businesses we believe are run by the Azteca cartel in Managua. It would be a typical bag job. Stake them out and grab one of the higher ups."

"There is one more thing though…"

"What is that?"

"We want Enrique Sanchez. He killed a DEA agent. He is untouchable in Nicaragua. If you get the chance to grab him, we want him for trial in the US."

"What if we see him and can't grab him?" Dan asked.

"If you can't grab him, kill him."

CHAPTER XXII

Pat stood under a banyan tree looking at the crude submarine. Despite his host's assurances it would be safe, he wasn't so sure. It looked like a fifteen-meter homemade coffin to him, but he figured he'd done riskier things in his life. He watched as the workers hit the boards comprising the dam with sledgehammers and the water from the stream flowed in and slowly lifted the vessel. There was a trench carved out to the sea and with the diesel now turning the prop, they were underway. They left in the afternoon as they had to travel a long way to get to the coordinates where Pat would disembark.

It was a mind-numbing trip as the hours passed in the cramped little vessel riding just below the height of the waves. The sun set behind the coast and the stars came out. Despite it being a partial moon, it was bright out on the sea with no running lights. When they came to the coordinates, the pilot stopped the U-boat. Pat climbed out of the hatch and sat atop the little sub in his solid black wetsuit. He tied the transmitter for his ScubaBecon mask to the sub. Since the boat could not drop anchor, this would guide him back. The skipper handed him his rebreather and fins, then his scooter and finally the net bag containing the explosives. Earlier in the day he set the timers in each box to go off tomorrow and siliconed the boxes shut even though they were supposed to be waterproof. The three great ships were easy to see in the west as they were fully lit up. Three great cities on the horizon. He took a compass bearing on the middle ship and entered the water. He dropped to a depth of twenty feet, clearing his ears as he descended. The water was warm and clear. The moonbeams filtered down to create a light blue aura. Looking up, he could see the moon above the water. Below was darkness. His mind could not help but think about the darkness. *Any big fish down there is going to silhouette me against the moon*, he thought. He engaged the scooter and it was like flying weightless through the atmosphere. His iridescent compass was his navigational guide and his depth gauge was his altimeter.

Halfway to the ships, he heard the high-pitched whine of propellers over his head. He stopped the scooter and looked up. A dark shadow passed over him with its wake lit up by the moonlight. The water was so clear he felt sure the boat must be going to hit him as it passed over. Its wake left a wash of iridescent green created by tiny phosphorescent plankton in the water column. *A glowing green trail must be good luck for an Irishman*, he thought.

He continued until by his watch he was sure he must be near the reef. He stopped his scooter periodically to listen. When he heard the distinctive sound of the reef, he knew he was close. The sound was tiny shrimp snapping their claws and fish biting at the reef, but it sounded exactly like the snap, crackle, and pop of Rice Crispies. This was maybe the most dangerous part of the trip. He had to find a way through the reef without being spotted. Using a light would have been the easiest, but that was a risky proposition. He chose instead to surface carefully hoping his black hood would hide him. The south entrance was not too far from him. He could hear the engines of one of the patrol boats behind him. He did not turn to look but took a quick glance to see where the biggest ship was moored and ducked back beneath the waves.

He dove quickly all the way to the bottom and turned south. He found the drop off for the channel and followed it in. He was able to navigate to the middle set of lights, the largest ship, and made his way aft. It was as dark as a coal mine under the great ship. He used the scooter to move in its shadow away from prying eyes. He easily found the great propellers underneath and magnetically attached an explosive where two of their shafts came out of the hull. Like a shark, he intended to take out his prey's ability for propulsion. There would be no getting back to dock tomorrow. He worked his way along the keel in the dark placing a charge approximately every ten meters. He attached some of his mines radiating out from the keel, so the pattern of the limpets formed a cross. He intended to not only flood the ship, but to break her back and sheer off the stern. *She should go down faster than most*, he thought.

Egress was the same process in reverse. Another patrol boat passed over, but he didn't stop this time. He knew he was invisible. The heads-up display in his mask started giving him directions as he neared the rendezvous point. The sub commander had been drifting and then cruising back to the GPS location since he could not drop anchor. He was surprised when Pat appeared pounding on the sides of the vessel. Pat climbed aboard and they headed south. With any luck, he would be out of the country by tomorrow afternoon with a priceless painting and a duffle bag full of cash.

Chapter XXIII

A round dawn Sam and Dan were back on the Santa Maria. Dan called Javier on their encrypted phones. He told him about the plan and asked him to reconnoiter the three businesses that logically seemed best for a kidnapping. That was a bar, a barbershop, and a restaurant. Javier said he would have a report in a few hours. This was not Dan's first snatch and grab operation. He'd hunted terrorists around the world, sometimes with host country support and sometimes without. He knew how to run an operation. He also knew the risk. He was busy hand picking the men he would take with him while Sam was briefing Morne who was having a cup of coffee with Johannes.

"Do you support the idea, Morne?"

"I do."

"Dan and I worked out the rough details on the ride back. He will lead the ground force and grab the target. I will lead the quick reaction force if they get in trouble. We will use two of the helicopters with the tail numbers covered for extraction."

"If it goes bad, what are the implications for ARC?"

"We will have to deny everything."

"Exactly, which is why you cannot go. You are too involved with the president and vice president. You have to do the damage control if it goes wrong."

"He's right," Johannes said as he looked at Sam's concerned face. "I'll run the quick reaction force."

"You sure?"

"You already got shot at once. Let me have some fun."

"Fine. Dan is in the war room." Sam said slightly disappointed in missing out on a potential fight.

Dan was briefing the snatch and grab squad and the quick reaction force on what he thought the plan was going to be. He really wouldn't know until he heard from Javier. They had a list going of what they thought they would need. Everything from zip cuffs to night vision was written on the board. They heard the ship's whistle and knew they would be leaving the dock in ten minutes. It was Thursday. Time for the great ships to put to sea for their weekly rotation. Dan and his team were not concerned. Johannes already had two of the ARC helicopters fueled and sequestered at the airport. They would pick the teams up from the Santa Maria's helipad and whisk them to the outskirts of Managua where Javier and the old Contra network would be waiting.

Two hours later, the first helicopter touched down on the helipad as gently as a dragonfly. Dan took the copilot's seat and the snatch and grab team piled in the back with their gear. He could not hear his phone ringing or vibrating over the whirring of the rotors. As soon as the door closed, the sleek helicopter rose slightly, dipped its nose, and roared off at its fastest speed. The second helicopter had an oil pressure problem on spin up, but it settled out. It was twenty minutes delayed getting to the ship. Johannes took the copilot's seat and the quick reaction force boarded. The airship cleared the helipad and streaked to the west. They had just crossed the beach when the radio came alive. Neither Johannes nor the pilot could believe what they were hearing. Johannes instructed the pilot to turn around. The Eurocopter banked hard to the left and everyone held on to keep from being thrown from their seats. Though it was sideways in the cockpit glass due to the steep turn, Johannes could see the nine-hundred-foot Niña was stern down in the water and sinking.

"Put us on her pad," Johannes exclaimed.

Chapter XXIV

A riela's idea was to use the piece of paper to keep the door from locking. She balled it up and shoved it into the latch hole in the bathroom door. She eventually got it to retain a rectangular shape. Now the plan was for the next time Leon came to take Zanita away, Zanita would covertly shove the paper into the latch hole of the bedroom door, thus preventing it from locking. Ariela would be able to leave the room while the two were away and try to find a way to signal Dan. If everything went well, it would be tonight.

Leon hid in the opening of the study listening to his father talk to the representative from the Mexican cartel. He was absorbing the minute aspects of the conversation, the inflections, the innuendos, the real and false intents. His father was angry. The Mexican was aloof and insolent.

"You owe me fifteen million US dollars," Gabriel Perez stated.

"We owe you nothing. We are merely the transportation conduit into the United States. You know we cannot guarantee one-hundred percent performance on every transit. That is why it is called smuggling."

"You guaranteed me you could get that particular shipment through."

"Señor Perez, you are a very experienced and powerful businessman. You understand better than anyone the risks we all take, but we get through much more than we lose."

"How do I know you did not just steal my merchandise?"

"You wound me, El Tigre. Our reputation is built on trust. We would never double cross you or any other supplier. We need you."

The Mexican smiled letting his gold tooth show.

"I don't think you need me like you used to. I think you have gotten very good at manufacturing methamphetamines. I think you are making even more money smuggling fentanyl from China into the US and Canada. And let's not forget your human smuggling operations across the border and your organ harvesting operations after you have worn out your whores."

"We produce a lot of money from these other things. Much more than we make from transporting your goods across the border. But I came here out of respect."

"I warned you what would happen if you lost my merchandise."

"Amigo, we all say things we later regret. We are not going to reimburse you for the loss out of our pocket, but let's move forward together. As partners."

Gabriel Perez, El Tigre, put his hand up to his face and rubbed his mustache. He seemed in thought when he held up two fingers. The Mexican never heard Enrique come up behind him and before he knew it, the crook of Enrique's overly muscled arm was around his neck cutting off his air supply. He tried punching Enrique in the head, but it was no good, it just opened up his neck more and the man with the tiger tattoo on his face simply squeezed harder. He started seeing twinkling specs in his vision as he pulled at the muscular arm choking the life out of him. He used his legs to push up and off the desk throwing Enrique off balance, but Enrique just rode the fall, never letting go of him. His vision narrowed as the blackness closed in and he passed out.

Enrique let the man's unconscious body slump to the floor.

"El Diablo?" He asked.

"Si. Summon the workers to come watch in one hour."

Leon was alive with excitement as he raced back to his room. El Diablo was going to be fed. He loved watching the terror in the eyes of the damned. He thought of how they screamed when they were thrown into the pit and how El Diablo would tear them apart. Some tried to fight back. Most just cowered against their fate. The whole thing aroused him and in that moment, he thought of Zanita. She tricked him into revealing part of his father's plan. Sharing in the glory of El Diablo's feeding would be her penance.

Ariela and Zanita could hear the brass bell. They both had seen it in the hacienda's courtyard but did not know what its ringing meant. For a moment, Ariela wondered if it could be Dan coming for her, but she pushed that hope back down. The knock at the door was loud. Ariela opened it. Leon stood there looking past her to Zanita.

"Come with me."

"What is it?"

"A gathering. I have a good spot for us to watch."

"What about Ariela?"

"She cannot come. Only you. Hurry."

Zanita pushed past Ariela with the wad of paper palmed in her hand.

"Take care of my sister," Ariela said to Leon distracting him as Zanita slipped the paper into the door jam.

The courtyard was full. The cocaine factory workers and the household staff were all present. In front of them, the two stone monoliths rose from courtyard floor in front of El Diablo's pit. Chained to each was a Mexican cartel member. The man with the gold tooth was on the left, his pilot on the right. Gabriel Perez stood between the two. Enrique was slightly behind him.

"These men stole from us. They stole the money that pays your salaries, buys the things you need, provides for your families. They have betrayed me personally and all of you. One of you will get your money back today," Gabriel said as he nodded to Enrique.

Enrique walked in front of the man with the gold tooth. He pulled his side arm and smashed the man in the mouth with it. It took two attempts, but he knocked the gold tooth out of his gums. Enrique held it up in the air and the workers hollered in support. They all threw their hands up hoping to be the one to catch the gold tooth when Enrique tossed it. The tooth flew high, but they all missed it. There was a scramble on the ground until one man stood and held the bloody gold tooth high. The mob cheered him, but soon the attention turned back to El Tigre.

"What is the penalty for stealing from the group?"

"Death," was the unanimous reply.

"What is the penalty for betraying me?"

"Death!"

Enrique unchained the man. His hands were still restrained in front of him. Enrique maneuvered him to the edge of El Diablo's pit where he looked down onto the striped back of El Diablo. He realized he was out of time.

The great cat paced back and forth below looking up at the man. He could smell the blood dripping from the man's mouth, and he breathed deeply as his belly roiled in hunger. He flexed the micro muscles in his paws and extended his claws. He released a deep roar and the crowd above him cheered.

"Por Favor, El Tigre!" We will pay the money. It was our fault the Americans seized your shipment."

Gabriel walked up behind the man and placed the gold-plated Desert Eagle against the back of his head. He pushed forward so the man was on the balls of his feet trying not to fall into the pit.

"I offer you mercy in the form of a bullet. What do you want, El Diablo, or the bullet?"

El Tigre said it without the slightest hint of compassion.

"Por Favor!"

"Choose."

"Bullet," the Mexican cried out as he stared down into El Diablo's yellow eyes.

Gabriel Perez pulled the trigger and the hammer with its heavy spring fell on the big gaudy pistol, but all that was heard was a loud click. The Mexican took a breath. His brain realized he had not been killed. He started to relax. He tasted the iron in the blood filling his mouth and he suddenly felt more alive than ever. The vines on the courtyard wall suddenly seemed greener. The sky was bluer. The tiger below him was no longer a threat, but a beautiful beast made by God Almighty. He turned around to see El Tigre smiling at him. Enjoying the joke. He smiled back with his bloody mouth missing its prized front tooth. Gabriel Perez took a step forward. He put his hand on the man's chest as if to reassure him. He felt the man's heart pounding methodically like a hammer through his thin dress shirt spotted with is blood. They stared into each other's eyes. There was understanding. Gabriel Perez was the alpha. He was the one in control from now on. The Mexican nodded slightly to Gabriel acknowledging the understanding, then Gabriel pushed him backwards relishing the wild look in his eyes as he went over the edge.

The man screamed and El Diablo leapt upward to meet him mid-air, sinking his claws into him and landing atop the man. With the fury of a tornado, the big cat tore into him.

Enrique appeared with the pilot at the edge of the pit. He pushed him by his neck to the very edge of the pit while they watched the great tiger tear apart his employer.

"Go back to your people. Tell them I want my fifteen million dollars," Gabriel said.

"Si, Señor."

Enrique spun the trembling man around. Gabriel looked him up and down. The front of his trousers was wet.

"I am sure your pants will be dry by the time you get back to Mexico. Take him to his airplane."

Zanita felt her heart beating fast as they hustled through the house. It was empty and Leon was being cavalier parading her through the open rooms. He led her by the hand to the empty kitchen and down a flight of stairs to the basement. The bell outside had stopped ringing and she could hear many voices hollering in the courtyard above them. He spirited her into the alcove hidden from anyone standing above. She marveled at the great tiger. The clear wall full of four-inch holes between them seemed flimsy. *Surely it could not contain such a great beast if it really wanted out*, she thought. She saw him from above when she was brought in, but this view was eye level. She could smell him. He was pacing back and forth looking up. He was the one they referred to as the bad tiger and he seemed to be time and a half bigger than the others she saw housed at the back of the hacienda. Gabriel was talking and the people above were chanting. Leon stood behind her deeper in the shadow. When Enrique moved the man to the edge of the pit, she gasped. Leon clamped his hand over her mouth.

"Shhh. Watch," he whispered.

His other hand moved inside her shirt up to her breast gently rolling her tenderness between his fingers. She wanted to protest but was frightened. Life was relatively cheap in Nicaragua, but she had never actually seen anyone killed. Her mind ran wild conjuring the fate of the man who stood above them with blood running from his mouth. She realized he was about to be pushed off the ledge, but relaxed when the man turned around. She let her guard down for a second and then to her panic she saw him fall backwards. He screamed as he fell. She tried to look away, but Leon kept her head facing forward. As the tiger leapt up and sunk its claws into the Mexican drug runner, Leon dug his hard, sharp thumbnail into Zanita's tenderest spot, twisting and pulling as he did. The pain was like a hot needle that would not stop penetrating her whole being. She could not get enough air through her nose and her breathing became rapid and shallow as the pain shot through her and she was forced to watch the carnage before her. It was as if the tiger was mauling her. Her muffled screams could not be heard over the dying man's. Leon kept her that way until he felt her start to go limp. He spun her around and she clung to him. She was compliant in her state of shock but started to recover as he pushed her down on the concrete in the shadow of the alcove. The sex was rough, but the crunching sound of human bones being broken and splintered behind her was a horror unto its own. She stared into the dark wild eyes of the demon living inside Leon and realized she had never been in control for a single second.

Ariela waited no more than a minute before she tried the door. She peered out into the empty hallway. She was barefoot to be as quiet as possible. She worked her way through the empty house quickly. She was frantic to find something to help their situation. She crept into Gabriel's study. The glass wall was open, and the sound of the waterfall sounded like freedom, but she knew they could never survive the jungle. She saw nothing immediately helpful but noticed a bag beside the chair in the location where she spent so many painful hours on her knees being questioned. Questioned and choked by that animal Enrique. The bag belonged to the Mexican man about to be fed to El Diablo. She rummaged through it and in the bottom was a satellite phone. She turned it on and the display glowed. It was useless inside the house. She ran out the doors to the pool. She watched the display while it attempted to pick up the satellites. It seemed to take forever. She could feel the blood rushing in her ears downing out the sound of the falls. Finally, the circle and slash came off the satellite icon and four bars took its place. She dialed Dan's phone number from memory. It rang six times and on each ring, she died a little bit inside. Finally, automated voicemail picked up.

"Dan, Zanita and I have been kidnapped. The cartel intends to sink one of the ARC ships. I don't know where we are, but I hope you can find us. It is a big house next to a waterfall. I love you. I love you so much…" was all she got out before the voicemail disconnected.

She stared at the phone and heard the chants of death coming from the courtyard. She tapped the log part of the display. It showed Dan's number. She highlighted it and deleted the call. She turned the phone off and returned it to the bag. She looked about the study and saw El Tigre's Santa Muerte grim reaper skull on the edge of the credenza. She walked over and knocked it onto the floor shattering it. She raised the gold cross from around her neck and kissed it, then with a mischievous smile she made her way back to her room and locked herself back inside.

Ariela had not been back long before the door opened, and Zanita came in. Leon was with her, and he kissed her gently on the forehead before closing the door behind him. Ariela could tell something was very wrong. When she asked, Zanita simply plopped down on the bed and said she saw a man eaten by a tiger. Ariela was aghast and moved to comfort her little sister. Zanita clung to Ariela but did not cry. She was in shock, but her base instincts realized she had to compartmentalize this trauma and bury it away forever. She assumed she deserved it for getting her sister into this. She feigned happiness when Ariela told her she got a message to Dan. She silently wondered if they would live long enough to be rescued. Leon was as big a psychopath as his father, maybe more so.

CHAPTER XXV

Captain Matthijs Mesmen was on the Niña's bridge with his first officer. They had just been served an after-lunch coffee. It was a beautiful day to be sailing. The sky was cloudless, and the high sun shone down through the clear Caribbean waters. The great ships white paint radiated an angelic glow as she gracefully traversed the blue liquid below.

Every week the Dutch captain looked forward to leaving port. Even if it was only for a few hours out into international waters, it served to ease the itch in him that was the call of the sea. He was just raising his China cup to his lips when he felt the shudder, then another and another like a ripple through his spine. His mind was trying to make sense of what he felt as the alarms sounded. All of the alarms. His teacup shattered as it hit the floor and he rushed the main console. The list of alarms was impossibly long. The electrical failures were massive and there were some fires, but what worried him most was the water sensors indicating the sea was rushing into the ship in multiple locations. The first officer silenced the alarms on the bridge although they rang through the rest of the ship.

"Did we hit something?" The first officer asked.

"Engine Room," the captain said to the first officer ignoring his question as he picked up the microphone and called all hands to general quarters, the command for everyone to move to the lifeboat positions.

"No response from Engineering, Sir."

"Go."

"Aye Aye," the first officer said as he left the bridge.

"All pumps at maximum."

"Sir, most of the pumps are offline," was the response.

"Do we have the ability to maneuver?"

"Negative, Sir. She's dead in the water," the helmsman responded.

Calls were coming in from everywhere about explosions and water pouring into the lower levels of the ship.

"Send the distress call. Get the other ships on the radio."

"Mayday. Mayday. This is the Niña. We are declaring an emergency," the captain heard as he grabbed his own radio and called Admiral Sharpe.

"Mesmen, What is the problem?"

"We are taking on water fast. May have to abandon ship."

"Good God, man . Do you have propulsion?"

"Negative."

"Understood. We are on the way."

The captain could feel the deck listing beneath his feet. The internal radio cut in. It was the first officer.

"Captain, Engineering is flooded and the water is rising. She is going down."

The captain stepped out onto the side viewing platform on the bridge. Ten minutes had passed, and the ship was already ten degrees down in the stern.

"Launch the lifeboats. Abandon ship."

Johannes and the quick reaction force bailed out of the helo leaving their guns behind. The helicopter pad was slanted already. People were everywhere on the deck. It was pure chaos. The quick reaction force ran down multiple flights of steps toward a group of panicked people. There were children with them. Johannes gave instructions.

"Take the kids to the helo. Stack 'em like firewood if you must but get them off this ship."

Johannes saw the helicopter lift off headed for the Santa Maria. He could hear another ARC helicopter coming in from the airport. His team started lining more people up to board the inbound chopper.

Johannes made his way to the bridge. Captain Mesmen was surprised to see him.

"What can I do to help, Captain?"

"Most of the crew is launching lifeboats, but we won't be able to launch the forward ones because of the angle of the ship. I need someone to check the school."

"I will make sure it is clear."

The captain pulled a rechargeable light from the wall and handed it to him.

"Good Luck."

Johannes worked his way through the crowd of nervous people gathered on the main deck. He could see the fear in their eyes. He pushed past the people coming up the stairs and worked his way down into the ship. The battery powered emergency exit lights were the only illumination. When upward rush of people thinned, he stopped the last person coming. The man was soaking wet and in full panic.

"Did you pass the school?" Johannes asked in Afrikaans.

"No. I just came up the stairwell. I barely made it to that level. It's all flooded below, and the water is rising fast. Don't go down there."

Johannes pushed past him. The sounds coming from the Niña were like a wounded humpback whale. She groaned a stressful call that started as a low baritone and grew higher and higher into a squealing pitch. She was dying and Johannes knew he had to find the school fast. He kept descending to the deck where he remembered the school being. The water was up to his knees and rising. He called out but got no answer. He waded through the dimly lit hallway to the door. There was a schoolgirl with a death grip on the door jam.

"Hello Darling," he said in Afrikaans. "I am going to get you out of here. Are there any more children inside?"

She just looked at him with big blue eyes and then launched herself to cling to his neck. He picked her up and looked inside. He could not see any more children inside, so he rushed her back to the stairwell. He put her on the stairs.

"Go up to the main deck. Don't stop. I'll be right behind you."

He waded back to the school rooms. The water was nearly to his waist and the floor was so slanted, walking was difficult. He went into the main schoolroom with his light. He saw no children in the first room. He made for the connecting door. There were no children in this room either. He sighed a bit of relief. He made it through the next connecting door and his foot caught on something under the water. Something soft. He shined his light down and saw the teacher's body. He pulled her up and saw a gash on the side of her head. Her eyes were open, and she was quite dead. He used the light to look around the room and saw three girls and three boys perched around the room in various states of panic. His brain started calculating his options.

"Come to me children."

Two of the boys and one of the girls came to him. He went and picked up the two remaining girls, one under each arm. He yelled at the remaining boy, but he was non-responsive. He held a death grip on a pipe. There was no way to carry the third boy with the two girls being incapacitated out of fear. He looked at the other two boys, but saw they were not going to be able to manage another child their own size. He would have to come back for the last boy. *He had time to make two trips if he hurried.*

"You three. Hold onto my belt. We are going to the stairs."

Johannes pushed through the water that was now mid chest on him. His powerful thighs and calves strained to move him forward. The children held on tight, but if the water rose much more, they would have to let go of his belt to keep breathing. With a tremendous effort, they reached the stairs. Johannes placed the girls on the stairs and instructed the boys to make sure the they got to the top deck. He watched them go up as he rested for a half-second before throwing himself back into the water. The water was clear and warm, and he could see the bottom by the emergency lights. When he was halfway down the hallway, it all went dark. The dying sounds of the Niña grew loud. His light was still on, so he used it to navigate through the neck deep water. He would be swimming the last kid out it appeared. He pushed into the last school room and took the child's hand.

"Hey there young man. We are going to have to swim out though. Do you think you can hold onto my back?"

"Yes, Uncle," the boy answered in Afrikaans.

"I need you to be brave. You must hold onto my shirt and hold your breath if we go under the water."

The boy nervously nodded as the ship moaned a primal dying scream.

Johannes was halfway to the door when the whole ship shifted. The shift meant the flow of water coming in was unstoppable and inescapable. Johannes made an instant decision and threw himself against the watertight door. He sealed it. If the seal worked, they would wait for rescue. A rescue that would have to come before they ran out of air.

Admiral Sharpe ordered Pinta and Santa Maria to the aid of the Niña. They both put their launches in the water while the ships closed the gap. They began towing the Niña's life boats back to the other ships.

The Niña's bow was clearly raised, and her stern was sinking fast. Admiral Sharpe was turned away when he heard the snap, the screams, and a great crash as the Niña's bow plunged back into the water. He turned back to see the stern completely broken away and submerging rapidly.

"My God."

The remainder of the ship, released from its sinking stern crashed back into the water initiated a wave that tossed the lifeboats about. Captain Mesmen wasted no time. The front lifeboats could now be released, and he ordered the crew to do so. The bulk of the ship began to settle in the water with a starboard list. There were many injured, and the crew loaded them onto the boats as quickly as possible. As the great white ship settled, the order was given to jump and most of the able bodied hurled themselves over the railing in their bright orange life jackets. They were picked up by the lifeboats and tenders. Captain Mesmen took one last look around the bridge. Seeing it was clear, he looked out to sea. The Pinta and the Santa Maria stood off the starboard side contrasted by the dark blue waters of the Caribbean like two angels watching a good friend die. He saw a white military ship closing from the horizon. He left the bridge for the main deck. Getting there was treacherous, but he made it. He was alone. He looked about for any passengers or crew. Seeing none, he looked out at the humanity being plucked from the sea. Above him, Dan's chopper hovered. It returned following the radio news as well. It descended towards him. It did not lower its landing gear but opened its rear door. Captain Mesmen struggled not to be blown down by the rotor wash, but when it was close enough, he leapt aboard. Dan gave him a thumbs up. Captain Mesman donned a radio headset taken from one of the operators in the back.

"Take me to the Admiral, please."

Chapter XXVI

T he leadership of ARC was not ready for this kind of mass casualty event, but their natural talents came into play quickly. Morne was triaging things from the highest levels. The admiral coordinated everything afloat including cooperation with a US Coast Guard ship that responded to the mayday. Marcus was overseeing air operations. Ansel and Jayden were managing emergency healthcare and international flights for any critically wounded. Katherine was trying to account for the missing and Sam was coordinating the search for survivors.

Sam put out an announcement on both ships and ashore for any certified divers to meet on the Santa Maria. He divided them into three teams, rescue, recovery, and support.

"Group one rescue divers are going down immediately. Two and three will follow in fifteen-minute intervals. Use your ears as well as your eyes. Listen for any banging. If we find survivors, they are going to get the worlds' shortest lesson in scuba diving.

"This is a tough environment. None of you are certified for this type of diving. Secure your guide ropes and don't stray far from them. If you find a corpse, note where the body is located so we can recover our friends later.

"The bottom is a hundred and ten feet. The stern is lying on its back. The rest of the ship rolled onto its starboard side. Air is not going to last long at these depths. The no-decompression time limit is fifteen minutes at that depth. Our friends have already been down there for over two hours. We will suspend tanks at sixty and fifteen feet so you and any survivors can decompress and get the nitrogen out of your bloodstream. We have jets standing by to take anyone that gets bent to Houston, New Orleans, or Miami for treatment. Move fast. Move efficiently. Be careful."

Sam clamped his teeth around his regulator's mouthpiece and back rolled off the patrol boat. He carried an extra scuba cylinder under his arm with a rope around the yoke. The regulator hose was held against the tank by a bungee cord. He pinched his nose and cleared his ears as he sank towards the wreck. His dive buddy was not a big man, but he had served in the Australian Special Air Services as a diver. He had consumed more compressed air than anyone else in the group and Sam figured he could handle himself. Sam chose him because he had the most important mission. Save Johannes and any children with him. Floating down, they were both aghast seeing the interior of the ship pointed up towards the surface. It was as if someone simply sliced the back of the ship off with a giant knife. The water column was awash with debris at different levels and Sam had to keep pushing paper and cloth out of the way as they descended. He said a silent prayer as his partner cinched a knot on the stairwell railing and they started into the wreck.

Once inside, it was pitch black. Sam was thankful the water was warm and clear. Their lights illuminated the inside of the passageways and rooms well, although in many of the rooms, the debris was suspended in the water to a degree they had to push their way through it. There were many pieces of jagged metal and glass and they had to be careful around the jumbled piles of furniture.

Sam knew exactly where he was heading. His hope was that Johannes was holed up in an air pocket telling stories to some children in the dark. As he and his buddy made their way closer to where the school was, anxiety started to build. The idea of losing his longtime friend was unthinkable. His mind wandered there and for a moment, he felt he could not get enough air from his regulator. *Calm the hell down*, he thought. *Save your air.* He held his breath to get his breathing under control. The school door was open and hanging from its hinges towards the ocean floor. Sam did a half-pike to enter the former doorway that was now a hole. The desks in the first room were all piled at the bottom and paper filled the room suspended in time and space. Sam was alone as his partner was tying the rope off in the hallway. The second door was also open and as Sam penetrated that dark space, his light illuminated the dead school teacher near the bottom of the room atop a pile of desks. His heart went out to her. He flicked his light around and did not see anyone else. He looked back and his buddy was behind him acknowledging the body.

The third door in the school was closed. It was a watertight door. Hope soared in Sam. He banged on the door with his light. There was no sound on the other side. A little bit of the hope died. He banged again and he heard a slight vibration in the water. He reached for the handle and opened the door letting it fall free on its hinges with a bang. He looked up and saw the line between water and air. He kicked up until his head cleared the water and he saw a boy clinging to an electrical conduit keeping himself above the waterline.

"Hello Son."

The boy started speaking Afrikaans and Sam had no idea what he was saying, but he could guess.

"Can you switch to English for me?"

"Yes."

"Ok. We are going to get you out of here…"

Sam showed the boy how to breathe with the regulator in his mouth. He put the extra mask on him and made him practice a couple of times with his face in the water taking the reg in and out underwater.

"We are going to swim out of the ship together. We can't go to the surface for a while, or you will get sick. We are going to breathe this whole bottle of air at sixty feet, then we are going to do some more at fifteen feet. Are you with me?"

The boy nodded with wide eyes. As Sam turned to his partner, his partner just said the word below. Sam stuck his facemask below the surface. He saw Johannes' body in the ruble. He had been trapped when the stern broke off and drowned. Sam looked back at the little boy and tried to control his emotions. He held the boy tight, and they dove under together. The three followed the ropes back to the stairwell and they ascended to sixty feet where the extra bottles hung. Sam looked at his own gauges. He was down to a third of a tank. Too little for what he was considering, but he could not stop himself. He handed the boy to his partner and dove.

Going into a wreck alone broke a cardinal rule. Going in alone with a single source of air was stupid. Going in low on air was suicide. He followed the ropes to the school. He made his way to Johannes' body. He could see the damage where something hit Johannes in the head. He freed his body from the wreckage and pulled him by the collar to the hallway. He looked at his gauges. The needle was deep into the red. He was about out of air. Following the ropes was the smart play, but he didn't think he could make it back along the ropes. He saw a phantasm of light deep in the hallway in the other direction, so he pulled Johannes' body down the dark corridor where there were no ropes. He was pretty sure this was where he was going to die. He could see a tiny bit of light coming through where the stern had been blown open by an explosive or torn open when it separated. Light meant life and he pushed on not looking at his gauges hoping there would be enough air in his cylinder. As he ascended the twisted metal hole, towing his best friend's body, his tank went empty. He tried to draw a breath and it was as if his esophagus was plugged. His lungs would not inflate. He kept trying as he franticly kicked towards the surface, never letting go of Johannes. He knew as he ascended, he should pick up a breath, maybe two from the little bit of air in the tank expanding. He picked up a half-breath at seventy feet and it gave him new energy. He only had to make it to the sixty-foot bottle suspended above. He spit out his regulator and salty seawater filled his mouth. He neared and reached for the waiting deco bottle and shoved the regulator in his mouth. The rush of the compressed air inflating his lungs gave him his life back. He closed his eyes, breathing deeply and rapidly filling his aching lungs. Starved for oxygen, his body felt heavy, but his soul felt heavier. Under sixty-feet of crystal blue water, he dangled on the line holding Johannes by the collar as his lifeless body pulled towards the deep.

CHAPTER XXVII

One-hundred-and-fifty-one people died in the attack. Although some drowned, most were killed instantly from the bombs strung along the hull of the ship. The body recovery took days. It was aided by the Coast Guard cutter USCGC Tampa with its gleaming white hull and prominent orange stripe. It appeared over the horizon after picking up the distress call from the Niña and its crew and capabilities were invaluable. They stayed on station for nearly a week until Admiral Sharpe told them there was little more they could do. He did not let them go before having all fourteen officers aboard the Santa Maria for the Admiral's dinner. The captain of the Pinta and the Santa Maria were present along with their first officers. Captain Mesmen and his first officer were not, although they had been invited. Both felt guilt and shame at losing the Niña and for the deaths aboard, even though there was nothing they could have done to save the ship or those lives.

Admiral Sharpe was tasked with preserving the bodies for burial. Morne was insistent there would be individual graves dug for each person. They began loading the bodies into the freezer units of the two great ships, but soon they were at capacity. The bodies recovered in the last couple of days were in bad shape after being submerged in the warm Caribbean waters. The bodies were wrapped in plastic and covered with ice in the hold of the tanker. It was the best they could do. Ashore the construction crew dug graves with their equipment and built coffins from lumber. There were three clergymen among the crew and they set about performing funerals as quickly as possible. Morne assigned board members to each minister so there would always be a board presence at each service. Captain Mesman attended every service he could. The funerals were held outside near the newly created graveyard and all of them were well attended.

The entire board was present for Johannes' funeral. His was the last held. The exhausted minister delivered a sermon as lively as if it was his first. Morne spoke of Johannes' contribution to ARC and of the man he knew. Sam held Anna on his right arm and Katherine on his left. Patson stood on the other side of Anna holding her hand. He was weepy at the loss of one of his step-fathers. Sam too was overcome with sadness, and he kept his sunglasses on to hide his eyes. Katherine and Anna were both dressed in black as was the rest of the board. Sam asked God to give him strength to get through the funeral. He needed to be there for Anna. When it was over, he turned to her.

"I'll never have a friend like him again."

"Me either," she cried as she buried her head in his chest.

El Tigre sat in his den watching the sinking of the Niña on CNN. It had been a week since Pat Callahan destroyed the ocean liner and left the hacienda with his payment and little more than a goodbye. Gabriel never thought he would see the actual sinking, but a US Coast Guard cutter responded to the distress call and arrived in time and filmed the sinking with its long range cameras. *No doubt the cutter was part of the American's attempt to keep his product from being transported through the Caribbean*, he thought. The video was thrilling. To see such a great ship go down was a triumph of his planning; a complete revenge for the killing of his men in the jungle. Now they would know the price for interfering with his business. He was concerned when he found his Santa Muerte statue broken on the ground. He feared it might be a bad omen, but the mission went perfectly.

He thought about the two women held prisoner in his home. He promised to let them go, but he was reluctant to do so just yet. They might make excellent pawns in case the African gringos decided they wanted to make war. Besides, he knew Leon was sneaking the youngest one out at night. *Why spoil the boy's fun before necessary*, he thought.

The war council convened in the admiral's quarters. Dan played the voicemail from Ariela for the men. She called to alert him before the explosions hulled the Niña. He hadn't gotten the message until he landed back on the Santa Maria.

"I called my friend, Jay Nobel, at the DEA and gave him the number of the originating phone and the time of the call. He called in a favor at the NSA. They traced the GPS coordinates of the phone to here, a valley in southern Nicaragua," he said pointing to the map rolled out on the table.

"Let me guess, El Tigre's hideout?" Sam asked.

"Yep. And it is a son-of-a-bitch."

"How so?" Morne asked.

"Here are the file pictures the DEA has on this place. All aerials. All shot from sixty-thousand feet, but with great cameras.

"There is a plateau up top with the usual heavy vegetation, but the runoff from the rain forms a good-sized waterfall that carved this valley. The water proceeds through the valley, around several different hilly formations and out to the sea. The vegetation in this long valley is really dense. No roads or no paths that can be seen. The compound sits next to the waterfall."

"What about defenses?" Marcus asked.

"Here are the thermal pictures. Atop the plateau on overwatch is a sand bagged machine gun. You can't land on that airstrip by the hacienda without falling under its fire. There are sentries on the airstrip and around the cocaine factory. The hacienda has guards at the entrance, some on balconies, and look at this…"

"What is that?" Marcus queried.

Dan dropped a color photo on the desk with a blow up of what Marcus was pointing to on the thermal image.

"That's a tiger. His guards use tigers instead of dogs."

"Nee Akkies," Marcus muttered.

"When were these photos taken?" Morne asked.

"Date is last year," Dan replied.

"Then we should assume there is a stronger force given what just happened."

"Show them our options for infiltration," Sam asked.

"There are four possibilities. We either come up through the valley, which is a two-day hike at best, we cross the plateau and come down the waterfall, we try to land on that landing strip, or we parachute in, preferably at night."

"Do we believe they have night vision?" Sam asked.

"We have to assume they do. They just sank an ocean liner. I don't think anything is beyond their capabilities. It may be some cheap Russian junk, but it probably works well enough."

"This guy has money. Their gear is going to be top-shelf."

"Objective one must be neutralizing that gun on the cliff. We can't land or evacuate via a helo with it operational," Marcus said.

"Agreed. That means we must land someone on the plateau."

"If we are going to do that, why not send the entire assault team in that way?" Morne asked.

"And then evac on the choppers," Sam added.

"And if it all goes to hell, it is a race down that long valley to the sea," Dan offered.

"I think this is our plan," Morne said. "Now, how do we make it easier? How do we lessen the resistance and make rescuing Ariela easier?"

"Diversion in the valley? Get them to send forces away from our strike force," Admiral Sharpe proffered.

"No. That will make the hacienda defenses tighter," Morne responded.

"We get him to leave the compound," Sam said.

"How do we do that?" Dan asked.

"We call a meeting," Morne replied.

"No disrespect, but he ain't going to meet with us."

"He will if the meeting is at the Presidential Palace," Sam said.

"We can't kill him at the palace, can we?" Marcus asked.

"No, but it might be our best shot at rescuing Ariela."

Sam and Patson sat next to each other on Sam's balcony looking out to sea. Both were thinking the same thing.

"I can't believe Father Johannes is gone."

"Me either."

"Why did it have to be him?"

"If he hadn't gone down there, those kids would have died. Your father knew the risks in going back for the last child. He died a hero."

"I wish I would have known the last time I saw him it would be the last."

"What would you have done differently?"

"I would have hugged him longer. I would have told him how much I loved him. I would have thanked him for all he and Ms. Anna did for me."

Patson's voice was shaky and his bottom lip quivered. Sam put his arm around him and pulled him close.

"He knew how much you loved him. You showed it all the time."

"Do you think so?"

"I know so. But, let this be a lesson for you. Never let things go unsaid between you and people you are close to. None of us knows when our last breath will be."

"I love you, Father."

"I love you too, Son. And I am very proud of the man you are growing up to be."

"I want that Gabriel Perez to pay for what he did. I want him to die, but I don't want to risk you."

"Those are strong emotions. I wish you didn't feel that way, but I understand. I am not going into harm's way. Morne and I are the decoys to get Gabriel out of his lair. Dan and the others will be the ones going into danger, but they are experienced and have a good plan. I suspect the Narcos won't know what hit them. While I am away, spend time with Ms. Anna. She needs our love and support."

Sam and Patson watched the darkness descend on the water as the sun set behind the ship. They ate dinner with Katherine and Anna and then Patson went to bed. He thought about his adopted father dying saving those children. He thought about how Johannes saved him when he adopted him out of the village in Mozambique. He became angry that a drug lord arrogant enough to call himself the tiger would attack a peaceful people trying to build something great. His anger filled his dreams, and he awoke the next morning with purpose.

Chapter XXVIII

Gabriel lounged by the pool reading the reports his bookkeepers sent him on the profits and expenses of his empire. His cigar was not lit, but he had chewed it such that the end was slimy and malformed. Enrique approached carrying a mobile phone.

"The president's chief of staff for you."

"Hello," Gabriel said taking the phone lazily into his hand.

"Señor Perez, this is Ernesto Ruiz."

"What does el presidente want?"

"He requests your presence at the palace tomorrow at 14:00 hours."

"Why does he want to see me? I am very busy."

"He simply asked me to make the call, Señor."

"If he wants to see me, he can call me himself," Gabriel said as he disconnected the call.

He smiled at Enrique and tossed the phone on the outdoor table. He crushed the end of his cigar between his molars and sucked the nicotine laden goo from it. Less than two minutes later the phone danced across the table with each vibration.

"Hello."

"Did you attack the ARC ship?"

"I don't know what you are talking about, El Jefe."

Beto Duran could hear the syrupy lie in his voice.

"Have you not seen CNN? It is everywhere."

"Was that the ARC people's ships? I didn't know they even had such things."

"Stop the pretense. It demeans us both. Are you in Managua?"

"No. I am at my country house."

"I need you to come to the Palace and meet with the ARC people."

"You want me to meet with them?"

"They asked for the meeting."

"Por qué?

"They want a truce. The ship was a terrible blow."

"How do I know this is not a trap? They might try to kill me. Or maybe you will have me arrested."

"I give you my word you will not be arrested. I will make them give their word not to try anything. I will even send my personal detail to pick you up and escort you to the palace."

"When?"

"Tomorrow. Fourteen-hundred hours."

Gabriel tossed the phone back onto the iron table. He was about to say something to Enrique when he saw Leon walking through the hallway. He called to him, and his son came out and presented himself before his father.

"I must fly to Managa in the morning. Do you want to go with me? I might stay for a few days."

"No Papa. I'd like to stay here if you don't mind."

"I'll bet you would, eh. Eh?" Gabriel goaded with a smile.

Leon never acknowledged what his father could be insinuating. He just stared back with the same impassive eyes his father passed down to him. He did not want to leave the hacienda. Not now. Last night he took Zanita to his room and was tender with her as he was the day before. He told her he loved her and made her say it back to him. He had something devilishly arousing planned for her tonight while her defenses were down, but if his father was leaving, he would be nice to her for another night. She would be even less suspecting tomorrow and if he were to be free of his father, he could release his inner demon unchecked. Gabriel dismissed his son and Leon left quickly.

"He is sneaking the younger sister out of their room at night," Gabriel said.

"Really?"

"Yes. He thinks he is getting away with it."

"If you are ok with him sneaking the younger one out, might I ask if..."

"Stop. I gave her my word. Besides, the fact the ARC gringos want to meet means we may have to return her. If the meeting goes badly, I promise you can have your way after I am finished."

Morne's Gulfstream carried he and Sam to Managua. The rest of the seats were occupied by members of Dan's security team assigned to protect the two board members. There was always a chance Gabriel Perez would try and assassinate them in Managua. When they touched down, Javier Cordova was waiting on them with the nephews. The Contra network had discreetly secured the FBO area of the airport and made sure there were no cartel members hanging around. The passengers were divided into two groups. Sam, Morne and four men went to the Intercontinental Hotel. The rest went to be housed in the barrio away from prying eyes. The meeting at the Presidential Palace was scheduled for tomorrow.

The ARC tanker was steaming south, over the horizon from the Nicaraguan coastline. Five helicopters were lashed to its deck. Two large construction helicopters and the three Eurocopters. In the crew quarters, the assault teams practiced their close quarter combat drills. Every man chosen for the mission was a volunteer and had combat experience, mostly from Iraq and Afghanistan. Although South Africa did not participate in either war, its Afrikaner sons enlisted in allied armies around the world and these men were experienced war fighters. Experienced or not, effectively taking down a building required precision and practice. Dan knew they would not be operating with the same precision as Delta or Dev Gru or even the FBI Hostage Rescue Team, but they would be good enough. They had to be. Ariela's life depended upon it.

He intentionally brought more men than he needed. He would pare down the group to the two assault teams on the ship. He didn't have time to do it before the tanker sailed and he needed extras in case someone got hurt during training. He'd been rough and brutally honest with the volunteers. He didn't have time to look at their files. He asked every man before they boarded, where did you see combat and how many of the enemy have you killed. He wasn't taking virgins on this trip. Only men who had pulled the trigger on another human being and were more than willing to do it again.

He drilled them time and time again taking down rooms, operating up and down stairwells, moving in covering formation and taking down targets on balconies. It was all pretend because they could not use live ammunition on the ship. Patson was their official timer with the stopwatch. He talked Dan into letting him come along after Sam left for Managua. Dan said no at first, but Patson reminded him Johannes was his father. Dan relented thinking that if Patson could be a part of the payback mission, he might get some closure, but he told him he was to stay on the ships and help the doctors who would be preparing to treat any casualties.

In between practice sessions, the men went over their gear and made sure they had what they needed. There was a wide variety of weapons to choose from as they brought a veritable armory with them on the boat. Most would carry M-4 rifles with suppressors and Trijicon red-dot scopes. The handguns were mostly their own personal preference. Some men carried grenades, others plastic explosives to breach doors and gates and destroy the cocaine factory. They all carried a hydration pack with a couple of protein bars and a personal trauma kit. They would all be wearing body armor and helmets when they went in. They would also be wearing electronic noise-cancelling earmuffs with integrated radios. The headsets would work until they started the assault, then the electronic jamming system they were deploying to cut off the hacienda's communications would make their radios useless.

Ariela was horrified when she saw the sinking of the Niña on CNN. Television was the one luxury in the girls' room. She cried all night after the story aired. Her guilt was crippling. There were few details. The video was provided by the US Coast Guard and there were only sketchy guesses about the presumed number of deaths. She wondered if Katherine and Sam were on the ship when it sank. She feared Dan died and no one would ever come to rescue them. She failed to warn them in time. If they were dead, it was her fault. She broke and told Gabriel Perez everything.

Zanita tried to comfort her, but it did little good as a perceptible distance had developed between them over the past days. To Ariela, something was different about her sister since she saw the man executed and she assumed the strain between them was a direct result. Something was different between Zanita and Leon too, but Ariela couldn't put her finger on it. Zanita seemed to get nervous when the time got close for Leon to come get her. She seemed to be relaxed, almost relieved, when she got back, but Ariela could still sense Zanita was trying to hide something. When Ariela asked her about how things were going with Leon, she simply said fine, you know how it is, then would smile demurely and turn away. The last time she did it, Ariela took her gold crucifix from around her neck and put it around Zanita's.

"Whatever is going on, Little Sister, this will protect you."

Zanita looked down at the cross and rubbed it with her fingers. She smiled up at her older, taller sister.

"Thank you, but really, everything is fine," she lied.

Sam and Morne travelled in the back of a black armored Mercedes driven by one of the President's security people. Behind them a black Toyota Helix pickup followed with four armed Presidential Guards. Unbeknownst to the security people, the Contra network kept trading off motorcycle riders behind the convoy never letting them out of their sight. Half a kilometer back trailed two trucks full of ARC mercenaries led by Javier Cordova ready to spring to the rescue if required.

The ride was uneventful, and they were deposited in front of the palace and escorted inside. Once inside, Ernesto Ruiz greeted them. He asked them to step through the metal detector and told them no phones would be allowed inside.

"Has Perez arrived?" Morne asked.

"He should arrive any moment," was the response and as if the man had said the devil's name three times, the front doors opened, and the notorious drug lord walked in as sunlight flooded around him. The security people took Gabriel Perez to a different area where they asked him to hand over his gold-plated Desert Eagle. Sam unlocked his phone and punched send on the text message he typed in the car. It was a single word. *Geronimo.* That text message went via radio signal into the nearest Nicaraguan mobile phone tower then to the Caribbean nodes of AT&T's fiber system and onto Miami. It routed itself through the US cloud infrastructure to the satellite phone providers system. It was then shot into space on a radio beam and delivered to Dan's satellite phone on the plateau overlooking Gabriel Perez's hacienda. It all happened before Sam walked through the metal detector.

CHAPTER XXIX

D an's phone pinged. He looked at the screen. Geronimo was the code word for go. Then he looked at Patson. Last night two cargo helicopters carried the assault team to their drop off point on the far side of the plateau, a night's hike from the hacienda. Dan was in the lead helicopter and when the second bird departed the landing zone, there stood Patson behind the second assault squad. The stream of profanity Dan leveled at him would have withered the hardest of veterans. Patson took it in stride. He knew it was coming. He also knew Dan could not bring the helicopter back.

"They killed my father."

"Well, what are you going to do about it?"

"I am coming with you," he said as he rested his hand on the Heckler and Koch .9mm holstered on his hip.

None of the men said as word as Dan leveled another profanity laced diatribe telling Patson he just endangered every man there's life by pulling this stunt and he should just leave him in the jungle. Dan then turned on the assault leader from the second helicopter.

"How did you let this happen?"

"He said you told him he could ride along on the helicopter. I don't know where he hid that pack and the gun. I never saw it."

"Well, Sargent Major, he is now your responsibility. He falls behind, kick him in the ass. He whimpers or whines, smack him in the mouth," Dan commanded as they started in the direction of the hacienda without turning back. Patson felt guilty now. What seemed like the right thing to do five minutes earlier was not feeling so certain with the entire assault team staring at him. He felt small and child-like, but then his pride bowed up under their stares and he realized he would show them he would not be a liability. That was dampened as the Sargent Major grabbed him by the collar and jerked him towards the cliff disarming him

184

of his pistol in one swift motion. The man ejected the magazine, racked the slide to clear it and handed it back to Patson.

"You brought it, you can carry it, Pup. Move out," he said in Afrikaans.

The assault team worked their way across the plateau during the night. The streams were the best way to make their way through the dense vegetation. As such, it was a long, wet night, but they were fairly dried out by the time the go message came. To Patson's credit, he kept up and had not muttered a word the entire night. Dan was thankful the only injuries were minor. A couple of twisted ankles of no consequence and some cuts and bruises. All night he struggled with what to do with Patson. Part of him wanted to keep the boy with him and protect him, but he knew he would be in the heaviest of the fighting most likely. Sam would never forgive him if the kid caught a bullet. He decided the best thing was to sit him on the sidelines with a protector, but it meant he had to pull a man from one of the assault teams. He had it figured out by launch time.

With the Geronimo call, two assaulters went forward. They already scoped out the path to sneak up on the machinegun nest atop the cliff. They watched the gunners switch out at noon. This would be their last watch. The assaulters got into position and put the red dots of their scopes on the back of the heads of the sentries. Two single suppressed shots and the sentries slumped over. The assaulters radioed for the rest of the crew to come forward. One of the men opened his pack and removed an electronic jammer. He dutifully lugged it and its big battery across the plateau in the dark and hoped he would never see it again. He connected everything. Dan looked at his satellite phone. It was useless, as were their radios now. He gave him the thumbs up.

The assault teams were divided into Alpha and Bravo. Alpha was the house team and Dan called out one of his members, Sargent Buser a combat veteran from the Afghan war.

"Modification of the plan. Buser, you and Patson are going to man this machinegun. If any aircraft other than ours try to land, you blow them out of the sky. Also, if either team gets in trouble, you cover their escape into the valley with this gun, call for the choppers to pick them up on the beach and retreat back across the plateau to our original LZ for pickup."

"Sir, that will leave you short-handed on the house assault," the soldier said disappointedly. He wanted some payback too. He wanted to kick some doors.

"I am aware. This is the right move though. I should have thought of it before. My poor planning. The gun is a two-man job, so having Patson here is actually a good thing. You instruct him on what to do."

Everyone, including Patson, was wondering if Dan meant this, or was saying these things to smooth over the situation for the soldier or more importantly for Patson. It was the latter, but he would never admit it. And while he was giving Patson a mission so he could feel like he participated, he wasn't going to be totally soft on him.

"Help Buser move these bodies out of the way so you can operate the gun properly," Dan instructed before he started towards the path that led down the cliff face. The Sargent Major of Bravo Team reached into his pocket and produced the magazine for Patson's pistol. He handed it to the boy and gave him a fist bump as he led Bravo team towards the path.

Sam and Morne were escorted into the conference room adjacent to the President's office. Beto Duran sat at the head of the table. His chief of staff stood next to him. Looking at the layout of the room, Sam intentionally approached from Duran's right side. He wanted to be seated at the old Sandinista's right hand to send a subliminal message to the drug lord. Duran did not rise, but offered Sam a wrinkled, liver spotted hand. Sam and Morne both shook it, and Sam hated every second of it. Dealing with a ruthless, bloody tyrant was not something he enjoyed, but they needed him for a bit longer. Two minutes later, Gabriel Perez was shown through the door. He sat down opposite Sam on Duran's left hand. He pushed his chair away from the table and casually crossed his legs.

"Thank you for coming," Ruiz said. "We will conduct this meeting in English as it is the common language between you two and I will translate for the President. I believe we can find some shared ground here today."

He was about to continue but stopped as he was interrupted by the opening door. The Vice President entered the room.

"Ah, I believe you all know the Vice President."

"Everyone knows our beautiful Vice President and First Lady," Perez responded.

Sam and Morne both rose. Gabriel was forced to stand as well. The President did not.

"Gabriel, so nice to see you," Isabella said as she offered her hand.

He bowed slightly and kissed it rather than shaking it.

"El Presidente, do you mind if I sit in?" She asked.

"Not at all," he responded in Spanish.

Gabriel expected her to sit by him and balance the table. She walked around her husband and stroked his shoulder as she did. She hugged Sam and then Morne. She sat next to him. The message was clear, and it infuriated Gabriel. *Puta*, he thought, and she saw the flare in his eyes.

"As I was saying, thank you all for coming. Let us work out some arrangements so everyone can get along," Ruiz continued.

"We want Ariela Sade returned. We know you have her," Sam said.

"So, you are Doctor Sam Harrington."

"I am."

"And you are Morne Delport."

"Ja."

"You have caused me no small amount of problems, Gentlemen. You call the DEA so they can intercept my merchandise. Then you murder fifty of my men. Good hard working family men on their way to work and you gun them down like animals. You are a plague on this land."

"And you are a piss-ant thug dealing in misery and death. Those men were there to murder our tower workers. And now you've gone too far sinking one of our ships," Sam said.

"You offend me, Doctor Harrington. I am simply a businessman, As for your ship, I am truly sorry to hear of your loss. Such a tragedy. Were there many deaths?" El Tigre said with a mild sweetness.

He relished the moment as he saw his lies crawling under the skin of the two men across the table from him. There was a noticeable pause. Perez was waiting on a number. He didn't know how many people he killed, but he was salivating and hoping for a big number.

"We were fortunate. We lost the ship, but no lives were lost. A few cuts and bruises, but no loss of life."

The disappointment showed on Gabriel's face. They were denying him the body count intentionally. It turned to anger he tried to cover with diplomacy.

"I find it hard to believe no one was killed in such a tragedy."

"Not one. Now, we want Ariela back and you stay the hell away from our tower crews and our concession granted by government."

"You will give me access to Honduras through those lands. I need it."

"No. And if you try to smuggle your merchandise through our area, we will see anyone armed as hostile and deal with them appropriately. Furthermore, any of your merchandise seized will be dumped into the ocean. We don't care how you move your product, but stay away from our areas and return Ariela unharmed," Morne said.

"I don't believe you have the ability to make me do any of those things."

Isabella leaned forward. "You are acting like a child. The ARC project is the future of Nicaragua. It is the President's legacy. It will be the greatest accomplishment of the Sandinista Revolution. You are jeopardizing all of that!"

"So, I am the past. Is that it? Never forget, we funded your revolution and we funded your coffers so you could stay in power."

"You have been and continue to be an important part, but we must adapt to changing times. You must adapt as well. You must make peace with ARC."

"I don't think that will be possible, Madam Vice President," Perez said in as derogatory a tone as possible.

Isabella switched to Spanish. Rapid fire and harsh.

"Don't screw with me, Gabriel. These people are a match for you. They have more money than you and they are tougher than you. Let me lay out some of the options. We can give ARC immunity from prosecution to do as they feel they must. We can send the army after you and seize all of your assets, or how about this. We call the United States and make some flowery overtures that we want to join the normal economy of the world and will they please help us get rid of one of our biggest problems, this evil drug lord. Do you want to see DEA helicopters at the Managua airport? Do you want to see their drones circling your hacienda? All it takes is a single phone call. Return the girl and stay away from them."

Sam and Morne had no idea what she was saying to him, but they loved the tone. The President sat silently looking at Gabriel. Gabriel returned the look but said nothing. The president's age was showing. It was clear to everyone Isabella was the real power in the room now. Gabriel stood, bowed to Beto Duran, and walked out.

Chapter XXX

The descent down the steep path was quick and quiet. Within fifteen minutes, the eleven assaulters were in the valley. The six members of Bravo held position while Alpha worked their way behind the waterfall to get on the side of the hacienda unseen. Dan signaled the First Sargent leading Bravo and both started their stop watches. Alpha was to have a head start to infiltrate the hacienda and see if they could free Ariela without raising an alarm. If Bravo heard one gunshot or any type of alarm, they would assault the factory and housing area taking down any military aged males.

Alpha worked their way to the wall surrounding the hacienda. They found the side door through the wall Leon used to sneak Zanita out to the waterfall. It was locked, but Dan produced his lock pick kit and opened in less than a minute. *So far so good*, Dan thought as he led the way inside the walls. They made their way stacked up in an assault formation to the nearest door, which was located at the back of the hacienda. The door was unlocked. They crept in quietly. The room was big and divided into what appeared to be floor to ceiling horse stalls. Dan's eyes quickly adjusted to the dimness of the room, and he approached the first stall. He peered inside and was amazed to see a tiger stretched out on its back in a pile of hay. The tiger simply looked at him without showing a sign of caring. The team fanned out. Three of the four stalls were occupied by great cats. The last was in use, but empty.

"Stay frosty. There is a big cat out there somewhere," Dan said.

Dan opened the opposing door and peered out. The interior of the hacienda was built around a two-story open courtyard with large living rooms on the bottom open to the courtyard. The second story was surrounded by a walkway with a low wall. There were multiple doors, presumably bedrooms, on the second floor. It was like assaulting a motel with a central pool. Assailants could come from any direction and from behind any doorway. He led the team through the door. He went left, the second man went right immediately, and the last three followed Dan. He paused as he looked for and identified the rear set of stairs. The team formed up on him and snuck crouched toward the stairs with the last man watching their six. Dan led up, his rifle's red dot always looking for a target. He peaked around the baseboard of the stairs and saw no one. He slowly rose. The landing went left and right. The wall in front of them was short so they could see down into the courtyard below, but it also meant anyone below could see them moving down the hallways. Looking across the second floor, Dan could see five doors on the left and right side. Dan took the man behind him right, left a sentry at the stairs as overwatch and sent the last two to the left.

Dan went to the first door. It had a hotel style door lock, an oddity for a home. He looked down the hallway and they all had them. If he kicked it in, everyone would hear. He tried it and it was locked. He slung his M-4 and drew his suppressed .45. He knocked softly. No answer. He knocked again. Still no answer. Next door he thought. He looked at the other team across the courtyard. They were moving to the next door as well. He knocked twice, no answer. He heard a man yelling in Spanish from below. Then he heard a suppressed shot and the yelling stopped. He took a knee with his partner, each of them facing a different direction waiting for a door to open. He heard another suppressed shot. The overwatch killed a man who saw one of the teams working the door and another coming out of a downstairs room with a rifle. Dan looked over the railing and saw the two dead men laying in the courtyard below. A door on the opposite side of the courtyard flung open and a man appeared with an AK-47. Dan's partner dropped him with two shots to the chest before he crossed the threshold. Dan cursed, turned, and kicked in the third door. He and his partner rushed in. It was empty. They backed out quickly and covered the other team while they kicked in their third door. They retreated and Dan and his partner moved to the fourth door. Before they made it, the wall plaster around them started flying off as 7.62 mm bullets began hitting all around them instantly followed by the roar and tale tell clattering of a Kalashnikov erupting from below. They ducked for the cover of the low wall. The overwatch moved towards the stairs to get an angle on the shooter. He encountered two men rushing up the stairs. He killed both and turned back towards the shooter. He was gone.

The sound of gunfire in the open courtyard filled the valley. Bravo team was ready for it. The three airstrip guards leaning against trees turned towards the house. Bravo team dropped them before turning their attention to the factory. They shot two guards standing outside the factory who were still wondering what was going on at the house. The team approached and split into two. One entered the factory while the other worked the parameter. The interior team encountered resistance immediately. There were no walls, so trees and tables provided the only cover. The workers, mostly women, hit the floor as soon as the first AK opened up towards the team. There appeared to be three gunmen working low amongst the tables, hiding as best as they could amongst the workers. One stuck his head up to shoot and the Sargent Major removed the top of his skull with the pull of the trigger. Women around the body started screaming and running half crouched out of the factory. The other workers panicked and followed. The interior team cleaned out the other two shooters with multiple chest shots. The Sargent Major was turning when he was knocked off his feet and he heard an AK fire from behind him. His men killed the shooter hiding behind a big tree. They rushed to the Sargent Major. One tended to him while the other kept watch. He was trying to reach behind him because it hurt, but his man pinned him on his stomach.

"Damn it. Hold still, Sargent Major," the soldier said as he started pulling away the man's body armor. He looked at the downed man's shirt and there were no holes. He ran his hands over his back. No holes. The body armor did the job. There were two flat round lead and copper bullets the Sargent Major's body armor stopped. He would be dead if it weren't for that. The soldier rolled the Sargent Major back over and showed them to him.

"Jy is 'n gelukkige bastard, Sersant Majoor."

The Sargent Major accepted a hand up realizing he was as lucky as the man said and put the flattened bullets in his pocket. He thanked God for the ballistic plates. Outside the trees, the other team was engaged. Workers were running towards the housing units. Armed men were running towards the factory. The team was trying to be careful not to hit any of the workers, especially the women. They shot the first few men that tried an uncoordinated assault. Then, incoming rounds started striking around them from the housing units. They retreated into the trees surrounding the factory. The first team started working south, the other team would work north, but not before they dropped a smoke grenade in the tree line to create a distraction. As they moved in different directions, they took targets as they found them. The cartel security forces were little match for the well-trained South Africans. It took less than ten minutes for them to clear everyone standing outside. Then they started going house to house as a single unit. They could not afford to leave anyone that would shoot at the helicopters when they landed. The buildings were mostly empty except for the old, sick, and young children. The workers scattered into the surrounding vegetation. They collected the weapons from the dead unloaded them and dropped them in an empty fuel drum which they lit on fire with kerosine from a nearby can. There was no longer any gunfire coming from the house. They reloaded and hoped Alpha had been successful.

Dan looked at his overwatch. The man gave him the OK sign after he exchanged magazines. They could all hear the AKs firing around the factory. Dan rose and kicked in the fourth door. He entered with his partner behind him. It was empty. They went back into the hallway. The second group kicked in their third door. It was empty. The dead man with the AK-47 lay in the doorway of room four. No one else was inside. Dan motioned for them to take down five. When the door was kicked in, AK-47 rounds started spraying from the inside. The Afrikaaner was able to duck back outside the door without being hit and the rounds flew across the open space striking the walls on the other side where Dan and his partner stood. He pulled a flash grenade from his belt and tossed it in. The concussion was loud, and the flash of light was beyond brilliant. The AK kept firing, but it was shooting all around the inside of the room. When they heard it run dry, they went in. The leader put two holes in the shooter's chest and one in his head. No one else was in the room.

Dan was amped as he approached door number five. He barely felt the resistance of the door as he crashed through the lock with his boot.

He and his partner were quick, guns up, fingers on triggers and ready to surgically remove any hostiles in the room. What he saw made his heart leap. He held up his left fist telling his partner to stop.

Ariela was crouched down in the corner using the dresser as cover. Dan pointed his rifle towards the ceiling and extended his left hand. Ariela raced to him and threw herself in his arms. The sound of AK-47s firing outside shattered the moment. Dan's partner turned around to cover the door. Dan tossed his rifle on the bed and stripped off his body armor. He put it over Ariela's head. She told him she did not need it, but he simply fastened the Velcro strips as tightly as he could around her.

"Where your sister?"

"Leon came and got her a while ago."

Chapter XXXI

Leon walked down the hallway with his arm around Zanita. Zanita hoped this would be another nice encounter. She'd seen the demon inside the man-child, and it terrified her. The last three days were pleasant with Leon being extra attentive as if he were trying to atone for the awful experience of the days before. She wanted to believe everything was going to be alright and she was beginning to lower her defenses, but she was still wary of him. She could tell it showed because Ariela kept asking if everything was alright. She repeatedly insisted everything was fine, even though she knew her sister wasn't convinced. She needed to be able to get out of that room and look for an opportunity to escape. For all they knew, Dan never received the voicemail, and he wasn't coming. Leon was the only way out of the room and if that meant giving her body to an emerging psychopath, then so be it. She was tough, but she had to keep it together. She realized they were not headed towards his room like normal. They were headed towards the kitchen, where the stairs were that led down to El Diablo's cage. Where she'd witnessed the great tiger tear the Mexican apart and where Leon had attacked her. She felt sweat prickle on her forehead and her cheeks flushed. The worms of fear began to writhe in her belly. Leon's arm around her felt like a python and even though we was whispering sweet things, her skin wanted to crawl. She tamped down her fear and whispered sweet things back. They stopped and hid behind a corner as a house guard passed by, then he snuck her into the empty kitchen. Leon kissed her by the refrigerator, and she kissed him back.

"Do you like your bracelet?"

"I love it."

"Good. I have another surprise for you, but you must put this on," Leon said pulling a blindfold from his back pocket.

"No. I don't want to."

"There is nothing to fear," Leon responded as he kissed her and then tied the blindfold around her head.

"Put both of your hands out together."

She complied and when she did Leon cinched a hemp rope around them that bit into the soft skin under her wrist.

"No!"

"Shhh. My darling. It is part of your surprise."

He opened the door and stepped in. He pulled Zanita towards him, and she yanked back hard out of fear. He pulled her forward by the rope and grabbed her firmly by the bicep.

"Step carefully."

"No," she said as she tried to pull away.

He jerked her forward and helped her control her clumsy descent down the stairs. She was afraid of falling and took a small solace when her feet were finally walking on flat concrete. She instantly knew the cage was not empty. She smelled the great cat.

The smell was so strong she knew he must have walked her in front of the glass. The glass that seemed so flimsy having so many holes in it. She wondered what horror she was about to witness. Instinctively, she tightened her abdominal muscles and tensed her thighs and arms. Her fight or flight instincts were coming out. Leon began to manipulate the bindings on her hands, then she felt her hands being drawn up over her head. She tried to pull down with her arms, but it was no use. She was held upright by a rope pulling her hands high. Leon bent down and removed her shoes. Her feet felt the rough concrete, then the rope tightened more until she was suspended on just the tips of her toes. The ridges in the cement bit into the pads of her toes. Her wrists hurt and her thighs and calves strained to support her. It was hard to breathe as her lungs struggled to inflate all the way. Leon pulled at her blouse, and she heard him cutting it away with a knife. She knew it was the carambit, that horrible sickle-shaped knife he carried on his belt. Her blouse fell away as did her bra. She heard the metal ting of Ariela's cross hitting the concrete below here feet. He cut through the rest of her clothes until she was naked. She began to cry.

"Shhh. Don't cry my love. There is nothing to fear. We are going to have some fun. You are going to show me how much you love me. You do love me don't you," he said as he kissed her trembling lips.

"Yes," she forced herself to say.

"Yes, what?"

"Yes, I love you," she said trying to keep her head in the game.

"I love you too," he replied as he kissed her again.

She could taste her own salty tears upon his lips. He kissed her until she started kissing him back. He rubbed her back and stroked her front until she relaxed. He retrieved a bottle of oil and used generous amount to coat her body and her tan skin shone like wet caramel. He ran his nails down her back and her sides, making stripes in the oil. He used his nails as the tiger would use its claws. The stripes on her body reminded him of the stripes on the great cat.

El Diablo found the events interesting. He stalked quietly to the edge of the glass and settled down on his belly to watch. Leon peered from behind Zanita to stare into the tiger's eyes as he dragged his nails down Zanita's torso. He saw the interest in the cat's face as she wiggled. He withdrew his carambit and slowly dragged the tip down Zanita's side and then up her inner thigh. When he pricked her with the tip, she made small yipping noises. Leon watched the great cat flinch each time. He ran the blade up her neck, and its edge was so sharp she didn't realize when he made a small incision behind each ear. Blood flowed freely down her neck, accelerated by the oil, and dripped from her chest onto the floor. El Diabo flared his great nostrils and silently stood looking at the sacrifice before him. His tongue hung over his canines as he tasted the scent of Zanita's blood in the air. Leon told Zanita to close her eyes as he removed the blindfold. She did as instructed, and she heard Leon moving somewhere behind her.

"Keep them closed."

The bite of the leather whip felt like a lightning bolt across her skin and the crack was as loud as one. Zantia threw her head back, her eyes shot open and she gasped in pain. El Diablo roared a great threatening growl and lunged at the glass at the same moment. The digits of his paw extended through the holes in the glass, and when she looked forward, she could see his huge, yellow claws trying to find a way through. Leon whipped her again and again. Each time, the tiger would roar, thrusting his great head against the glass with his nose squinched up and his fangs bared as Zanita struggled with the pain and to find a toehold to support her weight. She looked down and saw Ariela's cross on the floor below covered in her own blood. That became her focal point as her mind looked for a safe haven amongst the pain and terror.

Leon relished each lash and worked with precision to place each strike in a new place with as much speed and strength as he could muster. He loved not only the pain he was causing Zanita, but the torment of the frenzied roaring man-eater until on a back stroke he heard the sound of gunfire. He dropped the whip and rushed to the top of the stairs. He listened through the kitchen door as more gunfire erupted in the house. He flew down the stairs and ran past Zanita towards the exit at the other end of the pit which led up to the courtyard. As he passed the opening to El Diablo's cage, he flipped the lock and the seal cracked open. Zanita was left alone dangling before the hungry tiger as it paced back and forth smelling her blood, sweat and fear.

Dan and his partner appeared in the hallway with Ariela. The other three team members realized they had completed the mission and celebrated a tiny bit inside, but knew they still had to get out alive. They rendezvoused at the back stairwell.

"Ariela's sister is somewhere in here with a guy named Leon. He is El Tigre's son," Dan said.

"Orders, Top?" One man asked.

"Find the sister. Everyone else is a target."

The team put Ariela and Dan in the middle. Two men led; two men followed. They went downstairs and started clearing rooms. They could hear the firefight raging outside the hacienda. They hoped Bravo was holding their own, but there was no way to know with the jammer operating above on the cliff.

The team efficiently killed two guards that positioned themselves inside the study. They let a maid go that was cowering in Gabriel Perez's master suite. They were working their way towards the servants' quarters. There was a hallway that led to them and the kitchen. As the point man leaned around the corner to take a look, bullets came screaming down the hallway. He fell back around the corner. He'd been hit in the head. Dan was on him in an instant as number two took the defensive point.

"Are you OK?" Dan asked over the gunfire.

The man just started cursing. Dan did not see any blood. He moved the man's head and saw the mark left by the bullet on the helmet.

"Your helmet saved you," Dan said as he pulled him to his feet and pulled a flash bang from his belt. Dan pulled the pin and tossed it around the corner. When it went off, the new point man turned the corner to engage the defenders. He was met with a wall of lead and fell back. The flash bang had not made it down the hallway far enough to have an effect. Dan looked to the two men in the rear. Flank 'em was all he said, and the two pulled back and found a way out into the pool area where they could approach from the defender's side. They were crossing the pool deck when weapons fire came from a window. They ducked behind the stone columns around the pool for cover. They were up against the columns facing the opposite direction when the first man saw movement in the bushes. It was a tiger closing on them. He yelled tiger, catching his partner's attention. He raised his weapon and fired into the ground around the tiger. When he did, the window shooter opened up on his column throwing chucks of rock and plaster from it in a hail of gunfire. His partner spun around his column and killed the shooter. The tiger bounded into the house dragging its leash behind it. The tiger was going to get behind Dan and Ariela, but the man had no way to contact them with the comms out. He and his partner covered the distance to the window quickly and the first man there pulled a flash bang while the second covered him. He tossed it through the window and followed it with a frag grenade. They shot through the window at anyone moving inside after the frag went off. In the chaos, Dan and the rest of the team advanced forward and took out two of the defenders protected by the island from the frag grenade.

They cleared the kitchen and started towards the servants' quarters. They heard a muffled roar behind them. The tiger was in the hallway they just cleared. Dan took a flash bang from one of the men and tossed it at the tiger. He yelled get out of here just before it went off. After the flash, the tiger was gone. There was a door on the right side of the hallway and the point man stopped to listen. The electronic muffs he wore not only protected his hearing in the firefight, they amplified other sounds. He could hear a what sounded like a very angry tiger roaring. He looked at Dan who was hearing the same thing.

The point man opened the door and took aim. He saw stairs leading down. Ambient light was below. He took the lead as everyone followed. He ignored the naked girl hanging from the ceiling. He poked his rifle into the alcove as the number two man continued straight.

"Clear," he called.

"Clear," the number two man answered as he set up on the far steps leading up to another door. Dan was descending the stairs to the sound of El Diablo roaring incessantly. He saw the girl suspended and turned to stop Ariela, but it was too late. She saw her sister hanging from the ceiling and screamed. Dan grabbed Ariela by the shoulders and motioned with his head for the man behind her to investigate while he held her. The last man in line watched their six for any signs of danger.

"She's alive," the soldier said as he lifted her. The point man cut the rope holding her and they stood her on the ground. Ariela rushed to her.

"El Puerta," she said motioning towards the far end of the room.

Dan looked and saw the door to El Diablo's cage open.

"Close the cage!"

He approached and saw Zanita covered in blood on the front and whip marks on the back. The blood seemed to be coming from her scalp. Ariela was holding her, and they were both crying. He took the opportunity to look behind Zanita's ear. The cuts would need stitches, but that would have to wait. He grabbed her clothes and as he pulled them apart saw they were just rags now. He stripped his blouse and Ariela helped dress her sister. The rough cotton snagged at the whelps on her back and bottom. She bent down and grabbed Ariela's cross from the floor. She gripped it tightly as she slipped her feet into her shoes and dried the tears from her eyes with the sleeve of Dan's shirt.

Leon did not know what to do. We wished he had a gun. He had fired thousands of rounds from AK-47s and he wanted the security of one in his hand now. He covered his escape by opening El Diablo's door he thought. Whoever came that way would have to deal with a man-eating tiger. He felt nothing for Zanita. His only regret was that he had been unable to finish what he planned, and he was still extremely aroused, but that was fading fast with all of the gunfire. There was gunfire in the house and gunfire across the strip. The jungle offered protection, but he would have to cross a large open courtyard to get there. Behind the door he just exited was a corner where the outside wall met a large concrete planter. Vines overgrew the wall from the jungle outside and it was an ideal hiding place. He crawled behind the vines and kept silent.

Dan could see the sky through the glass wall of the tiger's cage. He knew the steps leading up would put them in the courtyard. All they had to do was clear it if there was anyone up there and get out the front gate. If Bravo had control of the other side of the field, they could call for extraction. The helicopters should be on station nearby.

Going through the door was essentially a frontal assault. The four men still wearing body armor exchanged their magazines for fresh ones and stacked up on the stairs. Shirtless Dan covered their six in case anyone came down the stairs from the house. The women were with him. The team burst through the door. The courtyard was empty. Two fanned out to provide outward facing fire, while two went to the main gate to investigate. Ariela appeared from the doorway supporting Zanita. The sunlight felt good on her face, and she realized the nightmare was about to be over. Dan emerged after the women and took stock. He looked about seeing the giant tiger head fountain on the wall across the courtyard and then glanced to the front gate, their next destination.

Leon realized he was the lone survivor from the hacienda. He wondered what his father would think. Would he be grateful his son was alive, or would be disappointed his son was a coward and survived by hiding? He held the carambit in his hand and formed a plan to solve both scenarios. The shirtless man was not looking his direction. He would rush from his hiding space and slash the throat of the gringo with his curved blade, then duck through the doorway before anyone knew what happened. He could run through the house, grab an AK and kill anyone that pursued. If not, he at least killed the man who appeared to be the leader of the group.

Dan was about to give an order to the two nearest men to move to the gate when his electronic muffs amplified a rustling sound behind him. He turned in time to see the man coming at him with a wickedly curved knife. He reached up and grabbed the man-child's wrist and swung him around with his own momentum. He let go when his would-be assailant was off balance and flying towards the tiger pit.

Leon's body hit the edge of the drop off and careened over. He flung the wicked carambit from his hand and grasped for the lip of the edge. The rough stones tore the skin from his fingertips and broke his nails, but somehow he was able to hang on. With his youth and fitness, he instantly began pulling himself up out of the hole. Ariela and Zanita turned to see his head emerging as he managed to get an elbow up onto the courtyard. Dan was walking towards him, but before he got there, Leon screamed as El Diablo jumped up and sank his three-inch hooked claws into him and pulled him into the pit. Leon screamed wildly as the tiger he befriended at times and tortured at others mauled him. Dan threw his M-4 up to his shoulder and pointed it into the pit. The tiger was on the boy and the white fur around his mouth and throat were already stained red with blood. He thought about shooting Leon in the head, but then he thought of Zanita. He dropped his weapon to his side and spit into the tiger's lair.

Alpha emerged from the hacienda grounds and made their way to the airstrip. Bravo was hunkered down on the other side. They exchanged hand signs over the distance and Bravo tossed a red smoke grenade onto the strip. Up on the cliff, Patson and the soldier saw the red smoke. Patson disconnected the battery from the jammer and waived down. Dan turned on his radio and called the two helicopters circling nearby. He told them the landing zone was secure and to begin the extraction. He asked Bravo about casualties. They reported none. He told Patson and the machine gunner to get down to the landing strip as soon as they saw the helicopters. It was but a few minutes before the beating of rotors filled the valley. Patson reconnected the jammer and they made their way down the cliff. Bravo set fire to the factory with diesel they found onsite. They did not burn the houses of the workers. The two big helicopters landed on the field. Patson rode with Bravo in the first helicopter while Alpha took the other with the rescued women. The helicopters gained altitude and headed for the ocean. Ariela held her little sister in her arms as she and Dan finally had a moment to make eye contact. They said not a word but understood each other perfectly.

Sam and Morne were aboard the Gulfstream. Sam suggested Morne give his pilots a little freedom to impress the victorious ARC warriors on the tanker they were searching for out in the Caribbean. Morne agreed and now both men were strapped in with their seat and shoulder belts fastened. The pilots had the great jet 200 feet off the water, and they were coming up on the tanker fast. She was steaming north with five helicopters lashed to her deck. The deck was full of waiving men as they passed, and they could see Ariela's long black hair blowing in the wind as she waved to the jet. It appeared as if they were having a party. Morne and Sam both wished the executive jet was equipped for sky divers because it looked like a good time. The pilot gave a short warning and pulled the yoke back and the Gulfstream climbed rapidly up. Both men felt the blood rush to their legs as the G force tried to crush them into the luxurious seats.

"You fighter jocks never lose it, do you?" Sam yelled at the pilot.

"No Sir! Yee Haaaww," he yelled back as he put the jet into a roll with the party below cheering him on.

Enrique approached Gabriel Perez by the pool at his Managua house. El Tigre had been brooding in a foul mood since he returned from the Presidential Palace.

"I have been trying to reach the hacienda, and no one is answering," he told his boss.

"What do you mean?"

"I've called the three house phones and the satellite phones carried by Juan and Carlos. No one is answering."

"Perhaps the stupid satellite internet service is down."

"That is what I thought, but why would Juan and Carlos not be answering? Their phones work independent of the internet."

El Tigre's blood ran cold. He looked at his watch. It was too late to fly to the valley. They would not make it there before dark.

"Keep calling and get the plane ready. I want to leave before sunrise tomorrow if we cannot raise them."

Chapter XXXIII

The sun was a half an orange ball barely above the horizon when El Tigre's King Air descended into the valley. It was still dusky, but light enough to see the strip. As the twin engine plane turned around at the end of the field, El Tigre saw people coming out of the housing area to greet the plane. He felt a sense of relief. Then he noticed there were no men in the group. It was just women and young children.

He did not wait for the pilots to open the door. He unlatched it while the plane's engines were still shutting down and leaped to the ground. He surveyed the area and saw the factory was burned inside. The great trees surrounding it and hiding it from the satellites were charred. He looked to the group of women coming forward. He knew the woman in front.

"Maria, what happened?"

"Men came. They burned the factory. They stormed the hacienda. Our men fought bravely, but they killed them all. They killed them and left on helicopters," she half cried.

"Where is my son?"

"We have not been able to find Leon."

"Did he get on one of the helicopters?"

"No. It was all strange men and two women."

Gabriel looked at the ground. Rage consumed him. He knew immediately who was responsible.

"What are we to do now, El Tigre?"

"Go back to your homes and mourn your husbands."

Gabriel hustled himself up the incline towards the house. Enrique was close behind. The gates to the hacienda stood open. He went through the front doors. Everything appeared fine until he saw bullet holes in the walls and scorch marks from the grenades. He found the head maid sitting at the kitchen table alone. She was exhausted from helping bury the dead men and scrubbing the blood from the floors and walls of the hacienda.

"Grace, donde esta Leon?"

She simply turned and pointed to the half-open door leading down to the cellar. He rushed down the steps. Grace and her maids had cleaned away Zanita's rags and blood. Everything appeared normal until Gabriel stared into the great cage he designed to hold El Diablo. He saw Leon's carambit lying on the floor. That gave him a start. When he saw the tennis shoe with his foot still in it, he turned and spit as if that would take the bile from his mouth. His creation of fear and intimidation had consumed his son. He looked at the tiger. It was magnificent and curled up in the corner on a pile of straw. Its eyes were seemingly lost in the stripes of its face until they opened and registered El Tigre standing outside the glass. It watched as Gabriel Perez opened the door to the cage and entered the enclosure. The tiger stood. For what seemed like an eternity, El Diablo and El Tigre stared at each other. The tiger could sense something was different. He took a step forward and Gabriel pulled his Desert Eagle from his belt. The tiger took another step and hunched its shoulders preparing for a lunge that would cross most of the cage. It recoiled as the first bullet hit, growling in pain and shock as it tried to gather its strength to attack. Another bullet and then another hit the tiger and each time it shrunk away. After the third bullet, the tiger found its rage and lashed out, launching himself at El Tigre. Two more .50 caliber bullets hit him in flight, and he landed with a thud on the floor of his enclosure. El Tigre put his final round into El Diablo's head. He did not move again.

Chapter XXXIV

Zanita lay sleeping in her bunk. Two doctors were aboard the tanker were prepared to treat battlefield casualties, but the injuries were light. They salved her whip marks and stitched up the cuts behind her ears. They were deep, but only about an inch long. Dan got Ariela to follow him up on the deck and they joined the men celebrating and thoroughly enjoyed the display put on by Morne's pilot. They were about an hour away from the colony when Dan took her aside.

"Tell me everything."

"I'm so sorry," she started and then burst into tears at the thought of the Niña sinking. She told him everything. She told him she tried not to tell El Tigre anything, but in the end the threat of him cutting Zanita's hands off made her give in. She told him about the brutal choking when she clawed at her own skin and Dan's blood boiled. The demon inside him flashed its eyes and Dan told it not yet. He remained calm as Ariela told him the entire story. Then he held her until she stopped crying. When she stopped, he recanted the story to her to make sure he had all the facts correct. He knew he would be debriefed upon their return.

The Board gathered around the table. Dan stood and gave an account of the raid. It was crisp and professional. He did not elaborate about Ariela and Zantia's treatment. When he finished, Morne thanked him and asked he and the admiral to leave. Morne and Sam gave a readout to the group about their meeting with Gabriel Perez. They were all interested in how the power seemed to shift from the President to his wife in the meeting. Eventually, the one remaining question came front and center.

"What do we do about Gabriel Perez?" Morne asked.

"What do you mean?" Katherine replied.

"Do we kill him, or do we let him live?" Sam responded.

"It is going to be harder to kill him now," Marcus said. "The question is what will he do next? Do you believe Isabella threatened him enough?"

"I think he is what he is, and no amount of threatening can change that."

"You believe he will attack again?" Morne asked.

"You were there. Don't you?"

"I believe he will be a nuisance. I don't think he will attack again the way he did," Morne said.

"We should kill him and be done with it," Marcus added.

"What happens if he attacks us again?" Ansel asked.

"The Vice President said she would send the army after him, turn a blind eye to us taking him out or call the US DEA for assistance in eliminating him," Sam replied.

"And he understood this?" Ansel asked.

"Perfectly," Morne replied.

"Then I think this is over. The consequences are too great for him to attack again."

"We just burned his factory, killed his soldiers and Dan threw his kid in a pit to be eaten by a tiger," Sam announced. "I think that has to be figured into the equation."

"And if we kill him, what happens in the power vacuum? Do we run the risk of getting someone more violent?" Jayden asked.

"More violent than a man that sank one of our ships and tried to murder an entire tower crew?" Sam responded.

"I think the risk is greater now to attack him. He will be prepared and the loss of one of our people in an attempt to assassinate this man is too great a loss," Ansel added.

The debate went on for ninety minutes. In the end, only Sam and Marcus voted to assassinate Gabriel Perez. The rest, including Katherine, voted to increase security and wait to see what happened. They decided killing him was an option they could invoke at any time. Sam broke the news to Dan who slammed his fist into the bulkhead. He wanted Perez dead for what he did to Ariela and for what he did to the people on the Niña.

The three of them lay in bed together that night. Ariela sleeping like she was dead; Dan fitfully trying to sleep in a tortured state; and Dan's demon who stayed awake all night whispering in his ear and goading him for vengeance. When Dan could take it no more, he got up and headed to the armory.

Patson emerged from the Santa Maria gangway headed for the bus that would take him to his job in the tool shed. The past few days had been the most turbulent of his life. He had still not fully processed the loss of his father, Johannes. He was glad he stowed away upon the rescue mission, even though his friend Dan cussed him in no uncertain terms. Dan surprised him by coming to his defense with Sam yesterday, but the dressing down he received in private from Sam was nothing less than humiliating. Sam was angry with him for being stupid and endangering his life and the lives of others. He was disappointed in him for not thinking through the ramifications, but mostly he was thankful Patson was safe, and everyone came home unharmed with the two women rescued. In the end, after a half hour of yelling Sam hugged him and told him he was glad he was safe. He also told him he was very brave, but to never do anything like that again.

As Patson walked sleepily towards the bus, Dan pulled up in his pickup. He told Patson to get in. Patson complied but was confused when Dan did not take the road up the escarpment towards his job. Instead, he took the coast road towards the docks where the patrol boats were tied up.

"You know how to find Aapo, right?"

"Yes."

"Good. I need his help."

"But I need to get to work."

"I already took care of that. Don't worry."

"Does my father know about this?"

"I'll take care of that too. You owe me, kid. You are coming with me," Dan said without blinking.

With his father's yelling still ringing in his ears and more than a bit of trepidation in his heart, Patson boarded the motorboat. He knew Dan was right. He owed a debt; one he could not easily repay. He also knew he would rather die than disappoint his father again. Dan started the engines and pointed the boat towards the mouth of the Coco River. As Patson watched the two great white cruise ships at anchor fade away he openly muttered the first curse word of his life in front of an adult, and it was the mother of them all.

The patrol boat appeared at the dock late in the afternoon with Patson and Aapo riding in the front. Aapo had not hesitated to get in the boat when Patson asked him to come with them. Dan opened the front passenger door of his truck for Aapo and Patson climbed in the rear seat. Patson saw Dan's backpack and rifle case in the floorboard. Dan drove across the dragon into Honduras to the airport. There were two helicopter pilots waiting beside one of the Eurocopters. They were more than a little surprised to see Dan arrive with a native wearing a loincloth and little else. Dan retrieved his pack and rifle case. Patson stood alone wondering what was going on, but he was certain he was not about to get on the helicopter under any circumstances.

"Tell your dad I've gone to take care of our problem. If he wants to pick me up, I will egress on the beach about where these guys drop me off. Five days, maybe longer. If he doesn't, I'll find my own way back. Thanks for helping me," he said as he tossed Patson the keys to his truck.

Dan instructed Aapo in getting aboard the helicopter and closed the door. The rotors began to spin and soon the sleek airship lifted off and spun south. Dan gave the pilots instructions to put the bird on the deck ten miles out so nobody would see them land on the beach.

After the helicopter left them alone on the beach, Dan gave Aapo a cigarette and lit it for him. He drew a map in the sand. It showed the valleys and hills they had to navigate to get to the hacienda. He wished he could have dropped in atop the waterfall again, but El Tigre would be expecting that, so that meant two or three days of hard walking through the dense vegetation. He rightfully assumed Aapo could get him there with the least amount of effort and thus he conscripted the little Indian.

Aapo seemed to understand and indicated by pointing to the sun, which was about to set they should spend the night on the beach and start at first light. Dan was good with that and built a small fire. He broke open two MRE packages and shared the contents with Aapo, who was delighted by some of the contents and less than enthused by the rest. When they finished, they shared a cigarette around the fire and went to sleep. Dan was tired from not sleeping the night before, and the demon inside him was satiated knowing its blood lust would be appeased soon enough. Aapo wondered what the goal of this adventure was, but he didn't have to guess what they were hunting. He knew it was men.

Sam was furious when Patson told him what transpired that day. He was hard on Patson, but also realized he didn't really have a choice. He sought out Ariela to find out what she knew. She knew nothing and he could see she was telling the truth by the fear in her eyes. She simply woke up that morning and Dan was gone. She spent the day with Zanita and Katherine. Sam sought out the helicopter pilots and they told him everything. They scrounged up the piece of paper Dan gave them with the GPS coordinates on them.

Sam was beyond irate at Dan for going off on his own and he was really furious he conscripted Aapo to help him. Now he was worried for both of them. He called Jay Nobel at the DEA.

"Our buddy has gone on a little trip, and I need to know what he might run into."

"Did our friend go to the zoo in the valley?"

"Yes, and we had a party there two days ago where things got kind of ugly."

"The lady was OK though?"

"Yes, her and her sister came home just fine, but the host has a lot of cleanup work to do."

"Understood. You have the latest pictures, but I can see what surveillance we have in the area."

"Anything you can do would be appreciated. I need to know if I need to order an Uber for our friend or just go join the party."

"Understood. Call you tomorrow."

Sam texted Katherine he would not be at dinner and asked Morne and Marcus to join him in the Admiral's quarters. A bottle of Angel's Envy bourbon was open when they arrived, and the Admiral fetched two more glasses. After the glasses clinked, Sam told them what was happening. Morne gulped his scotch and pursed his lips. Marcus sipped his and grinned. The Admiral sat not drinking but watching.

"What do we do?" Sam asked.

"What are the odds of him being successful?" Morne asked.

"Pretty good. He is a sniper by training, and I'd say he is one of the best ever."

"I guess our choices are to do nothing, somehow support Dan, or warn Gabriel Perez."

"We cannot warn Perez," Marcus declared.

"If you think about it, it might buy us some good will. Sam could call Isabella and have her warn him."

"And sacrifice Dan in the process," Sam said.

"We voted not to assassinate him. Dan went off on his own."

"We never voted to sacrifice one of our people," Marcus said as his face flushed.

"I am just talking it out. We could never sacrifice Dan. But what do we do? Nothing? Or do we try to help?" Morne asked.

"We do nothing," Sam said flatly. "He will get it done, or he will get himself killed."

"We need to be prepared if he is unsuccessful," the admiral said.

"Retaliation?" Morne said with a single raised eyebrow.

"Yes. If Dan gets caught, there will certainly be retaliation. Even if there was already going to be some, it will be bigger."

"And if he is successful?" Marcus asked.

"We are already on a defensive posture," Sam said. "I am not sure what else we can do at this point. We'll see if Jay Nobel comes up with any intel about what is going on at the hacienda, but I can tell you this, I am not going to leave my buddy out there alone."

Sam used his thumbprint to unlock his cabin door and saw Katherine waiting for him on the couch. Her body seemed listless, and he outstretched his arms. She slowly rose to him and welcomed the embrace.

"I missed you today. I spent most of it with Ariela and Zanita."

"How is the girl?"

"Strong. Amazingly resilient, but I suspect she is just pushing everything down inside. It will come back to haunt her."

"That is unfortunate. What about Ariela?"

"She told me everything. Perez and his henchman, the one with the tattoo on his face, stripped her nearly naked and choked her for hours. They did it with a belt around her neck and when she passed out, they woke her up and started again. She said she was resigned to die rather than give them anything, but when they threatened to cut off Zanita's hands, she gave up. She feels horribly guilty about the people that died on the Niña."

"She shouldn't feel that way. I went through SERE school in the army. Everyone has a breaking point. I guess that explains why Dan went to kill El Tigre."

"What?"

"Ariela didn't tell you?" Sam asked double checking Ariela's story.

"I don't believe she knows."

"He took Patson up the river to find Aapo and then had a helicopter drop him and Aapo off on the beach a couple days walk from the hacienda."

"Is Patson OK?" She asked with urgency as if he were her own.

"He is fine."

"Good. I hope Dan kills this…Tiger," she said with her Austrian accent.

"Yeah?"

"I didn't know everything I know now when we voted. I should have voted with you. I am glad Dan has gone to kill him."

"Yeah well, now I have to figure out how to help him."

CHAPTER XXXV

El Tigre buried what was left of his son, Leon. It was little more than the foot in the shoe and part of his spine. El Diablo was skinned by Enrique and his carcass was hauled on a wagon into the jungle.

The household staff busied themselves cleaning the blood stains from inside the hacienda and patching the bullet holes and damage caused by the grenades. They worked without instruction. The hacienda was their domain. Enrique worked over at the factory trying to get it back to operational status. The women there worked hard because they knew their very lives depended upon the generosity of Gabriel Perez. This did not stop Enrique from using the toe of his boot or the back of his hand to incentivize them to work harder. They were mostly nervous widows now. They were brought here by plane, usually as the wife of one of the guards to work in the factory. They didn't even know where they were geographically speaking and with no means of leaving, they were essentially slaves. Slaves to be worked, to be used and to be given to new men working for El Tigre as either a reward or for entertainment.

Earlier, Enrique found the radio jammer atop the cliff and reestablished communications for Gabriel Perez. Perez paced around the pool calling his lieutenants around Nicaragua and beyond. He was summoning an army to be brought to the hacienda. When Enrique appeared in the early evening hours, El Tigre instructed him to sit and poured him a glass of dark rum.

"I saw the plane and helicopter leave," Enrique said.

"I sent them to bring our soldiers here. We are going to attack the gringos. No mercy. No quarter. We will leave none of them alive."

"What about what the Vice President said? That she would send the army or call the Americans?"

"Do you think I care what that bitch said? Do you think I will lower myself before her and that decrepit old man? I gave her and her husband

213

their power! They would not be the leaders of the country without me! In fact, I believe it is time for a change of control within the government. You are my most trusted lieutenant. I want a plan to assassinate the President and Vice President as soon as possible," Perez said with a tone that was deadly serious.

Enrique dismissed himself quickly. He rubbed the tiger tattoo on his face as he walked outside. He looked up at the sky and could almost imagine a US Predator drone circling high above looking at him with its powerful camera. Would he even hear a Hellfire missile screaming down upon him from 30,000 feet? Probably, but it would be too late. He briefly thought about getting on the next aircraft leaving the strip and never coming back, but he realized that was a fool's thought. He was marked. He belonged to El Tigre. He just hoped his boss would change his mind.

Chapter XXXVI

At Beale Air Force Base near Sacramento, California Lieutenant Henry Davidson directed his team to zoom in and get a closer look at the goings on in the remote valley they were tasked with observing. They recorded small planes landing on an airstrip at the base of a cliff nestled between a grand hacienda and a burnt-out area surrounded by small huts. Zooming in they could see the cargo was mostly armed men, soldiers of the cartel, although some shipments brought food and supplies. Since the aircraft coming and going from the valley operated in the ungoverned zones of Central America, there was no air traffic control to tell the pilots that high overhead at sixty-thousand feet circled a U.S. Air Force Global Hawk drone. The fifty-foot drone with its enormous wingspan and great bulbous nose full of cameras and sensors loitered higher than anyone would suspect and was nearly invisible to those on the ground unless atmospheric conditions left a con-trail.

Special Agent Jay Nobel received a call from an Air Force Major giving him an update on what they were seeing in real time. El Tigre was amassing a sizeable force quickly. He called Sam to give him a brief update and promised a more detailed account. He'd been able to get time on the Global Hawk that was headed further south on a counter narcotics mission over Colombia, and it would stay on station over El Tigre's lair for an hour.

Sam found Admiral Sharpe on the bridge of the Santa Maria and asked if they could meet in his cabin again. Naturally he agreed and Sam invited Morne and Marcus via text message. It took forty-five minutes for Morne and Marcus to arrive as they were on shore working.

"We will get another report in a little bit, but right now it appears El Tigre is amassing a sizable force. The only logical conclusion is he intends to attack something," Sam said.

"You mean, us," Morne corrected.

"Yep. The tower construction groups or us here."

"How long?" Marcus asked.

"Don't know, but Dan is walking into an army."

"What should we do?"

"The admiral and I are going after Dan. The tanker weighed anchor fifteen minutes ago and is headed south. It is towing one of the patrol boats. We will join via helicopter later today. We'll use the boat or helo to pick up Dan on exfil."

"I'm going with you," Marcus declared in a tone that said there would be no further discussion on the subject.

Sam's phone rang while he was throwing a few things in a bag in his cabin. Patson sat on the couch listening.

"What do you know?"

"Not much different than when I called you earlier. Lots of little planes landing and dropping off men and supplies. They sent me some close ups. Mostly yahoos with AKs, but they sent us a picture of Enrique Sanchez standing in the open greeting the guys getting off the plane."

"Any pictures of Perez?"

"None. But listen. We want Sanchez. Dead or alive."

"If Dan makes contact, I'll pass that along, but I have to tell you. Sanchez tortured Dan's girlfriend. I can't see him getting out of this with his head still attached."

"That would make the DEA very happy. It would also be a nice feather in my cap."

"Is that bird headed back to California?"

"In about twenty-four hours."

"Can you get me another look tomorrow?"

"I'll see what I can do."

"I need a thermal picture. I am looking for a person on the perimeter."

"You figure Dan is going to be laying up waiting on a shot?"

"I would be," Sam said as he hung up.

Patson stood and Sam glanced in his direction.

"I want to go with you, Father."

"No."

"Please. I am invested."

Sam looked at his adopted son. Their eyes met and he could see the man he was developing into standing before him.

"I guess you are. You stay on the tanker though."

CHAPTER XXXVII

Dan was relieved to be standing at the edge of the jungle surrounding the hacienda. Following Aapo for two days was no easy task, but it was far easier than trying to navigate the terrain on his own. Periodically when he found an open patch of sky, he used his GPS to check their course. How Aapo kept his orientation through the terrain and vegetation was more magic than science it appeared. Aapo used the stream beds when he could, but parts of their journey were more mountaineering than hiking. Other parts were simply tediously hacking their way a foot at a time through the jungle with machetes.

The sound of the area around the hacienda was chaotic after the silence and bird songs of the jungle. Dan and Aapo heard a propeller driven aircraft coming from behind them and moments later a twin-engine Cessna sat down on the short runway and unloaded eight armed men. The plane never turned off its engines but spun around at the end of the runway and took back off. Dan saw a man emerge from the area where the factory worker housing was located to greet the men. He appeared to have a tattoo on his face. Dan shouldered his rifle and Enrique's head filled the scope. He placed the crosshairs on Enrique's nose and thought about how he strangled Ariela with his belt. His finger drifted to the trigger and pressed hard enough to feel the tension in it. A micro amount of pressure and Enrique's head would explode. *Not yet* he thought, and he relaxed his finger as he heard another twin-engine airplane full of soldiers approaching to land.

Jay Nobel's name appeared on Sam's mobile phone screen. He was standing on the bridge of the tanker. Sam's phone was connected to the satellite WIFI on the ship.

"I just emailed you the photos the Global Hawk took as it passed over on the way home."

"And…"

"Lots more people on the ground. All males, all armed."

"And the thermal?"

"Look at picture thirty-five. You will see a distinct yellow hotspot directly south of the main gate of the hacienda in a tree. It sure looks like a man to me. Looks like he is laying on a tree branch."

Dan had been laying on the branch of an enormous tree for several hours. His scope was zeroed in on the front doors of the hacienda. His range finder said the distance was three hundred and thirty-three meters. He was two tree layers deep in the jungle and wearing a ghillie suit made from a net and the leaves and twigs from the tree. Aapo sat below the tree. He seemed as patient as the forest itself. Dan gave him an MRE before he scurried up the tree. Everything was a waiting game now. With no spotting partner, it was Dan's responsibility to maintain a vigilant watch on the hacienda. The hardest part was keeping his mind focused, so he gave himself tasks. He started with sexual conquests, remembering each woman starting with his first and ending with Ariela. He found he could not remember all of the names. He decided there was no penalty if he had never known their last names, but he racked his brain for the last names of some he should remember. When he got bored of that, he turned to kills. Unlike the faces of some of the women he'd bedded, he could see the face of every man he ever killed up close or through a scope, and he remembered the events in vivid detail. He started this list in reverse with Leon. He didn't know if he would have helped him up, shot him, or just stepped on his fingers if he had gotten to him before the tiger. The screams from the boy had been blood curdling, but he had heard those screams before. Knowing what he did to Zanita, he felt no remorse about letting the tiger eat him. Dan ticked off the list of men he killed all the way back to his first. Of course, the first was the first of many that day in Mogadishu where he and his friends were fighting for their lives all day and all night. It was an embarrassment. The army asked the Clinton administration for a tank to carry out rescues in the city, but it was denied saying it offered poor optics. The helos were sitting ducks above the city, and they lost five that day as well as two crews and some damn brave Delta guys. Mike Durant was taken hostage and held for eleven days. He thought about his friend Mike. He should have died after having his leg broken in two places, two vertebrae crushed, being shot, and beaten bloody with his co-pilot's severed arm by the mob. He might be the toughest son-of-a-bitch Dan knew, maybe even tougher than Sam Harrington.

He thought about his entry in the army. It too was a bit of an embarrassment for him. He was a sophomore at Notre Dame and got caught selling alcohol to other students. Not just alcohol, but cases and cases of it. He and a friend would drive down to Kentucky, load up and bring it back. It was a great way to put themselves through school they figured. Dan got ratted out, but he would not squeal on his partner. The judge gave him a choice. Go to jail or join the army. If he hadn't pulled that stunt, he would have graduated with an English degree and probably be a teacher or something else respectable instead of lying in a tree waiting to put a bullet through a drug lord's skull.

Gabriel met with his top four lieutenants in his study. The tall glass doors were open, and the sound of the waterfall filled the room. He had an aerial map of the ARC site on his desk, and they were all gathered around. He asked for suggestions on how to attack the enemy's location. The prevailing thought was to load up their men in trucks and perform a frontal assault. The lieutenants were feeling their full machismo and arrogantly saying what they would do to the African gringos. Only Enrique was quiet. El Tigre asked him what was bothering him.

"We will get slaughtered in a frontal assault."

"We will not. Grow a set. Nobody can stand up to us. We are ruthless and our men are the best," one of his peers named Jose countered.

"You are an idiot. I've been to their territory several times. I led the raid on the tower workers. We never stood a chance. I lost fifty men in less than a minute to these Africans."

"Then what do you suggest?" Gabriel asked.

"If we intend to attack, we should create a diversion to draw their troops away from our forces so that we can get to their ships and the power plant with as little resistance as possible."

"How should we do that?"

"If we get one of the Honduran gangs to attack the airport in force, that would draw their forces away from the southern routes into their facilities. Once we get to the main area, we have three targets, both ships and the power plant. We give no quarter. We kill everyone."

"You see, this is why Enrique is my number two. He is ruthless, but he is also thoughtful. You can all learn a thing or two from him."

The five men spent several hours huddled around the map discussing what was needed to make the attack a success. More than a little resentment grew between Enrique and Jose whose ideas kept being squashed, not because of anything personal, but because the ideas were simply not practical. By the time they finished, it was getting dark. The planes had slowed in the afternoon, but Enrique knew they would start again tomorrow when the sun came up because the plan they developed called for one hundred and fifty men. Enrique wandered through the huts housing the factory workers. He listened to the conversations between the men about what they were doing in this isolated place, to the conversations between the women about what would happen to them next, and to the conversations between the men and women where they were finding each other's company a pleasant distraction. He had very little faith his plan would work, and he wondered if he was listening to the last conversations of dead men. He remembered what the Afrikaners did to the three truckloads of men he took to kill a handful of them at the tower site. How could these men ever compete with defensive tactics executed like that? Part of him wished El Tigre would simply take the loss and keep on doing business by avoiding the African gringos. Their losses were greater now with no eastern routes, but they were still making money hand over fist. He knew Gabriel's pride was damaged and he was mourning the loss of his son. More than that, he knew Gabriel feared looking weak in front of the other cartels and the gangs. That was the biggest driver for revenge, but this attack could be their undoing. A little thought flickered in the back of his brain that maybe he should just go to the hacienda and put a bullet in the back of El Tigre's head.

The bark on the big tree limb Dan lay upon was doing a fine job of chewing the skin off his sternum, belly, and thighs. He'd gotten down to sleep a little and share an MRE with Aapo when the lights went off in the hacienda. Aapo understood he was supposed to stay awake while Dan slept, and he silently stood vigil over the sleeping warrior until the birds began to sing their morning calls. Dan shared a bit of an MRE with Aapo and crawled back up into the tree before the hacienda and encampment came to life. He'd been up there all day watching for El Tigre to make an appearance. The twin-engine planes kept coming two at a time delivering eight armed men on each landing. He knew it was a two-hour trip because they would return every four hours. He saw Enrique three times that day and each time he put the crosshairs on his tiger tattoo and his finger on the trigger, but he wasn't willing to take a consolation prize. He wanted El Tigre. The only entertainment he got during the day was when the guards handling the tigers made an appearance. It was crazy to watch these men walking around with the great cats patrolling the perimeter like one would with a dog. He wondered if a tiger's nose was as good as a dog's. He wondered how fast they could run. He wondered what he would do if one got after him. He didn't wonder that long. It would be him or the tiger. Probably even odds he figured, then he figured again and decided he better not let a tiger near him. Midnight came without an appearance by El Tigre. When the lights went out, he shimmied down the tree and began the same routine as last night with his ever-present shadow, Aapo.

Admiral Sharpe had the captain of the tanker drop anchor ten miles north of the GPS coordinates Dan gave the helicopter pilots and five miles offshore. There was no protection for the ship, so it rocked with every wave. They were lucky the seas were relatively calm, and they did not take too much of a beating being anchored. He and Sam took the patrol boat to the GPS coordinates and stayed out past the surf line using binoculars to scan the beach. They slowly patrolled the coastline hoping any second to see Dan and Aapo emerge from the jungle.

Marcus stood by at the ready on the ship with the two helicopter pilots who brought Dan and Aapo here. He mounted an M-249 machine gun onto a strap from ceiling inside the helicopter and was ready to play the part of a door gunner if the patrol boat called for backup. They decided to keep the helo onboard the tanker as they did not want to alert anyone on land that something was happening by having it airborne searching for Dan. Patson dutifully sat on a stool in the bridge playing with his phone like a typical teenager waiting for the radio to come alive.

The admiral looked at Sam seated in the front of the patrol boat looking back at him. The day had been long and hot, but now the sun was gone, and the Milky Way was high above in its full glory.

"How about a beer?"

"Love one."

"Maybe we will make contact tomorrow," the admiral said as he handed Sam a cold one from the cooler.

"Hopefully. But I am willing to stay as long as it takes."

"Me too," the admiral replied as he discretely dialed down the light on his navigation screen to a dim glow and covered most of the screen with his hat. He'd thought about this little joke he wanted to play on Sam earlier in the day.

"By my reckoning, the ship is that way and I believe I can get us there navigating by these stars here on the horizon."

"If you can find a dark ship five miles offshore by the stars, I will be impressed."

"Prepared to be impressed my friend," the admiral said as he wheeled the boat around on its axis and headed North trying not to let his grin give him away.

Zanita lay on her stomach naked while her sister applied ointment to her whip marks. They were less raised than yesterday and had scabbed over into crusty stripes that frequently pulled open when she moved. The ointment kept them moist and provided insurance against infection. She had been distant since the rescue. She kept reliving the whole incident over and over wondering what she could have done differently. *What if she had refused to go with Leon? What if she had fought back?* The answer always came back the same, they would still be locked in that bedroom with the sunflower yellow walls unsure if El Tigre was ever going to release them. Letting Leon have his way was the only chance for her and Ariela to exert some level of control over their fate, and it paid off. Dan came and rescued them. The price for that chance though was that she kept seeing El Diablo lunging at her, so close she could smell his breath through the holes in the glass. So close, she could see his terrible claws scratching the plexiglass around the holes trying to tear through and get her. And in her dreams, she could hear the crunching of the Mexican's bones by El Diablo. While these things haunted her, on some base level she drew a kind of happiness from the fact Leon was dead. In some way, watching him be torn apart by the tiger was cathartic for her.

"Are you OK?" Ariela asked as she finished applying the ointment and helped her sister up off the bed.

Zanita pulled up her shorts and reached for her shirt.

"I am fine. Thank you for applying the cream."

"You know I am here for you."

"I know," Zanita said.

"I wish you had told me Leon was a psychopath. Maybe we could have stopped him."

"There is nothing we could have done. I had to give myself to that monster to give us a chance. Afterall, I was the reason you were there. I was the reason those animals choked you to a point where I thought I had just seen my sister murdered before my eyes. My sister, who always loved me, and always looked out for me. I let them use me to get you. I am the real reason these people lost their friends on that ship and the reason your man is in the jungle trying to kill El Tigre. I am just a fool. A stupid, stupid fool," she said as she started to cry.

"You were not a fool. Those men were evil. They used you and there is nothing you could have done," Ariela said. "The main thing know is that we are both free and these people have said we can stay here. We don't have to go back to Managua. Leon is dead and his father will soon be too. Dan will come back safe, and we can get on with our lives."

"Am I a bad person for relishing the sight of Leon being torn apart by El Diablo?" Zanita asked between sniffles.

"No. He deserved it. Just as his father deserves what Dan will do to him. It was justice."

"You know Leon said one time how beautiful you were. I told him you were too old. I said oh my God, she is nearly thirty," Zantia said with a smile that made Ariela laugh. "I didn't want him coming after you, too."

Ariela hugged her tighter.

"My brave little sister, you saved us. You did good. Now finished getting dressed. Katherine is taking us to a special spot on the beach for lunch."

Dan was up the tree before the sunlight crested the ridge of the valley. It was beautiful misty morning in the jungle today and he wondered if this was what his predecessors experienced in Vietnam. He used his scope to try and penetrate the fog into the open areas. There was activity going on, but he could not tell what was happening. By ten o'clock the fog had burned off and he could see everything clearly. Men were scurrying around in small groups. Some were checking weapons and others were involved in other activities Dan had seen many times before. They were preparing for war. At noon, all the men assembled on the airstrip. They formed three block formations with roughly fifty men in each block. There was a man at the head of each block, a leader of some sorts, but the one man pacing in front of all of them was Enrique Sanchez. He was shouting instructions Dan could not understand at this distance, but he certainly understood the tone. Dan watched as block by block they formed into a double-file line and marched up to the hacienda. Once inside, they assembled into the three block formations facing the front door. Dan chambered a round into the rifle.

Gabriel Perez sat at his desk going over the plan one more time alone. Enrique would be leaving that afternoon to fly to Honduras. Their Honduran gang partners were assembling a hundred men. They too had been harmed by the ARC control of the eastern part of the country and they were more than willing to throw in with the Azteca Cartel. Enrique would lead them in their attack upon the ARC airport. He would be taking some serious firepower with him including four rocket propelled grenade launchers and a large amount of explosives charges. The attack on the airport should be an excellent diversion.

His people in Managua assembled fifteen trucks and were driving them to a rendezvous point in eastern Nicaragua. There was a small landing strip nearby and he would be depositing his one-hundred-and-fifty-man force there tomorrow. His pilots hired three additional airplanes so they could move the entire force in a single day. If all went well, they would launch their attack in the early hours of tomorrow night.

His soldiers were equipped with an AK-47 and ten magazines, which gave them three-hundred rounds of ammunition. One group would attack the Santa Maria, another the Pinta and the third would attack the nuclear reactor. That group also carried explosive charges to make sure the facility would never be operational. His orders to the troops amassing outside were going to be simple. Kill everyone. There would be no quarter given. Kill the men, take what you want from the women, but kill them and the children when you are finished. Take whatever you want from the ships and when you are done, we will return and have a great fiesta. He looked outside the open doors at the waterfall and decided his message was not very original. It was, however, a message the great warlords of history had told their troops time and time again. And one that had proven very effective. When his troops finished with ARC, there would be no doubting his prowess among his competitors, and he would have revenge for the death of Leon.

Enrique interrupted his thinking as he appeared in the doorway.

"El jefe, the men are assembled in the courtyard."

"Then, let's not keep them waiting."

Dan's scope was trained on the front doors of the hacienda. He saw the door crack and his heart rate increased. He willed his pulse to slow down and controlled his breathing. He pushed the safety into fire mode with his thumb. The door opened and a great golden colored tiger appeared. It and its handler proceeded down the steps of the hacienda into the courtyard and stood next to the lieutenant at the head of the first block of men, the ones designated to attack the Santa Maria. Another tiger appeared, this one a dark copper color also accompanied by its handler, and they proceeded down the steps to take their place beside the lieutenant in charge of the second block, the ones assigned to attack the Pinta. A third great cat appeared with its handler, and they assumed their position in front of the group set to attack the nuclear power plant. The fourth tiger made its appearance handled by none other than Enrique himself and he stopped at the top of the stairs. The great cat sat down and looked at the spectacle below with the dignified grace of an emperor. Dan's scope tracked from Enrique's forehead to the open doorway. Gabriel Perez, the architect of the sinking of the Niña and the man who tortured Ariela was starting to emerge. Dan took up the slack in the trigger as the crosshairs zeroed in on the bridge of the drug lord's nose.

Gabriel Perez rose from his desk and called for the head tiger handler. He appeared walking with the slight limp he was known for; an old knee injury from when he was bitten by a tiger. With him was a beautiful copper colored tom tiger with great black stripes and large yellow eyes. He was the biggest tiger in the group now that El Diablo was dead.

"Enrique, I want you to be this tiger's handler today," Gabriel said.

"Why me?"

"Because you have proven your loyalty and you are my number two. I want the men to know when you speak, you speak with the authority of El Tigre."

"Gracias, Gabriel. You are most generous," Enrique said calling the drug lord by his first name which he rarely did.

"It is easy to be generous when you have such people as yourself, mi hermano. Now, let's go finish this business with these Afrikaners," El Tigre said as he motioned for the handler to bring out the rest of the cats.

The handler gave Enrique the chain leash. The tiger did not even look at him. The leash seemed flimsy with such a huge animal attached to the other end. Enrique knew he had no control over this animal, it was all about training and the cat's will. From what he knew of cats, the idea held little appeal. He felt small and foolish standing next to this beast with the chain in his hand. His thoughts from the previous day creeped back into his head. *Maybe I should just shoot Gabriel and end this madness. Would the men outside lynch me, or would they follow? If they follow, I could take over El Tigre's empire,* he thought. Then an alternative plan arose in his mind. *Maybe I have the Hondurans only half-ass attack the airport. Then the ARC forces will be better able counter the main attack. He might be killed. But after what he just said to me, how can I ...* Enrique's thoughts were interrupted by the opening of the front door and the parade of tigers exiting the house with their handlers.

Based on the range finder's lasered distance of three-hundred and thirty-three meters to the front door of the hacienda, Dan turned his scope setting up to three hundred when they first arrived. The extra thirty-three meters was inconsequential. His shot would be off by a centimeter or two from the exact point where he aimed.

El Tigre emerged from the front doors of the hacienda. One-hundred and fifty men chanted his name over and over. He walked into the sunlight and raised both of his arms to their adoration. Their chanting became louder. Enrique heard the supersonic crack of the bullet the instant El Tigre was knocked backwards off his feet. The sound of the rifle followed half a second later. Pandemonium broke out in the courtyard. The tiger Enrique was holding roared at the loud sound, but Enrique dropped the leash and bent down to check on Gabriel Perez. He was dead. The bullet went right through his sternum and blew apart his heart.

Dan cycled the bolt on the rifle. His next round was for Enrique, but only had seconds to make the shot. Enrique was kneeling over Perez, who appeared to be down permanently, but there was a big tiger shielding Enrique's torso and head from sight. Dan briefly thought about shooting through the tiger, but he could not bring himself to do it. The odds were long he would hit Enrique with a mortal shot having to pass through the great beast, and he didn't want to shoot a tiger. He took his eye from the scope and saw some men starting to assemble at the gate. One of the lieutenants was trying to rally them into the jungle. Dan put his eye back to the scope.

Above the tiger, Dan saw Enrique's raised palm facing the jungle. He slowly rose with his other hand above his head. Dan placed the crosshairs on his chest. Enrique lowered his hands until they were pressed palm to palm in a prayer in front of his chest. He lowered his head and closed his eyes. He stayed that way not moving, offering himself as a target. Dan's finger paused on the trigger as he took stock of what he was seeing. Enrique needed to die, but he was sending a message and Dan felt certain he knew what it was. Dan squeezed the trigger and slid down the tree as he saw at least thirty men rushing out the gates in their direction.

Enrique stood with his head bowed and his eyes closed. He was certain a bullet would rip through his body in the next second and his violent life would be over. He was startled by the window behind him exploding with the supersonic crack of a bullet passing by. The window was an answer to his message, and he started screaming at the men in the compound. He ordered them to stop and not go into the jungle. He ordered the lieutenants to get control of their men immediately. Two of the three lieutenants did so, but Jose, the one he became cross with during the planning, did not listen. He led thirty of his men into the jungle to find the sniper and he had the tiger handler assigned to his group by the collar and the tiger was running with them.

Even though he was expecting it, Aapo was startled by the first shot. He threw his quiver across his shoulder and picked up Dan's day pack. The second shot came no more than fifteen seconds later, and Dan came bailing out of the great tree. He seemed to barely touch the branches on the way down. Dan clicked the releases on the Uberti scope and shoved it in his pack. He would leave the rifle, but those scopes were too hard to come by. He ejected the bolt on the rifle and threw it into the jungle. He dropped the long gun and shouldered his pack.

"Let's go," he said to Aapo who accelerated into a quick pace as they heard the hoard of armed men exiting the gates of the hacienda. They were barely on their way when they heard the commands in Spanish to fire. Dan grabbed Aapo and pulled him to the ground as thirty men fired thirty rounds apiece on full automatic into the jungle. Nine-hundred sound splitting bullets swarmed over their heads tearing into everything around them. The instant they stopped, the two men were up and running. Dan's sniper training taught him to run in whatever direction the bullets were not coming from, but in this case, there was only one path, down the valley.

Even with the ringing in his ears, Jose could hear Enrique yelling his name from the steps of the hacienda. But he knew the whole world changed in the last minute. El Tigre was dead. Now there was a power vacuum, and he knew Enrique was going to wind up on top. Enrique wasn't going to keep him around, so the only way for him to survive was to capture or kill the sniper and gain enough followers to challenge Enrique for control of the cartel. He sent his men headlong into the jungle to run down the sniper. He followed behind with the tiger handler and his great cat.

Aapo moved like some kind of jungle spirit. He was fast and lithe retracing the paths they followed and forged getting to the hacienda. When the path was easy to follow, he would send Dan ahead and cover their tracks. When the path was difficult, he would lead the way and expect Dan to keep up. This was an endurance race, and the prize was their lives. Dan's life anyway. Aapo figured if their pursuers caught up to them, he would be able to slip away if Dan could not keep up anymore. But he hoped that would not happen. He did not want to explain to Sam and his son what happened to their friend. Dan was fit and they were making good progress. They were keeping ahead of the armed hoard following them.

Aapo sent Dan ahead at one point and started creating a false trail of broken branches and twigs. He was covering their tracks when he heard a terrible deep growl. It was like nothing he had ever heard before. It was not the high-pitched screaming of a woman like the jaguar, but something deeper and more sinister. He finished clearing their tracks and ran at top speed to catch up with Dan. Whatever it was, he did not want to run into it.

They encountered the first steep incline they had to traverse. They both knew their pursuers would gain a lot of ground when they slowed to climb, so they threw themselves at the mountain as hard as they could. They were climbing fast and using plants and trees as handholds to pull themselves upwards. The fastest of the pursuers reached the bottom when they were near the top. They heard the crack of the bullets whizzing past them and saw the debris flying from the mountain around them as the sound of the rifles carried upward. They got off their track into the cover and continued up. When they got to the top, they peered down. Dan offered Aapo a drink from his canteen. The first pursuers had already begun the ascent and the rest of the party had caught up. Aapo could see the great tiger below them being held by a leash. He realized it made the noise he heard earlier. He stared incessantly at it and then looked at Dan. He pointed at it and made his mouth like that of a jaguar bearing its fangs.

"Yeah. I see it. Let's get going."

They were on the other side of the plateau headed down as the sun was setting. Dan tore open the last MRE in his bag and gave Aapo half of the blueberry desert cake and half of the crackers so hard and flavorless they must have been packaged before the turn of the century. They licked their fingers and stuck them into the beef stroganoff powdered content package and sucked their fingers clean. They downed some water and headed down the slope. Their pursuers were still behind them. They were seven hours into the chase and showing no sign of letting up. Both men knew there would be no sleep tonight. They would run all night and all day tomorrow. Either their bodies would give out and they would die, or they would reach the beach. Dan prayed Sam would be waiting for them.

Sam and the Admiral were stationed off the beach again this morning in the patrol boat. They had spent the last two days slowly cruising up and down the coastline looking for Dan or Aapo. It was monotonous duty scanning the beach with binoculars from a pitching boat all day and they took turns driving and watching. This morning, Sam broke out the fishing tackle he found stored in a long cubby on the boat. The Admiral's patrol teams were rumored to have the ability to fish and now they confirmed it. Sam set the lines out behind the boat with two spoons trailing on each line. He figured they might catch some fresh fish for supper and break up the monotony with a little fun. They hadn't been trolling for more than ten minutes when the reel on one of the rods began to scream. Sam handed the binoculars to the admiral and picked up the rod. He set the hook and the reel screamed harder. The fish was on the run, and it was a good one. Sam kept his rod tip up as his forearms pulled on the hand grip of the rod and its base dug into his hip. The line coming off the reel was as tight as if it was made of steel. He and the fish were in a stalemate. The fish couldn't run, but Sam couldn't get any of the line back. One of them would have to give. Sam knew it would be the fish if he could just hold on.

"I've got something," Admiral Sharpe said.

"Me too. A big damn fish," Sam said through gritted teeth.

"I think I see Dan."

The sun was coming up for the second time since Dan killed El Tigre. The birds were beginning to sing their morning songs and the insects seemed to be coming to life with their buzzing and flittering about. Dan was on a runner's high. The demon inside him kept pushing him not to stop. He and Aapo had been on the run for nearly thirty-six hours with very little rest. Their pace was a fast jog, and his endorphin system was going full tilt to block out the pain and tiredness. He was scratched up and bleeding from superficial wounds but had no real injuries. Every time they stopped; he re-laced his boots tighter. They had rubbed all the leg hair from around the tops and his lower leg was rubbed raw, but they were the key to survival. He had to keep from turning an ankle at all costs. Aapo seemed to be timeless and tireless. He only had a couple of scratches and it appeared he could run forever. Their pursuers from the cartel were not far behind. No doubt they lost some of them along the way, but the remainder were still in pursuit. Dan found it hard to believe hired guns would work this hard to run them down. He'd heard a couple of shots during the night. He wondered if they were shooting snakes, shooting deserters or if it was simply an accidental discharge. He wondered how long a tiger would keep running? Alaskan sled dogs were the world champions of endurance running. Surely a tiger could not run for this long without stopping, but he really didn't know anything about tigers and the image of the great cat doing to him what El Diablo did to Leon was a great motivator to keep moving.

These thoughts ran on one frequency inside his brain while on a sub frequency Dan kept an internal chant going to keep his rhythm and pace. The metronomic chant was always there. Always pushing no matter where the rest of his thought process wandered. It was another key to his survival. Tight boots and the chant. Military lessons from long ago brought up and recalled to get him out of a dangerous spot. Both frequencies went silent when he heard the crash. Aapo paused in his tracks and looked back. Dan heard the crash again. It was the surf. If Sam Harrington was out there, they might make it. If he wasn't they might be trapped on the beach. The cartel men were minutes behind. Dan forgot about the chant and pushed Aapo into a sprint.

"ARC One to ARC Two, launch," the admiral called into the radio handset on the console before tossing the mic onto the dash.

"ARC Two, copy," came back Patson's voice loud and excited.

Sam looked up from the reel he was fighting to put line on to see two figures running on the beach. He reached down and grabbed the rubber bumper buoy for the boat. He looped its line around the reel and tossed the rod and bumper overboard. He cut the line on the other rod and tossed it into the floor. The admiral handed him the binoculars as he spun the boat towards the beach and throttled up. Sam zeroed in on Dan and Aapo. It was them without any doubt. They were sprinting with Aapo in the lead. He scanned south on the beach and saw men breaking through the vegetation line behind them. Sam swiftly moved to the front of the boat. He pulled the cover off the M-60 machinegun mounted on a tripod in the front of the boat. He pulled the charging handle back. A long belt of cartridges ran from the gun down to an ammunition box bungeed to the tripod leg. Sam settled in behind the iron sites as the Admiral increased the speed of the patrol boat towards the beach.

Dan felt the first round pass by his head as he heard the supersonic crack. It was instantly followed by the report of the rifle behind them. Aapo looked back but did not slow down. Another bullet whizzed by as Dan extended his long legs in a desperate sprint to catch Aapo, who was now running flat out down the beach. Dan's lungs felt they would burst, and his thighs felt like wet concrete, but he made up ground. The bullets seemed to be swarming around them. As he caught up to Aapo he reached for his bicep and they heard another sound, the sound of thunder coming from the patrol boat. Dan turned Aapo towards the surf and Aapo tried to jerk away. He had no intention of going into the ocean. Dan held tight and drug him into the water as the bullets seemed to fade away. He dragged Aapo into the water knee deep and turned back towards their pursuers. They were shooting at the patrol boat with a long flame spewing from the boat's deck gun. With that as his last sight, Dan plunged he and Aapo into the next wave and took them under the clear salty water.

Sam saw the lead pursuer stop and aim his rifle down the beach. He could not hear the man's shots over the screaming of the twin Yamaha two-fifties pushing the patrol boat, but he could see the smoke and flames extending from the barrels of the AK-47. Before he could react, the other men stopped and began firing as well. Sam swiveled the big black gun in their direction tracking them as the admiral closed the gap to the beach and angled towards Dan and Aapo. Sam remembered his M-60 training from long ago. This was not a gun to handle gingerly. You had to pull the trigger and pull it hard to keep it from jamming. He squeezed firmly and it roared to life. He sent a burst in the general direction of the shooters. It got their attention, but instead of retreating into the vegetation as he hoped, they opened fire on the patrol boat. Bullets were zipping past the boat and more than a few struck the vessel. Sam tracked the gun onto the shooters and yanked the trigger. He walked the front sight back and forth on the beach until none of the men were standing. The boat slowed and he glanced down at the water. Dan was swimming a side stroke carrying Aapo like a lifeguard. The admiral put the boat between the swimmers and the beach. Sam stayed on the gun watching for anyone to emerge from the jungle. The admiral reached down and pulled Aapo into the boat. He extended a hand and Dan was able to crawl aboard and flop down on the deck, his chest rising and falling with great effort as he stared up into the sun and closed his eyes. The admiral hit the throttle and pointed the boat out to sea. He wanted distance between them and the beach. Sam sat Aapo up on a seat and looked him in the eyes. He was tired but seemed unharmed. Aapo started jabbering on and pointing to towards the beach. Sam smiled and held up his hand. He moved to the back of the boat and stood over Dan as the boat slowed.

"You OK?"

"Peachy."

"Want a beer?"

"Water first."

"Wennie," Sam said with a grin as he directed the admiral with a nod of his head to get the men some water. "Did you get him?"

"Affirmative."

"What about tiger face?"

"Negative. I'll explain later," Dan said as the admiral appeared with a water and a beer.

Dan pulled himself up into a sitting position and accepted both. Faced with the actual choice, he popped the top on the beer. The coldest and best beer he ever tasted. He looked up as they all heard the rotors approaching from the Eurocopter. Sam retrieved the hastily tossed radio microphone.

"ARC Two, this ARC One."

"Go ahead."

"Recon the beach."

"Copy," was the response and the helicopter veered away.

The admiral put the boat into gear and turned to the north.

"I see your buoy," he said.

Sam retrieved the boat hook from its holder and leaned over the side as they approached. He snagged the line of the buoy and pulled it and the rod aboard. He started reeling in the line and he felt it was heavy on the other end. He reeled quickly to add as much line as he could on the spindle. When the fish felt it was being hauled to the surface, it put up as much fight as it could, but it was tired having fought Sam first and then the buoy. Sam had it in the boat within five minutes. It was a four-foot amberjack, and it would make an excellent dinner. Aapo had never seen a fish as large as this one and he began excitedly jabbering on about it.

The admiral pushed the throttles forward and the boat rose atop the waves and sped towards the tanker waiting offshore. Sam went forward and sat opposite Aapo. Dan moved on uneasy legs and sat next to Aapo. He put his arm around him and pulled him in. Aapo looked about at the wonderment around him and took a long drink of his beer. He laughed in nervous amazement. His smile was contagious and soon the whole boat was smiling.

The helicopter landed aboard the tanker and Marcus made his way to the bridge. Dan, Sam, and the Admiral were huddled together. They hadn't been back long. Patson was missing as he took Aapo below to help him rinse the salt water from his skin and possessions. It was to be his first hot shower.

"Did you get him?" Marcus asked.

"I did."

"Fantastic! That bastard needed to die."

"What did you see on the beach?" Sam asked.

"Nine dead. Your handy work?"

"Yeah. The sixty."

"Bad day to be those fellows. You don't want to be one the wrong end of a machine gun with the great Sam Harrington on the other end!"

"Gimme a break. Anything else?"

"Ja. We flew south and do you know what we saw?" Marcus asked stopping for a dramatic pause.

"No."

"A tiger! A tiger walking down the beach."

"No one was with it? No leash?" Dan asked.

"No. It was alone."

"Probably going to be hell on the local wildlife population," Dan joked.

The ARC board of directors convened aboard the Santa Maria. The mood was serious. Dan stood before them and told them what transpired in the valley, how he assassinated El Tigre and how he let Enrique Sanchez go. Naturally, there were questions.

"Why do you think Enrique was communicating with you?" Ansel asked."

"He held up his hands. I felt I understood what he was saying by the way he put his hands into the form of someone praying. A peace gesture if you will."

"How sure are you that is what he meant?" Katherine asked.

"I had my crosshairs on his heart. I believe he knew it. He was offering his life in exchange for peace with the cartel. Believe me, I wanted to pull the trigger. That animal nearly choked Ariela to death. It took all my willpower not to give into my instincts and pull the trigger. But I remember what Sam said after your last board meeting. You were afraid of who would fill El Tigre's role in a power vacuum. You were afraid of someone more violent, not that I think that was really possible. So, I let him live since he was offering peace."

"Thank you, Dan," Katherine said with an understanding smile.

Dan was dismissed and the council began their discussions on the matter. They unanimously agreed to wait and see what happened with Enrique Sanchez. They hoped Dan read the situation correctly and they now had a truce with the Azteca cartel.

"We have one more thing we must discuss," Morne said.

"What is that?" Jayden asked.

"We decided there would be no punitive action against Gabriel Perez after the raid that freed Ariela. Dan took matters into his own hands and defied the will of the board. We must decide if there are to be consequences for this and if so, what those consequences should be. Does anyone want to start the discussion?"

"I will," Katherine said. "If I had known the details about what happened to Ariela and Zanita, I would have voted to assassinate Gabriel Perez. I think Dan did what we should have voted to do."

"But that is not the question, Katherine," Ansel responded. "Are we a people that abide by the guidance of the board, or are we allowed to ignore that guidance? If we let Dan get away with...literally get away with murder, how will anyone respect us? How can we expect anyone to follow what we say?"

"Ansel is correct. We are a society built on an ideal. An ideal of creating a new home for our people and if our people see corruption from this b or ARC leadership, the entire endeavor will fail," Jayden added.

"Hold on a minute," Sam said. "First, murder is a strong word to throw around. We are talking about a man that killed a hundred and fifty of our friends. Yeah, Dan killed him, but he did not murder him."

"I agree, Sam," Morne said. "Murder is too strong a charge. There will be no more talk of murder. At best it was a non-sanctioned military operation."

There were nods around the table. Everyone sat for a moment in their own thoughts. The faces were solemn, many of the brows wrinkled as they thought.

"Let's start with the obvious question. Does anyone here make a motion that Dan violated company direction?" Morne asked.

"I motion that we recognize Dan Weston violated company direction by engaging in an unauthorized military operation," Ansel said.

Jayden seconded the motion, and a vote was held. It was unanimous. Every board member including Sam voted in favor of the motion.

"Since we are all in agreement, is there a motion that we should enact some kind of punishment?" Morne asked as he looked about.

Sam sat jaw clenched staring at Ansel and Jayden. Neither would look at him. Ansel was about to speak when Katherine cut him off.

"I would like to make a motion that we give Dan Weston a symbolic punishment for taking part in an unauthorized military action," she said feeling she could cleverly preempt something worse.

"You can't do that." Ansel replied.

"She can motion anything she wants," Sam said.

"We can't make a motion for a symbolic punishment and expect to be taken seriously. I motion we provide Dan Weston with a punishment equal to the offense, banishment."

"What?" Sam said in a voice that rattled the glass.

Marcus Odendaal began yelling at Ansel in Afrikaans. Sam could not understand the words, but from the tone it was clear Marcus might be about to commit an unauthorized military action right there in the boardroom.

"I second the motion," Jayden yelled over Marcus silencing the big man.

"Then we vote," Morne said. "All in favor of banishment for Dan Weston raise your hand."

Sam, Marcus and Katherine sat still as Ansel and Jayden slowly raised their hands. They were shocked when Morne raised his. Sam stared at Morne in disbelief.

"I am sorry, Sam, but Ansel and Jayden are correct. We must hold everyone to the same standards."

Morne lowered his hand and addressed the group. "The vote is a tie. Unless anyone wants to change their vote, the chairman will decide a tie vote. Does anyone wish to change their vote?"

No one did. Sam suddenly missed Johannes. The Board was designed to have an odd number of members to avoid a tie. Johannes would have voted with Sam had he not died. Dan would have been safe.

"Then as the chairman, I break the tie by approving the motion that Dan Weston will be banished from the colony. This banishment will be effective for three-hundred and sixty-five days."

Sam stormed out of the room. Katherine ran after him. Marcus stood and covered the space to Ansel and Jayden in two giant strides. There was fire in his eyes, and he was going to let them have his full wrath. Morne moved to intervene for fear the big farmer might actually harm the two men. He'd seen Marcus beat a guerilla to death with the butt of his rifle in combat. Neither the technology wiz, nor the banker were a match for him if he lost his cool.

Katherine called Sam's name twice, but he never turned around. He was headed towards his quarters and rather than create a spectacle of herself by calling after him anymore, she simply walked as quickly as she could with dignity. She did not knock, but simply pressed her forefinger to the biometric reader and entered his quarters. He was at the bar pouring himself a drink.

"Want one?"

"No thank you."

She was in uncharted waters. She had never seen Sam lose his cool. He was more than a bit scary.

"Do you want to talk?"

"Nope," he said as he gulped down the golden colored scotch whiskey.

She sat on the couch and looked at him. He stared back. He seemed like a mountain of granite.

"You know, I am as guilty as Dan. I killed nine men yesterday. Ansel would say I murdered nine men. But nobody dared bring that up, did they?"

"You were there to rescue Dan if he needed it, and that was sanctioned by the Board of Directors."

"This whole thing is a farce. I can't believe Morne voted the way he did. I get it, we all have to abide by the same rules and people have to believe in the system, but if it weren't for Dan, I would probably have been killed in Managua during the assassination attempt. If it weren't for Dan and Javier, we would have had a whole tower crew murdered. That has to count for something."

"It does. That is why he only gave him a one-year banishment. It could have been permanent."

There was a knock at the door. Katherine rose to answer it. She opened the door to a solemn looking Morne.

"May I come in?"

Katherine turned to Sam requesting his approval without saying a word. Sam nodded and she opened the door enough for Morne to enter.

"I just wanted to come by and say how sorry I am, but I had to vote the way I did. The people must know we are an open and honest society, and the leaders are not above them in any way. I hated the vote. I still do, but it was the right thing."

"I understand. It just seems we should have tried to figure out a better way."

"This was the only way, Sam. The rumors were already out that Dan went against the board. We had to set an example and it had to be harsh enough to send a message. You know we will open our arms to Dan in a year if he will be willing to return. He always has a place here."

"OK."

"If you will excuse me, I need to go find him and tell him about the board's decision."

"We should tell him together. Sit down and I will text him."

As Sam walked to his desk to retrieve his phone, Katherine stood and excused herself to leave. They didn't need her and she didn't want to be there. She took the route she thought would least give her a chance of running into Dan and went to find Ariela.

Dan stiffly came through the door of his quarters and saw Katherine and Ariela sitting on the couch. His face wore a mask of indifference, but both women sensed he must be upset. Ariela crossed the room and hugged him, his arms wrapping themselves in her long black hair. He stared at Katherine with impassive eyes. and she rose to speak.

"I am sorry, Dan. The board is wrong on this one."

"Actually, they are not. Morne explained it. I think he is correct."

"Well, that is not how I voted."

"Thank you, but it doesn't matter. Given the same choice, I'd have done it all over again."

Ariela pulled away from his chest and kissed him on the mouth with her pouty lips. She leaned back and they stared into each other's eyes.

"I am sorry."

"Don't be. Nobody gets to hurt you and get away with it. Nobody."

She hugged him tighter this time and Dan saw tears welling up in Katherine's eyes.

"I should let you two be alone," she said as she started towards the door. "When will you be leaving Dan?"

"The day after tomorrow. Sam wants to take Aapo home tomorrow while I get Ariela a visa through Jay Nobel. He owes me one for killing the biggest drug lord in Nicaragua. Then, Sam is flying us to his house in Texas."

This time Katherine knocked on Sam's door. He answered it and moved aside for her to enter. Morne was gone and Sam's suitcase was on the bed.

"Dan says you are taking him and Ariela to Texas. How long will you be gone?"

"I don't know. A while. I need some distance."

"I will miss you."

"Come with me."

"I can't. I have responsibilities here."

"Your Seconds can handle it, just like mine can."

"No. I must see it is done correctly."

"I understand," he said with a resigned tone.

She hugged him tightly and left without saying a word. She was halfway down the corridor before her tears began to fall.

The End

Epilogue

The patrol boat slowly snaked its way up the Coco River towards the spot where Aapo would disembark. Dan and Aapo sat in the front staring upriver while Sam stood alone at the helm. Aapo sported a new tattoo. It was an orange and black tiger's face, and it covered his right pectoral muscle. It was a fierce looking tattoo with fangs bared and nose snarled. Dan took Aapo drinking last night and sought out a woman who was a truly gifted tattoo artist on the Pinta. He told her it was a single night job, but her customer was tough. Aapo was strong, but Dan's whiskey seemed to help him through the ordeal. When it was completed, he was in awe of what he saw in the mirror. He motioned for Dan to sit in the chair. He produced his jade handled knife from the hidden pocket in his loincloth. Above where Dan's sleeve tattoos stopped on his shoulder, he scratched a border pattern into Dan's skin. It matched the tribal markings on his own arm. When he finished, he turned to the tattoo artist and motioned for her to fill in his scratches with ink.

When they reached the right spot, Aapo stood to leave the boat. Dan grasped his hand and pulled him close. When released, Aapo turned, and Sam did the same. The wiry little man launched himself from the front of the boat and landed on the bank. He slipped his quiver over his left shoulder so it would not rub on his new tattoo. He smiled and waved before disappearing into the rainforest.

Enrique was sitting at the desk in the hacienda. It rained the night before and the falls were magnificent. He had the tall glass doors open and the water was thunderous. One of his lieutenants entered and told him Jose had returned. Enrique rose, pulled the gold-plated Desert Eagle from the desk drawer, and stuck it in his waistband. He and the lieutenant walked into the courtyard. The man who Enrique previously argued with in front of El Tigre was ragged and led only a handful of men equally as ragged and worn out. He and his men stood in front of a courtyard full of armed mercenaries.

"Jose, you left with thirty men to chase the assassin, did you kill him?" Enrique asked.

"No. He escaped."

"Escaped? How?"

"By the sea. I sent my fastest runners after him, but he killed them on the beach and the tracks say he swam away. I assume he had a boat."

"Is this all that is left of your men?"

"Some already returned I assumed. We had to leave them behind during the pursuit."

"A few did return. They have been looked after. Where is the tiger you took?"

"I do not know. Its handler fell behind. I gave the leash to another man."

"Where is that man now?"

"Dead."

"So, you defied my orders and went after the assassin. You lost most of your men, lost a valuable tiger and you failed to kill the assassin."

"Why would I care about your orders? I only took orders from El Tigre," Jose responded defiantly.

Enrique pulled the gold-plated pistol from his belt. It hung loosely in his hand pointing at the ground. Jose was mesmerized by the light glinting off the gun. He knew these were the last few seconds of his life.

"Jose…I am El Tigre."

There was a great thunderous roar from the pistol followed by the chorus of chanting in the courtyard.

"El Tigre! El Tigre! El Tigre!"

Dan Weston opened the door of the barbershop owned by the Azteca Cartel on the outskirts of Managua. His sleeves were rolled up exposing his muscular tattooed arms. His Oakleys hid his eyes from everyone inside. When he stepped in, all activity stopped. A gringo had never set foot in the barbershop, much less one so menacing in appearance. Dan looked at the barber.

"Enrique Sanchez. Aquí. Mañana. Cero Ocho Cero Cero. No Pistoles. Comprende?" He asked.

The barber nodded twice, and Dan backed out of the door.

One of Julio's nephews was waiting for a haircut. He had a small pistol concealed in his waistband in case Dan needed backup. He listened as the barber got on the telephone immediately and told his superiors a tough looking Americano wanted to meet with El Tigre tomorrow morning at eight o'clock. The nephew couldn't hear the other side of the conversation, but he listened to the bravado being spewed inside the barbershop for another half hour before his haircut was finished. He and his cousins would sit on the place all night making sure the next morning would not be an ambush.

At ten minutes until eight o'clock, Julio's nephew drove the two Americans to the meeting. Dan and Sam knew Enrique was in the barbershop alone. Enrique did not want any witnesses to the parle. Dan handed the nephew his 1911 as they exited the pickup. They walked into the barbershop to find Enrique sitting in one of the barber chairs. Dan scanned for weapons and saw none. Enrique stood and met them in the middle of the room. He looked at Dan.

"You are the one that killed Gabriel Perez."

It was a question and a statement all at the same time.

"Yeah."

"Thank you. That will be our secret."

"OK."

"And thank you, for not shooting me. I am sure you wanted to."

"Still do."

Enrique smiled and the tiger on his face bared its fangs.

"But you did not, so I assume you understand what I am offering as our new relationship."

"We don't have a relationship," Sam interjected. "You stay away from everything to do with ARC, and we don't come after you."

"Agreed, Doctor Harrington."

"There is just one more thing we need from you."

"Yes?"

"The name of the bomber who set the mines on our ship and killed our friends."

Dear Friends,

I hope you enjoyed *Valley of the Tiger.* I had a great time writing it. Sam Harrington and friends will return in *The Dragon's Proxy.* It is a epic adventure you won't want to miss.

Until then, all my best.

Raylan Wayne

The Dragon's Proxy

Raylan Wayne

2024

www.ingramcontent.com/pod-product-compliance
Lightning Source LLC
Chambersburg PA
CBHW050731180626
46814CB00002B/695